I0775677

Also by the Author

The Erin O'Reilly Mysteries

Black Velvet
Irish Car Bomb
White Russian
Double Scotch
Manhattan
Black Magic
Death By Chocolate
Massacre
Flashback
First Love
High Stakes

Aquarium
The Devil You Know
Hair of the Dog
Punch Drunk
Bossa Nova
Blackout
Angel Face
Italian Stallion
White Lightning
Kamikaze (coming soon)

Tequila Sunrise: A James Corcoran Story

Fathers
A Modern Christmas Story

The Clarion Chronicles
Ember of Dreams

White Lightning

The Erin O'Reilly Mysteries
Book Twenty

Steven Henry

Clickworks Press • Baltimore, MD

First publication: Clickworks Press, 2023
Release: CWP-EOR20-INT-P.IS-1.5

Sign up for updates, deals, and exclusive sneak peeks at clickworkspress.com/join.

Ebook ISBN: 979-8-88900-008-2
Paperback ISBN: 979-8-88900-009-9
Hardcover ISBN: 979-8-88900-010-5

For my big brother Peter. Sorry about being a bratty kid
brother all those years ago.

White Lightning

Illegally-distilled corn whiskey; otherwise known as bootleg, firewater, moonshine, hooch, and many other nicknames.

Chapter 1

"I hate judges," Vic Neshenko said.

"I think you should tell Ferris that when we ask for the warrant," Erin O'Reilly replied. She squinted against the glare of the oncoming headlights on the Expressway. She spotted a momentary gap in the traffic and slipped her Charger sideways into the space, drawing an irritated honk from a New Yorker who felt she'd cut him off.

"I hate New York traffic, too," Vic said. "Doesn't that idiot know we're cops?"

"We're unmarked," she reminded him. The Charger was painted solid black and its flasher bar was low-profile, as befitting a detective's ride.

"And that was a legal lane change," he went on. "You had plenty of room. Hell, I could've parked a Suburban in that hole. I hate Staten Island."

"Maybe it'd be quicker to list the things you don't hate," she suggested.

Vic said nothing. Behind the driver's seat, in his special compartment, Rolf panted audibly. The German Shepherd loved car rides.

"Can't think of anything?" Erin asked after a moment.

"What? No, I'm already done," Vic said.

"You didn't say anything."

"Exactly."

Erin shook her head. "I shouldn't keep you up past your bedtime," she said. "You get grumpy."

"What are you talking about? It's not even ten o'clock. If it was late, we wouldn't be doing this. Anyway, you're the one who didn't want to wait until tomorrow. We could've done this nice and civilized, gone to see Ferris in his office."

"And let our guy knock over another café? No thanks," Erin said. "We were lucky nobody got killed last time. Next time might be different. This guy's a fatality waiting to happen."

"I'm just saying, it's a long drive," Vic grumbled.

"Would you have preferred the ferry? It goes straight to Saint George."

"No, I would not have preferred the ferry. I—"

"Hate ferries," Erin finished for him. "Why?"

"I get seasick."

"Really?"

"Well, I did once."

"Only once?"

"It's the sort of thing you remember. I've stayed off ferries since then."

Erin got off the Staten Island Expressway and headed north. "Quit bitching," she said. "We're this close to making an arrest. No time to waste."

"If Ferris had his fax machine turned on, we wouldn't have even needed to make the trip," Vic said, continuing to bitch. "I can't believe we're still using fax machines. Might as well saddle a horse and gallop the damn warrant over to him. He'd probably prefer that. I bet he switched it off on purpose."

"Could be a mechanical malfunction," Erin said. "Like you

said, it's an old piece of technology."

"Yeah, but old stuff *works*," he said. "It's the new crap that breaks down all the time. That's why you still see fridges from 1965 or whenever, but the brand-new ones go on the fritz after a year or two. Hell, take Ferris himself. How long's he been riding the bench?"

"I have no idea," Erin said. "Forty or fifty years, I think."

"And it's not like he was fresh out of law school when they put a robe on him," Vic said. "Now he's gotta be eighty or ninety."

"At least," she agreed. "How close are we?"

Vic looked at the directions on his phone. "Almost there," he said. "You want Fort Hill Park. Take a left on Victory Boulevard, then hang a right on Daniel Low Terrace and take it to Fort Place. Man, this guy lives at the ass-end of nowhere."

"It's the closest part of Staten Island to Manhattan," she said. "And if we'd taken the ferry, like I said, we could've taken the shortest route and we'd already be there. I hope it was worth it to your stomach."

"I don't even care," he grumbled. "Let's just get this done and get back to civilization."

"You've got the paperwork, don't you?" Erin said.

"I've got the damn paperwork. Warrant to search the apartment of one Dylan White, suspected of multiple armed robberies. Want to see it?"

"I'm driving. Show it to Rolf."

"He can't read."

"So what? He'll pretend to care."

They finally pulled up to Judge Ferris's house. As Vic had complained, it was remarkably remote, set back on a little road in a small patch of woods. The house had a vaulted roof with a shape that reminded Erin of a converted barn. It was a big place for an old man living alone, but hardly a mansion. She parked in the driveway, behind a blue Prius.

"That seem right?" Vic wondered aloud as they climbed out of the Charger. "Ferris never struck me as a Toyota man."

"He's not," Erin said, pointing at a big, black Buick further up the driveway. "That must be his. I guess he's got company."

"High-class call girl," Vic predicted.

Erin rolled her eyes. "Because they all drive Priuses."

Light glowed behind the shades on the ground floor. Erin buzzed the doorbell, hoping they weren't interrupting anything important. She didn't believe Vic's theory for a second; Ferris might live alone, but he'd never have engaged a hooker even when he'd been young enough to make full use of one.

After a few moments, just as she was thinking about hitting the buzzer again, she heard the bolt slide back. Then the door opened to reveal Judge Ferris's white-haired face. His lips cracked into a smile.

"Good evening, Detectives," he said. "I wasn't expecting visitors."

"We tried calling, Your Honor," Erin said.

"Yes, of course," Ferris said. "I had a problem with my telephone line. A repairman for the telephone company was out just a little while ago, tinkering with things, but he wasn't able to fix it. He'll be back in a day or two."

"That explains the fax screwup," Vic said.

"Oh, yes, it would," Ferris said. "You've got a warrant for me to sign, I imagine. Something urgent, or you wouldn't be calling at my home so late on a weeknight."

"That's right," Erin said. "We're working a string of café robberies, and—"

"Where are my manners?" Ferris asked himself aloud. "Come in and sit down. You can spare a few minutes before the drive back, and I can offer you a little refreshment. Please, I insist."

He stepped back and, to Erin's surprise, slid something long and black into his umbrella stand.

"Judge Ferris?" she said, cautiously stepping over the threshold. "Did you just put a shotgun in with your umbrellas?"

"Mossberg International Silver Reserve Two," Ferris said proudly. "Twelve-gauge over-under hunting shotgun, one of the best on the market."

"Nice," Vic said, impressed. He knew just about everything about every firearm known to man. "Slug or buckshot?"

"Buck," Ferris said. "My eyesight isn't what it used to be, so I need to dispense the law with a generous spread."

"Do you always answer the door that way?" Erin asked.

"Usually," he said. "I am rather secluded here, and a judge with my length of service does, of necessity, leave a great many enemies in his wake. I've served long enough that some of the men I put away on life sentences have been paroled by now."

"Yeah, but they're old men, too," Vic said. "You really think anyone's gonna come gunning for you?"

"If I can still handle a long gun, so can they," Ferris said cheerfully. "Come into my parlor. I'm sorry it took so long to answer the door. Roy Bean would normally have alerted me to your presence. But he seems to have taken a slight turn. He's been sleeping soundly all evening. He seems quite comfortable, or I would have taken him to the veterinarian by now. How is your dog, Detective O'Reilly?"

"Rolf's good," Erin said. "I left him in the car. I didn't think we'd be long."

They entered the parlor, which was lit by a pair of lamps and a cheerful fire in the old stone fireplace. Erin stopped short. A woman was sitting in one of Ferris's big leather armchairs in front of the fire.

"Oh," Erin said. "Excuse me, ma'am."

The woman got to her feet. She was a slender Latina who

looked to be a few years older than Erin. Her hair was still pure black, without a hint of gray, but the fine lines at the corners of her eyes showed that she'd been around long enough to have seen some things. Her hair was cut in a professional style and her clothes were those of a well-to-do, well-educated woman. Her movements were practiced and confident. In her left hand was a glass containing a small quantity of clear liquid.

"Good evening," the woman said. "I don't believe we've met."

"Erin O'Reilly," Erin said, offering her hand. "I'm a detective with Major Crimes. This is my partner, Vic Neshenko."

"Judge Miranda Rodriguez," the woman said, shaking hands. She had a cool, firm grip.

"Pleased to meet you, Your Honor," Erin said. Another judge; that explained it. Ferris was hosting a colleague.

"Now, what can I get you?" Ferris asked.

"What do you recommend?" Erin asked. "I can't get too hammered; I need to drive back to Manhattan tonight."

"Howard was just sharing the fruits of his hobby with me," Rodriguez said, holding up the glass in her hand. "You should give it a try."

"What is it?" Vic asked. "Looks like vodka."

"White lightning," Ferris said with a chuckle. "Moonshine, just like my father made during the Depression. He ran a speakeasy, did you know that? Made his own bootleg liquor in the cellar."

"You've got a homemade still set up?" Erin asked, interested.

"Of course!" Ferris said. "I inherited my father's apparatus. An old man's hobby more than a source of revenue these days, I daresay, but I'm quite happy with the results. I'll pour you some. Half a moment."

He disappeared into the kitchen. Rodriguez smiled at the detectives. "It's really very good," she said. "It has a smoky sort of flavor. He ages it in wooden casks, just the way you're supposed to. Now, if you'll just excuse me a moment?"

"Of course," Erin said. Rodriguez walked down a short hallway, presumably to the restroom.

Ferris came out of the kitchen, holding a pair of glasses. He held them out to Erin and Vic.

"Enjoy," he said. "It's the original family recipe. You can imagine you're walking the beat back in the Thirties, trying to get the cuffs on Lucky Luciano and Albert Anastasia and all the rest of the original Mafiosi."

"I don't think I've met Judge Rodriguez before," Erin said.

"You wouldn't have," Ferris said. "She presides over corporate cases, primarily, not the sort of thing you folks in Major Crimes would encounter. But she's very good."

Erin caught the glint of pride in the old man's eye. "Have you known her a long time?" she asked.

"She clerked for me when she was out of law school," he said. "I suppose you could say I've been her mentor. A very bright young woman, one of the best lawyers I've ever known. A legal mind like—"

The lights flickered. A cry came from the hallway. It was a short exclamation, of surprise or possibly pain, abruptly cut off. Then there was a meaty thud, a sound that brought Erin's police instincts to sudden, screaming life.

Before she fully realized what she was doing, Erin was running for the hallway. Vic was only a step behind her. Ferris, bewildered, stood in the middle of his den, blinking at them.

A strange smell filled the air; a wild, sharp odor. Miranda Rodriguez lay on the carpeted floor, one hand outstretched, legs crumpled beneath her. The woman's eyes were wide, staring straight up at the ceiling. She lay completely still.

Chapter 2

The glass of moonshine fell from Erin's hand. It shattered on the carpet with a muffled tinkle. Erin followed it down, going to her knees beside the judge. She put out a hand to the woman's neck, tilting Miranda's head toward her.

"No pulse," she said. "No respiration. Call a bus."

"You call them," Vic said, dropping down next to her. "I'll start CPR. I've got better arms."

Erin couldn't argue with that; Vic did a lot of weight training. She yanked out her phone and called Dispatch while Vic started chest compressions.

Judge Ferris stood to one side, staring at his protégé as Erin rattled off the address and a quick description of what had happened. Vic was counting in time with the compressions, pausing to breathe into Miranda's lungs before continuing. He'd keep at it until the paramedics arrived to take over, or until he couldn't do it any longer.

"First responders en route," Dispatch informed Erin. "ETA on Patrol units, six minutes. EMTs, ten."

Erin swore silently. Ten minutes was an eternity when dealing with what looked an awful lot like a heart attack. But it could have been worse. Ferris could have been alone with Miranda, and he was in no physical condition to do ten minutes of CPR.

She took the phone away from her ear and returned to Vic's side. "Six minutes on uniforms, ten on the bus," she told him.

"Shit," was Vic's terse verdict. He kept doing compressions, not taking his eyes off the downed judge.

"What can I do to help?" Ferris asked quietly.

"Talk to her," Erin said. "If she can hear you, it might do some good. I'm going to the driveway to flag down our guys."

First responders played the percentages. Anything that shaved a few seconds off response time might be helpful, as long as you didn't rush. She'd learned a saying from Ian Thompson, former Marine Scout Sniper: "Slow is smooth and smooth is fast." It might sound weird, but Erin understood: Efficiency saved lives. If the medics didn't have to waste time double-checking the address, it might give them the edge they needed.

Rolf saw her come out of the house. He sprang to his feet, ears perked, tail wagging. When she jogged past the Charger to the foot of the driveway, he stopped wagging and cocked his head, wondering what was going on.

It really wasn't a long time before the incoming sirens pierced the night, but it seemed like it to Erin. A brief eternity later, an NYPD blue-and-white pulled up and a pair of uniformed officers hopped out. Erin directed them into the house. Vic was still working on Miranda. Ferris stood close by, talking quietly. Erin knew she'd be no use there; they had plenty of willing hands. She returned to the curb and waited for the ambulance.

The EMTs were a touch early, arriving in nine minutes flat. Dispatch had given them a pretty good idea what to expect, so they waded in with their stretcher and portable defibrillator. In a matter of moments, they had Miranda on the stretcher and on her way to the ambulance, and then to the hospital. The ambulance drove off, lights and siren engaged, which told Erin everything she needed to know. When the paramedics rushed to the hospital, it meant they thought they might be able to save the victim, but it'd be touch-and-go.

Erin watched the EMTs depart. Then she turned back to the house. Ferris was standing in the doorway. The old man's eyes were hollow and haunted.

"I'm so sorry," Erin said. It sounded as cheap and useless as every time she'd said it.

Ferris stepped back. "Come in," he said. "Please."

Erin went in. Vic was in the hallway with the two Patrol cops. They were discussing who would need to file the incident report.

"You were the responding officers," one of the uniforms was saying.

"We weren't on the clock," Vic said. "You guys were the official presence."

"He's right," sighed the other uniform. "Anyway, these guys are Manhattan Major Crimes dicks. This happened in the One-Twenty, and it's not a major crime. Far as I can tell, it's not any crime at all. Heart attack lands it in our territory."

"You guys can fight about the paperwork later," Erin said in an undertone. "Don't you have any respect?"

"Sorry, Detective," the younger Patrol cop muttered. "Just trying to get things straight."

"I guess we better get your statements, then," the other uniform said.

"It looks like a heart attack," Vic said. "I mean, we didn't see it happen, but the symptoms match. She was standing in that room over there. Then she walked down this hallway. A couple seconds later she gave a yell and fell down. We found her lying on the floor, unresponsive."

"Was she showing any symptoms?" the older Patrol cop asked.

"No," Ferris said. "We were just talking and sharing a drink after dinner."

"Did you eat in, or go out?" the uniform asked.

"Out."

"Where?" Erin asked, forgetting for a moment that she wasn't conducting the interview.

"Ruddy and Dean," Ferris said. "On Richmond Terrace."

"That's a good joint," the younger cop said. "Best steak you can get on the Island."

"When was this?" the older cop asked.

"We got there around seven," Ferris said. "I guess we left at eight-thirty, give or take a few minutes. We came back here for a few drinks and some conversation. We've been here since."

"Did she complain of any pain?" the older cop asked. "Numbness, tingling, anything like that?"

"No," Ferris said. "Miranda takes good care of herself. She goes running four or five days a week. She's in excellent health. I can't imagine she was having heart trouble."

"Could've been something she ate," Vic said. He looked at the floor, where Erin's fallen drink had soaked into the carpet. "Or maybe drank."

"Any allergies?" the older cop asked Ferris.

"She's mildly allergic to shellfish," Ferris said.

"Ruddy and Dean's has clams and oysters on the menu," the younger cop said.

"She didn't eat clams," Ferris said. "She had the chicken parmesan. I had the filet mignon."

"Could've been the whiskey," Vic said.

"The lights," Erin said.

Everyone turned to her. "What about them?" the younger cop asked.

"They flickered," she said. "At the same time she cried out."

"What's that got to do with anything?" the younger cop asked.

"Nothing," the older one said. "This is an old house, I bet it's got old wiring."

"No, she's right," Vic said. "It was at the exact same time."

"What're you saying?" the older cop asked. "A ghost popped out and scared her into a heart attack?"

"I'm just saying it'd be one hell of a coincidence," Vic said.

"Miranda doesn't scare," Ferris said, giving a severe look to the Patrol cop. "She's got guts to spare, young man."

"And there was a smell," Erin said.

"Yeah, I noticed that," Vic said. "Smelled like ozone to me."

"Like what?" the younger cop asked.

"Ozone," Vic repeated.

"You mean that stuff everybody was worried about a few years back?" the Patrolman asked, raising an eyebrow. "With that hole in it? Over Antarctica or something?"

Vic snorted. "Yeah, that stuff," he said. "But it's also the smell you get after—"

"A lightning strike," Erin finished.

"You're saying our girl got hit by lightning?" the older cop asked, skepticism all over his face. "Indoors?"

"Of course not," Vic said. "That would've blown a hole right in the ceiling. Plus, our victim would have burns all over her. I'm just saying what it smelled like."

"A lightning bolt could send you into cardiac arrest," Erin said. "But we would've seen the flash."

"Hold on," Vic said. "You're not seriously suggesting she *did* get hit by lightning, are you? Indoors? On a clear night? Without a clap of thunder?"

"No," Erin said. "But something electrical, maybe."

"I don't see any exposed wires," the older cop said, looking up and down the hallway.

"Electricity can arc," Vic said. "But you'd need a contact point, a conductor. Looks like it's mostly wood and plaster here. That doesn't conduct electricity. The only metal I see is the light fixture, the hinges, and the doorknob."

"Yeah," the younger cop said. He reached for the doorknob.

"Don't!" Erin shouted.

"Huh?" the Patrol cop said. A half beat later, Vic grabbed him, flinging him across the hallway. Vic was considerably larger than the Patrolman. The little guy bounced off the wall and came back with his face turning an angry red and his fists coming up.

"Take it easy," the other cop said, putting an arm across his partner's chest. "He just did you a favor. Might've saved your life. You gotta think before you grab, kid."

Erin was already studying the doorknob, keeping a careful distance. "Where does this door lead?" she asked Ferris.

"Bathroom," Ferris said.

"Is there a window?" Erin asked.

"Yes, but the glass is frosted," Ferris said. "For privacy, you understand." Erin marveled at the way the judge was holding onto his composure. He was a tough old man, that was for sure. He had to be worried sick about Miranda, but he knew he couldn't do anything for her right that moment, so he was trying to help the police. They really didn't make them like that anymore.

"We can't open the door," she said.

"Why not?" the younger cop asked.

"Because it could be booby-trapped," Vic said. He'd come to the same conclusion as Erin. "Maybe it was a one-time thing, but maybe not. I'm not touching it."

"Me neither," Erin said.

"We could call an electrician," Vic said doubtfully.

"I was thinking Skip," Erin said.

"He's Bomb Squad," Vic said. "This isn't really his thing."

"A booby-trap with an electric component?" she said. "I'm thinking it'll be right up his alley."

Ferris laid a hand on Erin's arm. "Excuse me," he said.

"What is it, judge?" she asked.

His jaw worked, as if he had something tough and chewy lodged in his mouth. "You've been present at a number of situations like this one, I imagine," he said at last.

"Yeah," she said.

"What would you say Miranda's chances are?"

Erin had given false hope to a lot of worried friends and family members over the years. Ferris was looking at her steadily, his eyes dark and serious. She knew she couldn't bullshit him.

"Not great," she said, shaking her head. "If they could restart her heart with a shot of adrenaline on the way to the hospital then... maybe. But I don't think so."

"What about the defibrillator?" Ferris asked.

"No good," Vic said. "That'll only help if your heart's still beating, but out of rhythm. If it's a straight flatline, I don't care what they say on TV, a shock won't restart it. CPR and adrenaline, that's your only shot."

Ferris nodded. "Then I'll stay here and do what I can to help you," he said. "But I should call Miranda's mother. What hospital are they taking her to?"

"The University?" Erin guessed.

"Probably," Vic agreed. "It's closest."

Ferris started to leave, then paused. "My phone lines are down," he said. "Might I borrow one of your mobiles?"

"My what?" Vic said.

"He means your cell," Erin said.

"Oh, right." Vic handed it over. "Don't you have a cell,

judge?"

"I do, somewhere," Ferris said. "But the battery is probably dead. I don't like carrying the thing. It's bad enough being shackled to a landline. Carrying a phone in my pocket makes me feel like a convict dragging a ball and chain. Now, if you will excuse me for a few minutes?"

"Don't open any doors," Erin said. "Or touch anything metallic. And stay close. We don't know what's safe around here."

Ferris nodded and moved back to the den, poking at Vic's phone.

"That guy's as tough as they come," Vic said in an undertone. "If Zofia had gone down like that, I'd be climbing the damn walls."

"Miranda's a friend, not a lover," Erin whispered back.

"You sure about that?" Vic asked.

Erin didn't answer.

"Because if they're involved, that makes him a person of interest," he went on. "As you know perfectly well. And if he wanted her out of the way, then that'd explain why he's so calm."

"He's a judge!" Erin hissed.

"And no judge ever committed a crime," Vic scoffed.

"I'm calling Skip," Erin said. "And I think you're nuts. Ferris would never kill anybody."

"You're talking about the guy with a twelve-gauge in his umbrella stand," Vic reminded her. "Most people say they'd never kill anyone. And most people find out they're wrong if the shit hits the fan."

*   *   *

Skip Taylor was far too upbeat and cheerful to be a combat

veteran who dismantled bombs for a living. He was calm and careful around explosives, but otherwise he seemed like a remarkably ordinary young man, round-faced and friendly. He showed up in record time, hopping out of the Bomb Squad van less than twenty minutes after the call had gone out. He walked up the driveway with his bag of tools in hand and three technicians tailing him.

"You got here fast," Erin said.

"We were already on the Island," Skip said. "Some idiot called in a bomb threat at Miraj. That's the Islamic school just down the way. I knew there wouldn't be a bomb, but the religious thing makes it a possible hate crime, and we've got to roll on every call no matter what. You know how it is. Ninety-five percent of our calls turn out to be nothing. You're lucky we got done making the sweep right before you called."

"How'd you know there wasn't a bomb?" Vic asked.

"There's never a bomb when there's a threat," Skip said. "Bombers don't want you finding their bomb before it goes off. What'd be the point of that? Nah, this was just some limp-dick Christo-fascist loser trying to make a statement. We could've used your dog, Erin. Would've made the whole thing go faster. I keep telling them, we need a sniffer K-9 attached to my squad full-time, but I guess they're all guarding Yankee Stadium or some shit. What've we got here?"

Erin explained what had happened. Skip listened carefully. He asked Ferris a few questions about the house's power grid, to which Ferris knew only some of the answers.

"Okay," Skip said when she'd brought him up to speed. "First thing we're going to do is cut the power to the house. Cobb, you want to fetch some lights from the van? Easiest way would be the fuse-box. Any closed doors between us and it?"

"The basement door," Ferris said. "But I opened it just a little while ago. That's where I keep my distillation setup."

"It still might've armed in the meantime," Skip said. "We'll shut the juice off at the street."

"Don't you think you're overreacting a little?" Vic asked.

"Would you take a piss on the third rail if a guy you just met told you it was safe?" Skip replied. "We're doing this one by the book."

A few minutes later, after Skip and his team had set up three big battery-powered floodlights around the bathroom door, the bomb tech went back out to the utility box on Ferris's lawn. Then all the lights in Ferris's house, with the exception of the team's floods and the fire in the den, went dark. Erin and Vic had fetched their flashlights, in case they were needed. They flipped these on.

Skip walked into the pool of glaring blue-white light around the bathroom, pulling on a pair of heavy work gloves and putting on a helmet with a built-in lamp. He took a little plastic gadget out of his bag and pressed it against the door.

"What's that?" Erin asked.

"Ammeter," Skip said. "It measures electric current. I know I cut the power, but somebody may have gotten cute with a capacitor and it might still have some kick in it. Okay, looks like we're good. This is the most trouble I bet you've ever seen a guy take just to go to the john."

"Most of the guys I know don't even put the seat down," Erin said, drawing a chuckle from Skip.

He finally reached out and turned the knob, giving it a light push and stepping back and to one side. Nothing happened. Skip flicked on his headlamp and went in. The others stayed outside; it wasn't a big room and nobody wanted to get in his way.

"I see your problem," he said almost immediately. "Someone want to come take a look at this? It's safe, don't worry."

Erin joined him, easing around him. He closed the door

most of the way and pointed.

"See that coil?" he asked. "The one that's wrapped around the doorknob on the inside?"

"Yeah. What's it made of?"

"Copper, from the look of it. And there is a capacitor, like I thought, but looks like it burned out when it gave our victim her jolt. This was a one-shot weapon. They plugged it into the wall outlet right there. No anti-tampering measures. I can just pull the plug."

"How'd it get installed?" Erin asked. "Did the perp go out the window after he put it in place?"

"I doubt it," Skip said. "What'd be the point? All he'd have to do is close the door without touching the knob. Just grab it around the edge and swing it shut on the way out."

Erin nodded, but she played the flashlight over the window just in case. "It's not latched," she said, surprised.

"Wonder why," Skip said. "It's been cold at night. I doubt our homeowner has been cracking his windows."

"We can ask him," Erin said. "Judge Ferris?"

"Yes?" Ferris said. He was right outside.

"When's the last time you opened the bathroom window?"

"I don't open the ground-floor windows."

"Would you have left it unlocked?"

"Never. It's wired into my alarm system."

"What sort of system do you have, sir?" Skip asked.

"LifeShield," Ferris said. "All the windows and doors are wired into a burglar alarm."

"Second-story, too?"

"Yes."

Erin was impressed. Most people didn't bother to wire the upper floors.

"Somebody's tampered with it," Skip said. "See there, by the frame? Looks like they cut this window out of the network.

They'd have to have done that from the inside."

"Who's been in this house within the past day?" Erin asked Ferris.

"Miranda and me, of course," Ferris said. "And Roy Bean."

"Roy Bean?" Skip asked.

"His dog," Erin said.

"And the telephone repairman," Ferris said. "I told you about him."

Everyone looked at him. "Did you get a look at his credentials?" Erin asked.

"No," Ferris said. "I may have made a foolish assumption. My phone stopped working and the gentleman showed up a short while later and said he was here to figure out the problem. I let him in without a name, and with a bag full of tools."

"That was understandable," Erin said.

"I'm not some senile pensioner, Detective," Ferris snapped. "I'm a sworn member of New York's judiciary. I've presided over cases in which con men take advantage of senior citizens to invade their homes and rob them blind, or murder them in their own living rooms. I knew better than this, and Miranda paid the price. Damnation."

"That's a little harsh," Erin said. "Would you know the telephone guy if you saw him again?"

"I never forget a face," Ferris said grimly.

"We can sit you down with a sketch artist. Would you be willing?"

"More than willing." Ferris's anger was cold and contained, but Erin could feel it radiating off the old man.

"I guess we can call this a homicide," Vic said.

"Definitely," Skip said.

Chapter 3

"This was supposed to be a routine paperwork run," Lieutenant Webb said. "Now we're talking about someone assassinating a judge?"

"Sorry, sir," Erin said. "Thanks for coming down so late."

It was almost midnight. The CSU guys were bagging evidence in the bathroom and dusting for prints. Webb had been home when Erin had called him. Now the Major Crimes Lieutenant was on scene, tattered trench coat and all, looking like he'd much rather still be in bed.

"If I'd wanted a nine-to-five job, I wouldn't have put on a shield," Webb said wearily. "I've had later nights. But I'm missing my beauty sleep."

"That's okay," Vic said. "Your beauty was a lost cause anyway."

Webb gave him an unamused look. "Where's the judge?"

"Which one?" Vic asked.

"Ferris went to the hospital half an hour ago," Erin said. "He's meeting Judge Rodriguez's mom there."

"Any word on the victim's condition?" Webb asked.

"They called it just before you got here," Erin said. "I don't think she ever had a chance."

Webb nodded. "That makes it our case, then," he said. "This isn't a garden-variety homicide. This is premeditated murder of a judge."

"It was the wrong victim," Erin said. "I think this was meant to kill Ferris."

"Unless Ferris is our perp," Vic added.

"Why would you say that?" Webb asked sharply.

"Think about it," Vic said. "He's got access to the house. He knew she'd be here this evening. They have a lover's quarrel. He invites her out for dinner to make up, brings her back to the house. He knows the bathroom is rigged. He gives her some booze. Then she needs to go, and bam! If he gets lucky with the autopsy, it'll present like a heart attack. Perfect crime."

"I don't think so," Erin said. "First off, they weren't lovers."

"Says Ferris," Vic said.

"Ferris is almost ninety years old," Erin said. "You really think he's getting it on with a forty-something woman? I know he's in good shape for a guy his age, but seriously?"

"Hugh Hefner's about that old," Vic said. "And he's got all those Playboy models running around. Viagra's one hell of a drug."

"Second, Ferris is a respected member of the judiciary," Erin said, refusing to be drawn into a discussion of the merits of sexual pharmaceuticals. "His record is squeaky clean."

"He's handled dozens of murder trials," Vic argued. "He knows how it's done. And he knows we'd never suspect him."

"You suspect him," Erin said.

"Yeah, but I suspect everybody," Vic said.

"Ferris wasn't nervous when we turned up," she said. "What if one of us had needed to use the can after our drive?"

"There's a pleasant thought," he said sourly.

"And there's plenty of evidence," she went on. "Ferris never could've gotten away with it."

"He would've cleaned up the evidence before anybody searched the place," he said.

"There's the window latch," she said. "And the compromised security system."

"Well, yeah," Vic said. "That way he could pin the whole thing on this mysterious telephone-repair guy."

"You just said he was setting this up to look like a heart attack," she said. "Not a murder. Your conspiracy theories are tripping over each other."

"Okay, Sherlock," Vic said. "What's your theory?"

"I agree, this was supposed to look like a heart attack," she said. "But Ferris was supposed to be the target, and he was supposed to be alone."

"What does being alone have to do with it?" Webb asked.

"I think it was the telephone guy," Erin said. "He cut the phone line so he'd have an excuse to come to the house. And if Ferris didn't die right away, he wouldn't be able to call for help. Our guy probably asked to use the bathroom while he was here. Then he messed with the security system, unlocked the window, and rigged the door. After that, he walked right out like he owned the place."

"Why bother with the window if he wasn't going to use it?" Vic asked.

"Because he was planning on coming back," Erin said. "If Ferris had a heart attack and died alone, he'd have plenty of time."

"Time for what?" Vic asked. "Burglary?"

"Time to remove the evidence," Webb said, nodding.

"Exactly," Erin said. "I think his plan was to circle back during the night and take out the electronics he put in. Then, even if the autopsy showed Ferris had been electrocuted, we'd have no way of knowing how it had happened. His body wouldn't have been moved, there'd be no electronics nearby. It might not be written up as a heart attack, but we'd have no way to prove it was murder, either. It'd be one of those mysterious deaths that find their way into medical textbooks."

"Clever," Webb said.

"So where is this asshole?" Vic asked. "Why didn't he come back?"

"I expect all the police cars and flashing lights spooked him," Erin said.

"But if he could see us..." Vic said.

"Then he was here," Erin finished. "Watching the house. And maybe he still is."

"If this guy's some sort of electronics whiz, he's smart," Vic said. "Nobody like that would be dumb enough to hang around with all these cops."

"Maybe, and maybe not," Webb said. "I think O'Reilly's on to something. A bunch of emergency vehicles might have showed up if his plan had worked. A smart guy would want to know whether he'd succeeded, and would definitely want to know how much we knew."

"Rolf's in my car," Erin said. "Probably going stir-crazy by now."

"Then I think you'd better let him out," Webb said. "Take Neshenko with you. If this guy's a professional assassin, he's likely to be armed and dangerous."

"So are we," Vic said.

*　*　*

Rolf had given up on them, settling down after the sirens had gone quiet. Erin found him curled up in his compartment, fast asleep. But when she popped the hatch, he came instantly awake and alert, springing up and out, stiff-legged, tail wagging. She snapped his leash to his collar and quickly strapped on his K-9 body armor. As she fastened the Velcro, her hand brushed the patch of short hair on his chest that was growing over his most recent scar. He'd taken a bullet a couple of weeks ago, in the course of apprehending a dirty cop. He'd been lucky not to lose his leg, or his life.

She swallowed the lump in her throat and tried to focus on the job at hand. "We don't know what our guy smells like," she said to Vic. "I could take Rolf through the house, but he'd be just as likely to pick up Ferris's smell, or yours, or Rodriguez's. We'll do better searching the woods. You're a tactical guy. If you were watching this house, where would you be?"

"In the trees," Vic said, studying the darkened landscape. "Not too far in the woods. I'd want a decent line of sight. And I'd want to be fairly close to the road, so I could get away in a hurry, but not so close that I'd get spotted by some pain-in-the-ass civilian. I'd be over there somewhere."

He pointed into the middle distance, near the southern edge of Ferris's property.

"Okay, we'll start there," Erin said.

"No flashlights," Vic said. "They'll help him more than us. Keep low, so we're not silhouetted. Go careful and watch your step."

It had been a slow, boring night for Rolf. He was prancing with excitement at Erin's side. Wearing the vest meant he was finally on duty, and he was more than ready.

"Rolf, *such!*" Erin said, giving one of his favorite commands, his "search" order. And with that, the Shepherd was off, snuffling eagerly, the two humans close behind.

The night woods were full of exactly the sort of smells that fascinated a dog: squirrels, rabbits, feral cats, and the markings left by Ferris's Labrador. But Rolf was a professional. He'd been trained to sort through the scents and disregard the normal odors. He'd been ordered to find any humans in the area, dead or alive, so that was what he was doing.

Nobody knew exactly how good a dog's sense of smell was, but everyone agreed it was orders of magnitude beyond anything a human could hope for. Rolf had no need of light. His twitching nostrils gave him plenty of information.

It was impossible to move quietly through the underbrush. Their legs caught on tangled branches. Autumn leaves rustled underfoot. Erin snagged a long, thin bough, which whipped back across Vic's face. He cursed quietly but emphatically.

They finished one pass. Erin turned closer to the road and started back. They'd gone only a few steps when Rolf went rigid. Erin felt the sudden tension on the leash. She knew what it meant; he'd caught a scent.

The dog lunged forward, throwing his shoulders into the motion and pulling Erin with him. She put a foot wrong, stumbled, caught herself, and kept moving. Vic, surprised, hurried to catch up. They made a tremendous racket in the brush, thrashing their way forward.

The sound of their own movements drowned out the other noises in the woods, but Erin caught a hint of motion to her front, a patch of slightly blacker shadow against the darkness. The shape was indistinct, but it was moving rapidly toward the road.

"Freeze!" she shouted. "NYPD!"

She didn't really expect the figure to stop, and it didn't. The dark shape sprang away, running now.

"Show me your hands!" Vic shouted. That was pretty optimistic of him; in the near-pitch blackness, neither of them would have had any idea whether the target was holding up its hands or not.

"I have a K-9!" Erin yelled, trying to keep up with the fleeing figure. "He'll bite you! Stop running!"

The retreating figure burst out of the underbrush onto the shoulder of the road. Clear of the trees, he was able to move much faster than the detectives. As he passed under a streetlight, Erin saw him from behind. He was wearing a camouflage jacket and hat, just like a Green Beret or something. She caught a glimpse of gray hair between hat and collar.

She'd had enough of this. She'd given him an order and a warning. What happened now was on him. *"Fass!"* she snapped to Rolf, unclipping his leash.

The dog sprang into pursuit, loping through the trees like a furry, toothy guided missile. It didn't matter how much head start the man had, or how fast he could run; Rolf was faster. Given ten seconds, he'd be on the man and it would be all over.

But Rolf didn't have ten seconds. The man skidded to a stop beside a parked car, flung the door open, slid into the driver's seat, and gunned the motor. Gravel crunched under the tires and the car roared away into the night. The Shepherd kept running. There was no way he could outrun a car, but he intended to try.

"Rolf, hier!" Erin shouted, calling him back. Rolf turned so abruptly that he lost his balance. He made a complete somersault, scrabbling to regain his footing. Then he was up again and bounding back to her, tongue hanging out, uninjured. She stopped running, standing on the side of the road, watching the taillights disappear into the Staten Island night.

"You get the plates?" Vic asked.

She shook her head. "He'd turned off the plate lights," she said. "Damn it!"

"I'll call it in," he said, pulling out his phone. "Our Patrol boys can get after him. Make and model?"

Erin shrugged helplessly. "Sedan. Dark-colored."

By the time a blue-and-white got underway in pursuit, the mystery vehicle was out of sight, leaving a man, a woman, and a dog standing on a dark road, staring into the night.

*　　*　　*

"We were right," Erin reported to Webb. "He was out there."

"But he got away," Vic said gloomily.

They were in Ferris's den, in front of the fireplace. Skip had turned the power back on, but the fire was warm and comforting. Rolf had taken one look and immediately lain down on the hearth as close to the fire as he could get without bursting into flames. The dog had started panting almost immediately, but stayed right where he was. Roy Bean, Ferris's Labrador, snoozed nearby.

"Something's wrong with that dog," Erin said.

"Maybe he's just lazy," Vic said.

"He's not that old," she said. "You think our guy slipped him a mickey?"

"Wouldn't be the first time," Webb said. "Housebreakers do that all the time, give drugged meat to guard dogs. If he's not dead, he'll be awake soon enough. Don't worry about it."

"Easy for you to say," Erin said, bristling. She liked the average dog more than the average human.

"We've got bigger problems," Webb said. "Did either of you get a description of our guy?"

Erin and Vic glanced at one another. "Too dark," Erin said. "Camouflage clothes and a military-type hat."

"I think he was a white guy," Vic said. "I saw the back of his neck. Gray hair, probably."

"Oh, great," Webb said. "We can put out a BOLO for John Rambo. He'd be about the right age, wouldn't he?"

Their target had been either smart or lucky enough to evade the immediate pursuit. Dispatch had put out the word, and every Patrolman on Staten Island would be looking for a dark sedan with its rear plate lights turned off, but the detectives knew their guy could easily have switched rides by now. Alternatively, Vic said, he could have just re-engaged the lights and driven on his way like any New Yorker.

"I had a shot," Erin said.

"Me too," Vic said. "Why didn't you take it?"

"Because we couldn't be sure," she said. "Maybe it was some idiot trespassing, or just a civilian who got spooked when we started yelling. We can't shoot a guy in the back on suspicion."

"Yeah," he agreed. "But if we'd tagged him, and if we'd been right, we'd have solved this thing right off the bat."

"And if you'd been wrong, you'd have seen your last sunrise as officers of the NYPD," Webb said.

"I know," Vic said. "Why do you think I held fire? I like being a cop."

"We'll have CSU canvass the area where he was hiding," Webb said. "If we're lucky, he left something behind. In the meantime, I want to go through Ferris's caseload."

"Current cases, or past ones?" Erin asked.

"Both," Webb said. "Neshenko, you and I will take prior cases. There'll be more of those. O'Reilly, you look at what he's currently got in front of him. You know what to look for: violent offenders who are currently not incarcerated, known associates with histories of violence, links to major criminal organizations. Prioritize guys with a high degree of technical proficiency. This wasn't some punk with a Saturday-night special. This hit took planning, patience, and skill."

"What about Dylan White?" Erin asked.

Webb blinked. "He's never been in front of Judge Ferris," he said. "Not that I know of."

"I mean, what about our warrant, sir?" she asked. "The reason we came here tonight in the first place."

"Oh," Webb said. "Right. I don't suppose you got Ferris to sign the thing before all the excitement."

"Slipped our minds," Vic said. "Probably on account of the dead judge and the lethal booby trap."

"A murdered judge takes precedence over some numbnuts knocking over cafés," Webb said. "But you're right, we should get that warrant. O'Reilly, go to the hospital and talk to Ferris. Find out about his current cases. And while you're at it, see if you can get his signature on the warrant."

"Yes, sir," she said with an inward sigh. It didn't look to be a pleasant meeting.

"And see if he seems guilty," Vic said. "Watch for shifty eyes and—"

"I know, Vic," she said, cutting him off. "I am a detective, you know."

"I'm just saying, I still like the jealous lover angle," he said.

"I'll keep that in mind," she said.

Chapter 4

There were worse places to be than hospital emergency rooms. Erin had been in many of them; morgues, drug dens, and murder scenes came to mind. But ERs were right up there, especially after midnight. The cold, glaring fluorescent lights and the way they reflected off the sterile, institutional floor tile; the patients, some screaming, some too quiet; the smells of disinfectant and body fluids. She didn't have the slightest idea how her brother, the trauma surgeon, could stand it day after day and night after night.

The University Hospital ER was fairly quiet on this particular night. The waiting room was nearly empty. Erin saw a gaunt, hollow-eyed woman clutching her own elbows and rocking rhythmically in one of the chairs, mumbling to herself. A little boy and his mother sat as far from that woman as they could. The boy was clutching a dishtowel in one hand and a plush dog in the other. The dishtowel was pressed against his leg and was stained dark red. Tears rolled slowly down the boy's cheeks. He couldn't have been more than seven years old. He didn't make a sound.

As Erin and Rolf crossed the room, the boy's streaming eyes tracked them. He stared at the dog and squeezed his toy tighter. Erin thought, *he's not much older than Patrick*, then wished she hadn't. She tightened her jaw and kept moving.

She spoke to the nurse on duty and got directions. She tracked down Judge Ferris easily enough, with the help of another nurse. He was in the hospital chapel with an old Hispanic woman. They were sitting side by side in a pew. Erin and Rolf came up behind them, Erin deliberately scuffing her shoes on the floor so she wouldn't take them by surprise.

They were holding hands, sitting in silence. Ferris turned his face toward Erin. His eyes were dry, his face as stiff and stern as if it had been carved out of one of the pews. The woman paid no attention, continuing to stare straight ahead.

"Judge," Erin said quietly.

"Detective," Ferris said, nodding once.

"I'm sorry to disturb you, Your Honor," she said. "And sorry for your loss. I just have a few questions for you. Is this an... acceptable time?" She had intended to say "good," but caught herself.

"Maria," Ferris said to the woman. "May I have your permission to step outside for a few moments?"

Now the woman did turn toward Erin. She was younger than Ferris, probably in her mid-sixties, but sudden grief had made her features crumble so that she looked as old as the man beside her. She blinked at Erin.

"Maria, this is Erin O'Reilly, of the New York Police Department," Ferris said. "Detective, Maria Rodriguez. Miranda's mother."

"Ma'am," Erin said. "I am so sorry for your loss."

Maria tried to say something and failed. She cleared her throat, licked her lips, and tried again. This time her voice came out, though it was faint and hoarse.

"You are finding out what happened to my Miranda?" she asked.

"Yes, ma'am," Erin said.

"And will you catch the man who did this thing?" Maria asked.

"That's our job," Erin said.

"Then I will pray for you," the older woman said with surprising firmness. "And with God's help, you will succeed."

Erin wasn't quite sure what to say to that, so she just nodded and said, "We'll do everything we can."

Ferris stood up and extricated his hand from Maria's grasp. Then he walked slowly out of the chapel beside Erin and Rolf. Erin was struck by the fact that he didn't use a cane. She didn't know many men his age who walked without additional support. But at this moment, it appeared he could have used it. He was putting up a good front, but he was trembling slightly, whether from exhaustion or emotion.

Erin put out an arm. "I've got you, sir," she said.

He took her upper arm. "Thank you, Detective," he said softly.

They found a pair of chairs in the hallway outside. Ferris sank into one. Erin took the other. Rolf sat beside her chair, keeping his head up and alert. He was still wearing his vest, which meant he was definitely still on duty.

"You ought to have a guard on you, Your Honor," Erin said. "I'll ask Patrol to assign someone."

Ferris waved a hand weakly. "No need," he said.

"I beg your pardon," she said. "But there's absolutely a need. A man out there is trying to kill you. We nearly had him outside your house, but he slipped us. He's in the wind, and we have no way of knowing what he'll try next."

"Do you know how many death threats I receive?" he asked. "Never mind, I was being rhetorical. I've put hundreds of bad men, and more than a few bad women, behind bars. They and their brothers, fathers, and sons have sworn vengeance on me. I made my peace with that a long time ago. I keep my twelve-gauge by the door, I keep my alarm system armed, but I sleep just fine at night. Or I did. I think I may spend the night at the courthouse. I have a fold-out bed in my office. The thought of staying in that house tonight..."

He shook his head sadly. "I never thought Miranda might pay the price for me. That is a terrible thing to bear. It was quick, at least. I hope she felt no pain, just a sudden, blinding flash of white, and then... eternity."

"I hope so," Erin said.

"But that, I suppose, is a question for the theologians," he said. "And one to which we will all, one day, learn the answer. I hope I learn it considerably sooner than you. As to the bodyguard, I suppose you have to do it. If you didn't, and if I was then killed, you would get in trouble, I imagine. Very well, I won't be difficult. Now, to business. You have questions?"

"I need to know about your ongoing cases," Erin said. "Who do you think might have tried something like this?"

"I've been asking myself the same question," Ferris said. "There's the Tarkov case, of course."

"That sounds a little familiar," she said. "I think I saw something about it in the paper."

"Yes, it's been in the news," he said. "Anatoly Tarkov, accused of the rape and murder of a teenage girl. We were set to hear closing arguments tomorrow, after which it will go to the jury who will, barring unforeseen circumstances, find him guilty in approximately the time it takes to boil an egg."

"Would it have been a mistrial if..." she said, her voice trailing off.

"If I had been killed instead of Miranda?" Ferris asked with a bitter smile. "No. The trial would have been adjourned until a new judge was appointed. The same goes for the other cases on my docket, some of which are already known to you. You've heard, I think, of Gabriel Vitelli."

"Angel Face," Erin said, nodding. "He's out on bail, isn't he?"

"He is indeed," Ferris said. "I wanted to hold him without bail, but the case is weak on account of that incident with the state's star witness. I set the bail at five hundred thousand dollars, which of course his father put up immediately. Fifty thousand cash, the rest secured through the normal channels."

"Do you think Old Man Vitelli could have done this?" she asked.

"Maybe. But to what point? I half expect the District Attorney to drop the charges altogether, in which case, of course, there would be no reason to attack me."

"Anyone else?" she asked.

"I think you should talk to my secretary," he said. "Julia Lockhart. She will have the files on all the cases I have pending. I would suggest you go to the courthouse in the morning, or whenever you arise after this late night. I may see you there."

"You're going to work? After what just happened?" Erin was appalled.

"Indeed I am," Ferris said. "Detective, I will not allow thugs and hooligans to dictate the process of the law. As long as I am breathing, you will find me performing my duty. And on that subject, I believe you had a warrant for me to examine?"

"What? Oh, yes, that's right, sir," Erin said, startled by the sudden shift. "Here it is."

Ferris perused the document, nodding to himself. "Yes, this all appears to be in order," he said. "Here is my signature. Will there be anything else, Detective?"

Erin hesitated. Ferris raised one white eyebrow.

"Go on," he said. "Spit it out."

"I have to ask," she said slowly. "Was anything... going on between you and Miranda?"

"I've known Miranda Rodriguez since she was twenty-six," he said. "That's sixteen years. I was her mentor and her friend. She was a lovely woman; intelligent, capable, and fearless. I loved her *as a daughter*. Do I make myself clear?"

"Yes, sir. I'm sorry."

"Don't be sorry," he said. "If you didn't ask, you wouldn't be doing your job. And if you have any further questions that will aid your inquiries, don't hesitate to ask them. Don't spare my feelings. I gave up worrying about those decades ago. But for now, I should go back to be with Maria. She was so proud of Miranda."

Ferris shook his head sadly. "What a damned awful waste," he said, half to himself. "It should have been me."

*　　*　　*

The original plan had been to swing by Ferris's house, get the warrant, and knock on Dylan White's door. They'd hoped to find evidence he'd been robbing Manhattan cafés. The crimes had been brazen, committed in broad daylight by a lone gunman wearing a ski mask. Major Crimes had gotten involved after an off-duty Patrolman had swapped bullets with the guy. Most criminals couldn't shoot worth crap, but it turned out this guy could. The cop had come off worst and had ended up in Bellevue Hospital with two bullets in his chest. He'd survived, but the incident had kicked the so-called "Coffee Bandit" up the NYPD's list of priorities.

In spite of the blatant and obvious style of the robberies, it hadn't been easy to put a face on their perp. He operated alone, which meant they couldn't identify and lean on his associates. He stole only cash, small unmarked bills which were impossible to trace. Someone had come up with the bright idea of seeding coffee shops with plainclothes cops. That had seemed like a brainstorm until someone else had realized there were over three thousand cafés in New York. The NYPD didn't have anywhere near the manpower they'd need to cover that much territory.

Eventually, Erin, Vic, and Webb had gone to a brute-force tactic. The security camera footage of the café where the gunfight had taken place showed their guy shooting it out with the poor Patrolman. It was Vic's opinion that the Coffee Bandit moved and handled his weapon like a man with military training. Erin figured their guy was too smooth and calm to be new at his job. So they'd gotten a list of every single guy in New York City who'd been charged with armed robbery and cross-checked it with military service records.

They'd come up with a ridiculous number of names. But it had been a start. From there, they narrowed it down based on height, build, and ethnicity. This led to four frustrating days knocking on doors and interviewing young, angry, violent men, many of whom probably belonged back in prison, but none of whom were a perfect fit.

Dylan White was a guy who'd had a tough life. Born in Queens, he'd gone into the system as a kid, bouncing back and forth between abusive foster homes and juvenile detention facilities until he turned eighteen, at which point an exasperated judge offered him a choice between three years in the military and five years upstate. It was just after the start of the Iraq War and America needed more bodies to throw onto the battlefield.

White, to his own surprise, discovered he was good at being a soldier. He deployed to Iraq, won medals, got promoted. In a supreme irony, due to lack of oversight by the Pentagon, he wound up serving as a military policeman guarding an armory.

Unfortunately, it also turned out he'd been selling US military equipment, up to and including heavy machine-guns and rocket launchers, on the local black market. That resulted in a dishonorable discharge and fifteen months in the stockade. So he'd ended up in prison after all.

After his release, White found himself back on the New York streets with no money, no prospects, and nothing to show for the past four years except the best training Uncle Sam could provide. Accordingly, he got his hands on some cheap guns and started robbing armored cars. Unfortunately for White, one of those cars was crewed by a pair of fellow combat veterans, one of whom was an expert pistol marksman, and the two vets weren't about to let their cargo get ripped off without a fight.

The following seven years provided White with a lot of time to think about what he'd done wrong. The first three months were the longest, while he lay in the prison infirmary waiting for his shattered leg to heal from the three bullets his former comrade had pumped into it. He decided his biggest mistake had been to try for too much money at once. The big money had protection. It'd be smarter to hit smaller, softer targets.

It was the wounded leg that got Major Crimes onto him. Erin and Vic, after hours scrutinizing grainy surveillance video, concluded that while their guy was experienced and moved like a pro, the slight hitch in his stride indicated an old injury to the left leg. That drained their pool of suspects to a manageable depth. An interview with White's former cellmate at the Attica Correctional Facility proved fruitful enough for them to finally take the name to Judge Ferris.

The case had been a headache, but it was almost over. Erin had been looking forward to getting the goods on White and, with any luck, locking him up again. All that had just gone out the window with Miranda Rodriguez's death. Now they had a judge's assassination to solve, and another judge to protect. A disgraced ex-soldier with a bad leg just wasn't that important anymore.

With those thoughts running through her head, Erin left Judge Ferris at the 120th Precinct, in the care of a bunch of cops and a police sketch artist, and headed off Staten Island. It would be an hour or two until Ferris finished the facial reconstruction with the artist, so she thought she could get more done from her home station. Erin didn't know where their suspect had gone, but if she could figure out who he was, she might be able to guess where he'd go next.

Chapter 5

"You know, once upon a time, I *liked* working the dog watch," Erin told Rolf.

The Shepherd raised his head and blinked sleepily at her. He decided it was a false alarm and lowered his chin back to his paws.

Erin, Vic, and Webb were back in the Major Crimes office on the second floor of Precinct 8. It was after two in the morning, the very worst time of night. Erin was on her third cup of strong coffee. Vic was slowly building a wall of empty Mountain Dew cans on the edge of his desk. And poor Lieutenant Webb was stuck without his drug of choice, a prisoner of New York's anti-smoking regulations. All three were staring at their computer screens. None of them were happy.

"How many guys has Ferris locked up?" Vic said in hopeless tones.

"Either too many, or not enough," Webb said. "Depending on how you look at it."

"We've got hundreds of suspects," Vic said.

"I don't suppose any of them are electricians?" Erin suggested.

"Unfortunately, they're not filed by technical skills," Webb said. "These aren't resumes and we're not a job fair."

"So it's manual search," Vic said.

"You have somewhere you'd rather be, Neshenko?" Webb asked.

"Somewhere? Anywhere."

Erin concentrated on Ferris's current cases. She knew he had several pending, but she was planning to ask his secretary about those, as he'd advised. The Tarkov case was promising. Anatoly Tarkov was a nasty piece of work, a level three sex offender with a liking for teen girls. Tarkov had an airtight alibi, however; he was being held at Riker's Island until his trial was over. Unless he'd somehow managed to slip out of the prison and down to Staten Island without anyone noticing, he couldn't have broken into the judge's house.

He did, however, have a brother. Andre Tarkov also had a record, and it was a very interesting one.

"I think maybe I've got something," Erin said.

"Give me good news," Webb said.

"Andre Tarkov," she read aloud. "Twenty-eight. Convicted as an accessory in two of his brother's sex crimes. Looks like he drove the van his brother used for his... you know."

"Activities," Vic said sourly. "So?"

"He also used to work as a custodian at a high school," she said. "He got fired and arrested when they found out he'd installed hidden cameras in the girls' locker room. He had the camera feed set to go to his brother's laptop."

"And this guy's not in prison now?" Vic said. "Seriously? Why do we even wear shields?"

"He was," she said. "He just got out last month. He didn't actually participate in any of the assaults."

"He just filmed them," Vic said. "What a guy. So why are we looking at this sleazebag?"

"Think about it," she said.

"If he could set up spy cameras, and if he could get through building security, he's got technical skills," Webb said, nodding.

"And his complicity in his brother's crimes suggests the two of them are pretty close," Erin said.

"In a creepy-ass way, yeah," Vic said.

"So how do you think Andre felt when he got out of prison and found out his beloved brother was about to spend the rest of his life behind bars?"

"Motive," Vic said.

"And he's out there somewhere right now," Erin said. "That gives him opportunity."

"Let's get Ferris's sketch and compare it to this mope's mugshot," Webb said. "With any luck, they might vaguely resemble one another."

Vic and Erin nodded agreement. They knew from unhappy experience that sketches were only a match for real faces about thirty percent of the time. Even the notoriously unreliable polygraph tests were more solid than that. But it was better than nothing.

"Put him on the board," Webb said. "And keep looking. There's bound to be somebody else out there who doesn't like our judge and knows how electricity works."

About an hour later, the ancient fax machine in the corner came reluctantly to life, coughed, and spat out the sketch from the artist on Staten Island. The Major Crimes detectives clustered around Erin's computer as she called up Andre Tarkov's mugshot.

"Might be him," Vic said. "And might not."

"The jaw looks right," Webb said. "But the nose is a little iffy. Tarkov's nose is straight. This one is crooked."

"I wish he wasn't wearing that baseball cap," Erin said. "We can't see the hairline."

"That was probably deliberate," Vic said. "A hat can really screw up identification."

"And the mustache, of course," Webb said. "The facial hair is all wrong. But that's easy for a guy to change. I guess we'd better pick him up. I'll put out a BOLO."

"I'll go get him," Vic said with enthusiasm.

"According to his PO, his address is Brooklyn," Webb said. As a convicted felon, Tarkov needed to file his whereabouts with his parole officer. "And you've been up for something like twenty straight hours. I'll put together a warrant and have ESU grab him and bring him in."

"I never should've transferred," Vic grumbled. "ESU has all the fun."

"As I recall, it wasn't entirely up to you," Webb said. "Your CO was glad to see the back of you, and I'm starting to understand why."

"Let me go down there," Vic insisted. "I can... you know, liaise."

"Do you even know what that word means?" Erin asked. "Because I've got the feeling you'd translate it as 'put on my tac gear and kick down Tarkov's front door.'"

"That's not what liaisons do?" Vic asked, feigning surprise.

"No," Erin said.

"But then, what about that movie?"

"What movie?"

"*Dangerous Liaisons.*"

Erin and Webb looked at one another. Both of them opened their mouths. Neither was quite sure what to say.

Erin recovered first. "Have you *seen* that movie?" she asked.

"No," Vic said. "Why?"

"I have," she said. "They remade it as *Cruel Intentions* a few years back."

"Oh, that one I did see," Vic said. "That's the one about the guy who wants to sleep with his step-sister, right?"

"Yeah, that's the one."

"Oh. What's that got to do with liaising?"

"Liaison can also mean a romantic encounter," Webb said.

"How come he knows that and I don't?" Vic demanded.

"Because I used to have romance in my soul," Webb said. "And you don't have one."

"I've had way more than one romantic encounter, for your information," Vic said.

"Sorry," Webb said. "I was unclear. I meant you never had a soul."

Erin had the misfortune to be taking a sip of coffee as Webb said that. She spit it halfway across the room.

"That wasn't very nice, sir," she choked out, rubbing the back of her hand across her mouth.

"All right, fine," Webb said. "You can go down to Long Island. But if you're going, so are the rest of us. Someone needs to keep an eye on you."

*   *   *

Getting the warrant required waking up another judge. Ferris couldn't sign it because he was directly involved with the case and therefore needed to recuse himself. However, upon learning their suspect might have killed another judge, the replacement they got out of bed was only too happy to sign.

After that it was time for a trip to Brooklyn. Vic took Webb in his Taurus, while Erin and Rolf rode in her Charger. Traffic wasn't bad at the ungodly hour of 3:30 in the morning, so they made good time, arriving on site before four. It was a three-story brick apartment in a low-rent neighborhood. The streets were deserted. Even the drug dealers had gone home for the night.

Alternatively, Erin thought, maybe the presence of the ESU assault vehicle was putting a damper on the local criminal element. The Lenco Bearcat looked like what it was, which was basically a black-painted, armor-plated military vehicle. The ESU team was clustered around the 'Cat when the detectives arrived, putting the final touches on their loadout.

"Lieutenant Lewis," Webb said.

"Lieutenant Webb," Lewis replied, shaking hands. "Neshenko. O'Reilly. Good to see you again. What're we dealing with here?"

"Just the one guy, as far as we know," Webb said. "Did you get his jacket?"

"Yeah, I looked at it," Lewis said. "You really think this guy rates ESU? He's not a violent offender."

"If we're right about him, he just killed a woman with a booby trap," Webb said. "We have to assume he's got his place rigged. We don't want to just knock on the door."

"Electrified doorknob," Erin explained.

"That's a nasty trick," Lewis agreed. "Okay, here's what we'll do. His apartment's on the second floor, on the back side, so he won't have seen us roll up. I've already got Twig covering the back. We'll have Diaz go to the basement and access the circuit breakers. Once we're stacked up, we'll have him cut the power, just to that unit. That should take care of any electric surprises this jerk may have for us. Then we'll go in with infra-red."

"Where do you want us?" Erin asked.

"I want you and your K-9 right there with my team," Lewis said. "Your dog doesn't care if it's dark or not."

"What about me?" Vic asked.

"Sorry, we don't have any spare NVGs," Lewis said.

"Don't worry," Vic said. "I've got my own." He popped the Taurus's trunk, rummaged around for a moment, and came out with a bulky set of night-vision goggles.

"Don't tell me," Erin said, rolling her eyes. "You got those from some mail-order military-supply store."

"Yeah," he said. "I've been wanting to try them out."

"What *don't* you have in there?" Erin asked.

"A flamethrower," Vic said.

"Okay," Lewis said. "You know ESU protocol. Is this guy likely to be armed?"

"We have to assume so," Webb said.

"Get your vests on," Lewis told them. "We go in five."

Erin strapped Rolf into his K-9 body armor, to the Shepherd's delight. Then she put on her own vest. She had a flutter in her stomach, but she told herself it was probably all the coffee she'd drunk. The ESU guys, in addition to their own vests, were wearing bulky helmets that reminded her of World War II Stormtroopers. The front guy carried a bulletproof shield and handgun. The rest of the team sported assault rifles. One of them handed Erin an earpiece, tuned to the unit's frequency. She pushed it into her right ear. Then it was time to go.

The team made entry through the lobby, which was completely deserted. They brought the elevators down to the ground floor and locked them in place. Then they headed up the stairs. They moved more slowly than SWAT teams did in the movies, taking their time, checking their angles. Nobody wanted to get ambushed.

The second-floor hallway smelled like old cigarette smoke and mildew. The lights were on, but several bulbs had burned out and hadn't been replaced. The ESU team moved with practiced smoothness, taking up position by the door to unit 219. Lewis nodded to the second guy in line, who pulled out a narrow fiber-optic camera.

The man got down on his knees and snaked the tip of the thing under the door. He fiddled with it, looking at the attached monitor. Erin waited, her Glock in one hand, Rolf's leash in the other. Time slowed to a crawl.

The cameraman looked up at Lewis and nodded. He'd found no sign of booby-traps on the door.

Lewis passed on the nod to the front man, who hefted a sledgehammer. This was a no-knock warrant, which Vic joked actually meant you knocked once, but you did it really hard. Since their suspect was believed to be dangerous, and capable of setting lethal traps, they weren't about to give him the chance to set up any surprises.

"Diaz," Lewis said. "You copy?"

"I copy." Diaz's voice crackled in their earpieces. "All set down here. 219, correct?"

"219," Lewis repeated. "Cut power now."

"It's done," Diaz said. The lights in the hallway didn't change. Erin hoped he'd gotten it right.

"Go in three..." Lewis said very quietly into his helmet's microphone.

Erin got set. Vic, beside her, worked his jaw to let out some of the tension.

"Two..."

Erin held her breath. She could feel her pulse in the palm of her hand where it met the pistol's grip.

"One..."

The silence seemed deafening, as if her ears had stopped working. Rolf was watching her, waiting for orders. His ears were perked all the way forward, the dog's whole body rigid. His tail quivered slightly.

"Execute!"

The sledgehammer slammed into the door just over the knob. There was a splintering crash. Some doors were hollow-core and just came apart at the first real impact. This one was sturdy, hard wood. It held together, but the force of the blow tore the lock-plate clean out of the woodwork. The brass plate spun to the floor, screws twisted and bent. The door flew open.

They had no reason to think Tarkov knew they were there, or was even awake. That didn't matter. ESU training was specific on the point; doorways were kill-zones. If you hesitated in a doorway during an assault, you died. The squad poured in fast and hard, clearing the doorway, checking the corners.

The apartment was pitch-black. Erin hung back, letting the guys with the night-vision go first.

"Living room clear!" somebody said.

"NYPD!" two men shouted. "Show me hands! Hands!"

"Bathroom clear!" someone else called.

"Bedroom, give me two!" Lewis said. A moment later the reply came from two voices in near-unison.

"Bedroom clear!"

"K-9!" Lewis called.

That was what Erin had been waiting for. She reached down and unsnapped Rolf's leash.

"*Such!*" she told him. It was his search command, not an attack order. From the sound of things, either Tarkov was hiding, or he wasn't home. In either case, Rolf wouldn't need to bite.

The K-9 dashed into the room, snuffling eagerly. More ESU chatter filled the airwaves as the team secured the apartment. For about a minute there was a flurry of activity. Then there was a lull.

"Okay, we're clear," Lewis said.

"Lights?" someone asked.

"Negative," Lewis said. "There still might be traps. Go to flashlights. Secure NVGs."

A moment later, three flashlights clicked on and Erin could see again. She found herself looking at a dingy, cheap bachelor pad. It was dirty and there was an unpleasant, sickly-sour smell in the air that she associated with Vice busts from her Patrol days. She hauled out her own flashlight and played it around the living room. The beam caught Vic standing in the middle of the room. He had one hand on his hip, the other holding his rifle on his shoulder.

"What a dump," he said. "And a washout. Nobody's home."

"Talk to me, people," Lewis said. "What've we got?"

"I got a bunch of electric shit in the bedroom," one of the ESU guys called. "Wires and cables and God only knows what."

"What's it for?" Lewis asked.

"Hell if I know. I don't even know how to program a VCR."

"Hopper, nobody uses VCRs these days," another guy said. "I don't think they make them anymore."

"Like I know that," Hopper replied.

"Don't touch any of it," Lewis said. "We'll have Skip Taylor go through this whole place, top to bottom."

Vic knelt down and peered at a cheap-looking desk in the corner of the living room. "I got a computer!" he announced.

"Laptop or tower?" Lewis asked, hurrying over. Erin joined them.

"Tower," Vic said.

"Leave it alone," Lewis said. "It could be rigged."

Rolf returned to Erin's side, whining unhappily. He hadn't found anybody, which meant he might not get his chew-toy. This was a disaster.

"Good boy," she told him, rubbing his ears. He wagged his tail and leaned into the contact. As Erin stroked her dog's head, she moved the flashlight slowly around the room. All she saw was peeling wallpaper and pin-ups.

"Bunch of dirty DVDs on top of the tower," Vic reported. "*College Coeds Gone Crazy* or some shit like that. This place is sketchy as hell. The CSU guys are gonna want full-body condoms for their own protection. Maybe they can put on those suits they wear when they're searching meth labs."

Erin nodded absently. Hanging around places like this was part of the Job. Vic knew that perfectly well; he just liked to gripe. Everyone had their own ways to cope with the everyday unpleasantness of wearing a shield. Dark humor was the most common method.

She paused. There was a glitter of reflected light from the corner of the room. Her flashlight had caught something shiny, near the ceiling.

"What's that?" she said aloud.

Vic crossed the room and craned his neck, shining his own light up at the thing.

"It's a camera," he said. "In the air vent. That's not creepy or anything."

"Son of a bitch," Lewis said. "Everybody out! Now!"

"Wait, what?" Erin asked. It had been a long night, she was tired, and she didn't have the slightest idea what was going on.

Vic grabbed her by the shoulder and bodily hauled her out of the room. Before she quite realized what was going on, Erin found herself back in the hallway. Her feet were barely touching the ground as the big Russian hustled her down the hall away from Unit 219.

Rolf didn't understand either. If some random guy had manhandled Erin like that, the K-9 would have taken him down. Rolf knew Vic and liked him. Vic had once given him a burger in a pub after he'd been an especially good boy. But Rolf still figured he ought to tell him that nobody did that to his partner. He started barking fiercely, hackles bristling.

"Put me down!" Erin snapped indignantly. "What's the matter with you?"

Vic let go. "Keep moving!" he said. Behind them, the ESU team was rushing out of the apartment.

A few more steps got them to the stairwell. Finally, when the heavy fire door swung shut behind the last ESU man, Vic relaxed a little. Rolf was staring balefully at him. The dog's hackles were bristling.

"I think we're okay," Vic said.

"Agreed," Lewis said. He keyed his radio. "Dispatch, Lieutenant Lewis, ESU. Get me the Bomb Squad."

"Vic," Erin said. "If you don't start explaining, I'm going to kick your ass."

"Think about it," he said. "We're looking for a guy who likes to set traps, a guy who killed a judge. We find a camera in a deserted apartment. Suppose that guy's in his car a couple blocks away, watching us bust down his door on live video. Suppose he's got a remote detonator sitting in his lap. What if he's just waiting for us all to settle in before he pushes that big red button?"

Erin went cold all over. She should've seen it herself. "We have to evacuate the building," she said. "Now."

Chapter 6

"I like when a girl calls me back," Skip Taylor said. "But twice in the same night is kind of clingy, don't you think?"

"Ha ha," Erin said. "You'd better go in, before we have a riot on our hands."

The street was full of irritated, groggy New Yorkers. Nobody was happy to be dragged out of bed before the sun came up. The grumbling had started immediately and had only quieted down when the Bomb Squad van arrived with its crew of increasingly tired demolitions experts. Now the apartment's residents were speculating about possible terrorist plots. The half-dozen Patrol officers on scene looked almost as edgy as the civilians.

"This the same guy as at the judge's house?" Skip asked as he hefted his equipment bag.

"We think so," Erin said. "We already cut the power, but he might have a cell-phone detonator or something. He's got a hidden camera in the vent in the living room, to the left of the door."

"Gotcha," Skip said. "Murray, turn on the jammer."

The technician climbed back into the van and came out with something that looked like a black suitcase bristling with antennas. He fiddled with it for a moment.

"How do we know if it's working?" Erin asked.

Skip winked and held up a finger.

A murmur of confusion spread through the crowd. It rapidly turned to outrage and anger. About half the people on the street were holding phones. All of them were now staring at their devices, shaking them and cursing.

"It's working," Skip said with a grin. "Between that and the power cutoff, we should be safe from anything remote. Let's get to work, people."

Erin, Vic, and the ESU team watched the Bomb Squad go into the building.

"You couldn't pay me enough to do that," Officer Parker said.

"You knock down doors all the time," Erin said. Parker was the biggest guy on the team, the one who usually swung the sledgehammer. His head was shaved smooth and he had an impressive array of scars and tattoos.

"I don't mind if they shoot at me," Parker said. "Bombs and booby traps are cheating."

"Yeah," Vic said. "How come the criminals never play fair? We've got the Patrol Guide. They ought to play by the rules."

"If they played by the rules, they wouldn't be criminals," Erin said.

"This suits me fine," Officer Carnes said, leaning back against the wall. "I'm pulling overtime and I get paid no matter what."

They waited. It was a long wait. A news van arrived with an indecently chipper blonde reporter. She wanted a statement from the officer in charge.

Lewis gave her a polite smile. "The NYPD doesn't comment about ongoing investigations, ma'am," he said.

The blonde answered his smile with a flirtatious one of her own. She was very pretty, in an overly made-up way, and in spite of the cold night air, the top two buttons of her blouse were unfastened.

"I have a source who says the Bomb Squad was deployed to Staten Island earlier tonight," she said. "And a judge was taken to the University Hospital."

"The NYPD doesn't comment about ongoing investigations, ma'am," Lewis repeated in exactly the same tone of voice.

She pouted prettily. "Come on, Lieutenant," she said. "There has to be something you can tell me. Maybe over a cup of coffee?"

"I'm on duty, ma'am," Lewis said.

The blonde looked past him for easier targets. Vic met her gaze with a scowl so fierce that she blinked. Then she saw Erin and Rolf. Her eyes lit up.

"Oh, crap," Erin muttered. But there was nowhere to hide.

"Detective O'Reilly, isn't it?" the blonde said, extending a hand. "Holly Gardner, Channel Six News. Let me say, I am a huge fan of yours! You've brought tremendous visibility to women in law enforcement, and I think that's amazing. You helped foil that attempted bombing at the Civic Center. Is there another bomb here?"

Erin hated dealing with reporters. She glanced around at the other cops. They were watching her with interest. She cleared her throat. Holly Gardner leaned forward eagerly.

"The NYPD doesn't comment about ongoing investigations, ma'am," Erin said with slow, malicious relish.

Holly's face fell. She turned back to her camera crew, taking a moment to adjust her blouse and her hair. She'd think of something to say, Erin thought sourly. They always did.

"It'll be getting light soon," Vic said once the reporter had moved off.

"Yeah," Erin said.

"If that jerk comes home, he'll see all this and head for the hills," Vic predicted.

"I know. But what else could we do? We can't risk blowing up the ESU team." But Erin had been thinking about this. "Rolf didn't alert," she added.

"So there aren't any bombs?"

"Not that he could smell."

Vic nodded. "On the other hand, we've got no proof this guy uses bombs. It was an electric device at Ferris's house."

"Right," she said.

"It could be some other kind of trap."

"Definitely."

"So I guess we have to do it this way," he said gloomily.

The front door of the apartment swung open. The Channel Six cameraman locked on immediately. Skip Taylor walked out. He was carrying a cardboard box piled high with what looked like a tangle of cables.

"Clear," he said, walking up to the waiting officers.

"Good," Erin said. "So we can let these folks back inside?"

"Sure thing. No traps in the place. Just a whole lot of camera equipment."

"Okay, people!" Vic shouted. "It's all over. You can go home now!"

The bathrobe-clad New Yorkers began moving back toward the building. They still weren't happy, but the complaining was minimal. A couple of older gentlemen even paused to thank Skip before going inside.

"So, what do you think?" Erin asked him. "Same guy?"

Skip shrugged. "I need to take a closer look at this stuff," he said. "And I really ought to show it to one of our computer guys.

I'm a hardware geek, not a hacker. But from what I can see, he had the whole apartment rigged with spy-cams. I found five."

Vic made a face. "Even the bathroom?"

"Especially the bathroom," Skip said. "Found a waterproof lens right under the shower head."

"What a creep," Erin said.

"What do you expect?" Vic replied. "This guy and his brother are sex offenders. You don't get in the registry for helping old ladies cross the street."

"But you didn't find anything that matched the wiring at Ferris's place?" Erin asked.

"I'll turn this stuff over to CSU," Skip said. "They can answer that better than I can."

"Excuse me, sir?"

Holly Gardner was there, wavy blonde hair, bright smile, and all.

"Hi," Skip said, giving her an appreciative look.

"Holly Gardner, Channel Six," she said, offering her hand.

"Skip Taylor, Bomb and Arson," Skip said, shaking hands.

"What can you tell me about the bomb threat tonight?"

"What bomb threat?" he replied.

Erin made meaningful eye contact with him and drew her finger across her throat in an emphatic gesture.

"I mean, no comment, ma'am," Skip muttered, looking away. "It'll all be in my report."

"We done here?" Vic asked Erin in an undertone, as the crestfallen reporter went looking for bystanders to interview.

"Pretty much," she said. "CSU needs to go over the apartment, see if Skip and his guys missed anything. But I don't think you and I need to be here."

"Good. I'll go back to the Eightball and crash on the couch until it's time to go to work."

"I'd better go home and change, maybe grab a quick shower," Erin said. "Then I'm going to hit the courthouse. I need to talk to Ferris's secretary."

*   *   *

The last time she'd been to court, Erin had gotten in a gunfight. She had no reason to expect danger this time around, but she hadn't known it was coming the first time, either. Therefore, when she and Rolf climbed the courthouse steps, both of them were wearing their body armor.

She reluctantly handed over her weapons at the security checkpoint, showed her shield to the courthouse cops, took a moment to examine the map in the lobby, and headed to Ferris's chambers.

"How come everybody else has offices but judges have chambers?" she asked Rolf as they went upstairs. "What's the difference?"

Rolf didn't have an opinion. Neither did the cops guarding Ferris's door.

A secretary was sitting in Ferris's outer office. She was a middle-aged, competent-looking woman, conservatively dressed. She reminded Erin of her high school math teacher.

"Good morning, Officer," the secretary said, taking in the shield at Erin's belt, the bulk of the Kevlar vest under her coat, and the police K-9 at her side. "How may I help you?"

"Julia Lockhart?" Erin asked.

"Yes, that's my name," Lockhart said. She was a little startled. "If you have business with Judge Ferris, he's actually sleeping in his office right now. He left instruction not to be disturbed unless it's important. He had a late night."

"I actually came to talk to you," Erin said.

"Why? Is something the matter?" All the horrible possibilities flitted behind the secretary's eyes. A police officer only sought you out if there was a problem, and usually that meant an accident or a crime.

"You're fine, ma'am," Erin said hastily. "Judge Ferris gave me your name. He said you could help me with something."

Lockhart's face cleared. "Of course," she said briskly, putting on her business manner.

"I need to know about the judge's current caseload," Erin said.

"Certainly," Lockhart said. "What's this about?"

"It's an ongoing investigation, ma'am."

Lockhart nodded and poised her hands over her keyboard. Then she paused. "You're not investigating the judge, are you?" she asked.

"Why would I be doing that?" Erin couldn't resist asking.

Lockhart frowned. "If that's the case, ma'am, I'm going to need to see your credentials," she said coldly.

"It's nothing like that," Erin assured her, unclipping her shield and presenting it. "Detective O'Reilly, Major Crimes. Somebody tried to kill your boss last night. I'm trying to figure out who."

"Oh God," Lockhart said softly, putting a hand to her mouth. "Is Howard... the judge, I mean... is he all right? There was a note on the door when I got here, so I thought he was okay, but..."

"Yes, he's fine," Erin said. "But one of his friends was killed." There was no harm in sharing what would be in the newspapers.

"He's not injured, is he?"

"No, he's fine, like I said. We need to know who might have wanted to hurt him."

"Yes, of course." Lockhart started typing with rapid, practiced fingers. "There's the Tarkov case. That's currently taking up most of his time. And he'll be hearing the Vitelli case shortly."

"I know about that one," Erin said grimly. She ought to; it was her squad that had arrested Gabriel Vitelli for murdering his fiancée.

"He hears a very large number of misdemeanor cases," Lockhart went on. "And there's quite a few that are pled out. I can print you a list."

"Please," Erin said.

"Do you know if he'll be working today?" Lockhart asked. "The Tarkov trial is supposed to be going on, but if there was an assassination attempt, isn't it unsafe for him to be here?"

"I think we'd need to tie him down to stop him," Erin said, smiling. "He's a tough old guy and he doesn't scare easy."

"No, he doesn't," Lockhart agreed.

"Besides, the courthouse has metal detectors and armed guards," Erin said. "And that's on top of his security detail. He's safer here than almost anywhere else he could be."

"That's true," Lockhart said. She blinked as a thought struck her. "You'd like the threat folder, wouldn't you?"

"Absolutely," Erin said, feeling foolish for not asking for it herself. Of course a public figure like Ferris would receive the usual assortment of loony death threats. She blamed her lack of sleep for her sluggishness.

"We give those to the courthouse officers," Lockhart said. "They ought to have them downstairs."

"You handle Ferris's mail, don't you?"

"Yes."

"So you sort out the threats?"

"Yes." Lockhart shuddered slightly. "It's not the most pleasant part of my day. Some of those people are really awful. They say the most terrible things."

"Did you see any recently that stood out to you? Anything that seemed particularly serious, like they might actually go through with it?"

"No. I don't really read them. As soon as I can tell what they are, I set them aside. One of the officers told me not to handle them more than I had to. I think he was thinking about fingerprints, but I can't help thinking of anthrax and that sort of thing. I know we have scanners to check for that, but seeing the way some of those people think and talk... it's dreadful."

"I'll bet," Erin said.

Lockhart's laser printer hummed and ejected several sheets of paper. Lockhart scooped them out of the tray, neatly snagged them with a binder clip, and handed them to Erin.

"There's everything on the judge's agenda," she said. "Is there anything else I can do to help? I'd like to do what I can. Howard isn't just a boss. He's a friend."

"Thanks," Erin said. "He's my friend, too. I'll let you know if there's anything we need."

*   *   *

Erin knew it was probably a waste of time looking through the threat folder. While it was illegal to threaten a judge, plenty of people did it. Reasons ran the gamut from anger at a particular case's outcome, to attempts to influence an ongoing case, to paranoid-schizophrenic craziness regarding imagined persecution. The whole thing would probably just add up to a lot of white noise that would interfere with their efforts to find the genuinely dangerous person who'd killed Miranda Rodriguez.

All the same, it was a necessary step. A detective had to waste some time if she wanted to generate leads. It was just part of the Job. So Erin took Rolf back downstairs to talk to the courthouse cops.

She'd just gotten to the ground floor and was looking around for the best person to talk to when she heard a familiar voice.

"Detective O'Reilly!"

The distinctive Jamaican inflection of her name identified the speaker before she'd finished turning toward him. Kingston Schultz was coming toward her, hand outstretched, teeth flashing a broad smile across his dark, handsome face.

"Morning, King," Erin said, shaking hands with him. They had a complicated but mostly-amicable relationship stemming from Schultz's work as family lawyer for the late Mafioso Matthew Madonna and his son.

"It is so good to see you," Schultz said. "What brings you to court today?"

"Working a case," she said. "What're you doing here?"

"A preliminary hearing for Alfredo's little problem," Schultz said. His smile faded. "I am attempting to obtain a change of venue."

"What's wrong with this place?" Erin asked, gesturing at the building around them.

"Nothing," Schultz said. "Except for the little fact that my client was nearly murdered the last time he set foot in it. Until I can be assured of his personal safety, Mr. Madonna does not step into this courthouse."

"I thought he'd already be sentenced," she said. "Wasn't that supposed to happen a couple weeks ago?"

"I obtained a postponement," Schultz said. "But every clock eventually strikes the hour."

"Are you in contact with Alfie?" The Madonna kid had gone off the grid after members of his organization had tried repeatedly to kill him. Alfie was facing parole-violation and weapons charges, which could, and probably would, send him back to prison.

"Of course," Schultz said. "I am his attorney, after all. Do you have a message for him?"

"I mostly want to know if he's okay."

"He is quite well, thank you."

"He pleaded not guilty, didn't he?"

Schultz shook his head. "He pleaded *nolo contendere*, Detective. He did not contest the charges, but that is not the same thing."

"So he shows up for sentencing, and then what? He goes to prison, right?"

Schultz gave her a pitying look. "I have been investigating Vincenzo Moreno's business, as have you, I think."

Erin glanced around. Nobody was within earshot, but she was still nervous. "King, I don't think we should be talking about this here," she said.

"I have a couple of names for you," Schultz continued. "Nina Bianchi and Carlo Peralta. Do they mean anything to you?"

"Yeah," Erin said. "Nina died in prison."

"She was *murdered* in prison," Schultz corrected. "By a mutual friend."

Erin nodded, recognizing that was as close as Schultz was going to come to identifying Vinnie the Oil Man. "And what about Carlo?" she asked.

"I would think you would be informed of his fate," Schultz said.

She felt a chill. "You don't mean..." she began.

"If Alfredo goes to prison, he will be dead within a week," Schultz said flatly. "*That* is what I mean, Detective. You know as well as I that certain men have influence which reaches into our houses of correction."

"Then why bother with the change of venue?" she asked.

"It is my job to safeguard the interests of my client," he said. "This includes keeping him alive as long as possible. Hence both the postponement of sentencing and the requested change of venue. I would like him to survive the legal process, at the very least."

"We can protect him," she said.

"How?" Schultz asked with a sad smile.

"We can get him special treatment behind bars," she said. "Or we can try again with WitSec."

He was already shaking his head before she finished. "He will never accept that bargain," Schultz said. "Not after what happened to him the last time."

Erin didn't have an answer to that. A Federal Marshal had been critically wounded and two hitmen had been killed at the supposedly safe house where they'd stashed Alfie.

"You and I both know the only way this ends," Schultz said more quietly. He stepped in close, pitching his voice very low. "As long as Vincenzo Moreno is breathing, the boy will never be safe."

Chapter 7

Erin took a step back, staring at Schultz. "What did you say?" she demanded, moving to the side of the corridor. He came with her, staying only a couple of feet away.

"I stated a fact," Schultz said, unruffled. "Don't act so shocked, Detective. I know what you are."

Her mind reeling, Erin found herself thinking, oddly, of undergarments. Specifically, she thought of her special brassiere, the one with the recording device sewn into its underwire. Unfortunately, that was a bra she was not currently wearing. She hadn't expected to need to record a conversation about the Mafia here in the courthouse. But here she was, talking with a lawyer about assassinating a Mafioso.

"That's not so easy to do," she said carefully, reminding herself that she was playing a role. Schultz thought she was a contract killer. It was all part of the undercover game.

"Do?" Schultz said with feigned surprise. "Nobody suggested a course of action. All I did was identify a threat to my client. Do you disagree?"

"No," she replied. "You're absolutely right about that. What do you want from me?"

"I heard about that unfortunate schoolteacher," Schultz said. His eyes flashed. "From what the papers said, the poor woman's parents had to bury a closed casket. There was scarcely enough of her to identify."

Erin stared at him, trying to hide her revulsion. Kingston Schultz had always been polite and pleasant toward her. It was so easy to forget he worked for the Mob, as had several generations of his family.

"I never thought you would be squeamish," Schultz said. "And I thought we were friends."

"We are friends," she said, forcing the words out through a throat that was suddenly very dry. She remembered her lessons in Mob etiquette; when in doubt, go on the offensive. "If you don't like the way I do business, that's your problem. But I get results. I think maybe I need to talk to Alfie."

"Toward what end?" Schultz's voice was sharp with sudden suspicion.

"Look, if I wanted him dead, he'd be dead," she said. "I'm the reason he's still alive. You have to trust me, at least a little."

"I will see what I can do," Schultz said. "I will be in touch. Good day, Detective."

He offered his hand again. She shook it mechanically. "Good luck with the change of venue," she said.

"Thank you," he said, showing his brilliant, charming smile again, as if they'd been talking about nothing more unpleasant than the weather. "It would have many advantages."

"Besides keeping Alfie alive a few more days?"

"A new judge might be no bad thing."

"What did you say?" she asked for the second time.

He blinked, surprised. "You know perfectly well who Judge Barberis answers to," he said. "And you know that releasing Alfredo upon recognizance was no act of charity. Detective, what is the matter? You have the look of a woman who has seen ghosts."

"It was something you said," she said absentmindedly. "You'll see what I'm thinking about. It'll be on the news if it isn't already. Thanks for your time, Mr. Schultz. I'll catch you later."

She left the mystified lawyer standing there in the courthouse hallway. It was time to get back to her own business.

*   *   *

"Any luck?" Vic asked when she walked into Major Crimes.

"Depends on what you mean by luck," Erin said. She detoured into the break room and emerged a moment later with a cup of coffee and half a donut. Rolf had the other half of the donut in his mouth. The Shepherd trotted happily beside her, plopped down next to her desk, and started eating.

"I swear those aren't good for dogs," Vic said.

"They're not good for us, either," she said with a shrug. "He's a police dog. Of course he gets donuts."

"You're holding some papers," Webb observed. "So you came back with something."

"I've got about four dozen death threats," she said, holding up the documents. "And Judge Ferris's schedule."

"That's worth looking into," Webb said. "Neshenko, do you want to start weeding out the crazies?"

"That's simple enough," Vic said. "They're all crazy. Sane people don't threaten a judge."

Webb gave him a look.

"I mean yes, sir, I'd be happy to, sir," Vic grumbled.

"That's the spirit," Webb said.

"Any word on our BOLO for Tarkov?" Erin asked.

"Nothing," Webb said. "He's probably gone to ground somewhere. He'll turn up. We're not talking about a criminal mastermind here."

"Right," Erin said. "Vic, while you're checking out the nutjobs, how about seeing if any of them have military training? I mean, like Special Forces stuff. They teach those guys how to set booby traps, don't they?"

"Yeah," he said. "I'll look. You remember the last combat engineer we dealt with? He almost blew up One PP."

"I don't think any of us are going to forget that," Webb said sourly. "Good thought, O'Reilly."

Erin nodded, but she was already thinking about something else. She was remembering what Kingston Schultz had said. Carlo Peralta was one of Vinnie the Oil Man's muscle guys, a Mob assassin. He'd tried to kill Alfie Madonna and had succeeded in killing Alfie's dad, but had taken a bullet to the gut in the attempt. He'd refused to flip on his employer, and Erin had last seen him in protective custody at the hospital. She'd never followed up with him, mainly because she knew it would be a waste of time. Carlo was either too loyal or too scared to turn on his boss.

She went into the prisoner database and punched in his name. The computer informed her that he was currently incarcerated at Riker's Island. This was typical for guys awaiting trial on serious criminal charges in New York. But if that was the case, why had Schultz mentioned him?

Maybe the database needed to be updated. Erin picked up her phone and called the prison. After wasting a couple minutes sorting through the automated menu, she reached a bored-sounding Corrections Officer.

"Riker's Island," he droned. "Visiting hours are Wednesday and Thursday, one to eight PM, and Friday through Sunday, seven to two."

"I'm Detective O'Reilly," she said. "Major Crimes. Shield four-six-four-oh. I'm calling to check on the status of one of your prisoners."

"Go ahead, O'Reilly," the man said, sounding marginally less bored. "Name?"

"Peralta," she said. "First name Carlo. Awaiting trial on Murder One, plus assorted other charges."

"Just a sec," he said. She heard keyboard keys clacking in the background. "Okay, I've got your boy here. Looks like we had him in the infirmary, recovering from GSW."

"That's right," she said, noting his use of the past tense. "Where is he now?"

"Dead."

"When? What happened?"

"Overnight. Don't think they've done the autopsy yet. Hell, the body won't even have cooled off. I don't know what happened. Let me call down to the infirmary."

"I'll hold."

Erin drummed her fingers on her desk and waited. A few long minutes later, the CO came back on the line.

"I'll patch you through to the doc," he said. "I think he can explain it better than I can."

There were a few seconds of silence, then the phone rang. A new voice came on.

"This is Doctor Birch. Is this Detective O'Reilly?"

"Yeah. I understand Carlo Peralta was killed last night?"

"I wouldn't put it that way, Detective," the doctor said. "I haven't nailed down a specific cause of death. He may have passed of purely natural causes."

"Natural causes? He was shot."

"Yes, I know that," Birch said, speaking slowly, as if talking to a dull student in class. "I meant that there may be no further contributing factors. Peralta was recuperating from a life-threatening injury. Complications are hardly unusual."

"What did kill him?"

"As I just told you, Detective—"

"Yeah, I know you haven't done the autopsy yet," she interrupted. "If you had to guess."

His exasperated sigh was clearly audible. "I don't like to guess in matters of medicine, Detective. But if you insist, it is my opinion that he suffered an air embolism, resulting in a fatal stroke."

"How does that happen?"

"It's a common symptom of decompression sickness," the doctor said. "But given that the patient was not doing any deep-sea diving, that's unlikely. A much more likely possibility is the accidental introduction of air into his circulatory system via syringe, IV, or catheter."

"Accidental," she repeated flatly.

"I don't like your tone, Detective," Birch said. "I understand you are conditioned, by your profession, to presume homicide as a cause of death. But Peralta was on a great many medications. He had numerous injections, an IV drip, and a catheter. Any one of these could have caused the embolism."

"So even if it was deliberate, it'd be impossible to prove?" Erin asked.

"I'm afraid so. Now, was there anything else? I'm a busy man."

Erin considered a few choice replies, but discarded them. "Can you forward the autopsy results to me once you've completed your inquiry?" she asked as politely as she could.

"I'd be happy to," Birch said, with an unspoken coda that he'd be even happier if his answer would shut her up and get rid of her.

"Thank you," she said. "Have a good—"

The phone beeped in her ear as the call disconnected.

"—Day," she finished.

"What was that all about?" Vic asked.

"Remember our old pal Carlo Peralta?" she asked.

"What, the Mafia goon that killed Mattie Madonna and Paulie Bianchi?" Vic said. "The guy they call the Hyena? Of course I remember him."

"He's dead."

"Good."

"No, Vic. Not good."

"Why not? He was a jerk."

"True."

"And a murderer."

"Also true."

"And we didn't kill him."

"Right again."

"So what's the problem?"

Erin shook her head and said nothing. She wasn't comfortable talking about Alfie Madonna in the Eightball, not after a Mafia witness had died in one of their holding cells under suspicious circumstances.

"Was he on Ferris's list?" Vic asked, flipping through the papers. "Hey, yeah, he was! But his trial wasn't set to start until sometime after New Year. You think he had something to do with this?"

She shrugged. Anything was possible. Carlo was absolutely capable of killing a man, or having one killed.

"It's a little weird," she said. "Him and Judge Rodriguez dying almost simultaneously, both in ways that look like natural causes on the surface."

"So now we're looking for two killers?" Webb asked doubtfully.

"Wouldn't have to be," Vic said. "That's the beauty of traps. You don't have to be there when they go off."

"But our guy was," Erin said. "We saw him in the woods."

"But maybe not at the prison," Vic countered. "How'd Peralta get his?"

"The doc said it was an air embolism."

"That's why they squirt that bit of fluid out of their needles before sticking you," Webb said. "To make sure there's no air in the tip."

"Seems like a kind of chancy way of killing a guy," Vic said.

"It's pretty effective," Webb said. "And the nice thing is, it doesn't leave much evidence behind. There's no poison to show up on tox-screenings."

"Yeah, the doc said it would look just like an accident," Erin sighed. "And maybe it was. It could be sheer dumb luck."

"The bastard had it coming," Vic said. "Maybe the universe just decided to get back at him. Karma."

"That's not actually how karma works," Webb said. "Karma is the spiritual balance you carry over into your next life, not your current one."

"You a Buddhist now?" Vic replied.

"I'm an aging cop," Webb said. "I don't believe in anything. But I'll say this much for Buddhists. They've got a fine sense of cosmic justice. If you're patient."

"Hey, Erin, how come you were looking into this Peralta punk, anyway?" Vic asked.

"His name popped out at me," she said, which was more or less true. She'd assumed Alfie Madonna's problems had nothing to do with her own case. But now, she was starting to wonder.

What the hell was going on?

Chapter 8

The rest of the day faded away in a haze of old arrest reports and criminal files. The sleepless night was really starting to catch up with Erin; her head was pounding and her vision was blurring, in spite of the caffeine she kept pumping into her system.

"I'm getting too old for this," she muttered.

"That's my line," Webb said.

"With all respect, sir, you actually got some sleep last night."

"Not very much. I got dragged out of a very pleasant dream to go to a murder scene."

"I don't believe that for a second," Vic said.

"That you two woke me up?" Webb replied. "You'd better believe it."

"No. That you have pleasant dreams."

That actually earned Vic a weary smile from Webb. "Good work today, both of you," he said. "Go home, get some sleep."

"We still need to serve the White warrant," Erin said.

"It can keep until tomorrow," Webb said. "Both of you look like warmed-over death."

"You sure know how to make a girl feel beautiful," Erin said. "What's Ferris's status?"

"He's got a protection detail," Webb said. "Plus a couple Patrol units staying at his house. He'll be fine."

"You sure about that, sir?" she asked. "That guy may make another play for him."

"Only if he's suicidal," Vic said. "This isn't some dumbass action movie. He's not gonna blow through four cops."

"I thought you liked action movies."

"I do. But I can tell the difference between them and reality."

"You're one of those guys who critiques all the weapons and tactics they use in movies, aren't you," she said.

"Hey, it's not my fault they get half the stuff wrong. And actors have the worst trigger discipline in the world, especially the ones from the Eighties."

"I rest my case." Erin stood up. "I'm going to take you up on that offer, sir. I'm out of here."

Rolf bounded up. He still had energy. But then, he'd been napping most of the day.

"Go to bed," Webb advised. "We'll serve the White warrant tomorrow. Get out of here. That's an order."

*   *   *

Rolf had missed his customary morning run, so he was ready for action. Erin, despite her fatigue, looped north to Central Park to take the edge off the K-9. She let him off leash and tossed his rubber Kong ball for him. He chased it down in long, easy running strides, snagging it on the first or second bounce. He bounded back to her and dropped the ball at her feet every time, prancing in front of her, tail wagging, begging for more. It was almost as much fun as running down bad guys.

She indulged the Shepherd for half an hour. Then she headed home. She parked across from the Barley Corner a little after six. Even as she crossed the street toward the pub, she could tell it was hopping with activity. The walls were thick and solid, but she could hear the muffled noise of the crowded bar through the plate-glass windows.

Erin really didn't want to hang around downstairs. The light and noise of the Corner made her headache flare up the instant she opened the door. But she was hungry, too. She figured she'd order a burger and take it upstairs.

Carlyle was at the bar, on his usual stool. He caught her eye and stood to meet her.

"Evening, darling," he said. She could barely hear him over the background noise. "Difficult day?"

"Yesterday was," she said. "If you haven't been to sleep, does a day ever end?"

"How may I be of assistance?"

"Food, a drink, and some peace and quiet."

"Just tell me what you're wanting and I'll fetch it up for you." He kissed her cheek. "I'll not be but a moment."

"Thanks."

Upstairs, she gave Rolf his dinner, then stripped off her work clothes and climbed into the shower for the second time that day. By the time she got out, clad in a dark blue bathrobe with a towel wrapped around her wet hair, Carlyle was in the dining room. A fresh, hot cheeseburger and fries were also waiting there, accompanied by a pint of Guinness. Rolf was lying just far enough away from the table so it didn't look like he was begging, but he was watching the food.

"You're a lifesaver," she said to Carlyle, sliding into the chair he held for her.

"I heard about that business with the judge," he said, sitting opposite her. "I assume that's what you're investigating?"

"What's on the news about it?" she asked.

"The usual," he said. "No comment from your lads, naturally. There's some question as to whether the unfortunate colleen was murdered."

"Oh, it was murder," Erin said between bites. "No doubt about it."

"Poison?" he guessed.

"Electricity."

He raised his eyebrows. "That's an unusual method. How was it done?"

"The bastard hooked up some cables to a doorknob. When she grabbed it, zap!"

"Seems a mite complicated, especially when the killer presumably had access to the premises. Why not a bomb, I wonder?"

"He wanted it to look like a heart attack," she said. "Only problem was, Judge Ferris wasn't alone, and his guest was the one who ended up riding the lightning."

"You're presuming Ferris was the intended target?"

"Of course. It was his house. He's the only one who knew he'd be having company. And it was just dumb luck Vic and I showed up when we did. If it'd gone according to plan, I think he'd have been home alone. The killer hacked the alarm system. We figure he did it so—"

"He could come back and remove the evidence," Carlyle said. "But for that to be the case, he'd have to be watching the place to know when the judge died."

"He was." Erin took another bite of her burger. Rolf watched with silent longing, a thin stream of drool trailing down to the floor.

"But he got away?"

"Yeah. And we didn't get a look at his face. It was definitely a guy, though. I could tell from the build."

"That rules out half the populace, I suppose," he said dryly.

"This guy's weird," she said. "He's not your standard killer. He's methodical. He plans things and he sets them up so they don't look like murder. And Rodriguez wasn't the only one who died last night."

"Who else? I've heard nothing."

"That's because it could've been an accident," she said. "Carlo Peralta clocked out at the Riker's Island infirmary. Air embolism, that's what the doc told me."

Carlyle was rubbing his chin thoughtfully. "It needn't be connected," he said. "But if it is, you know what that means."

"It means the Lucarellis are behind it," she said grimly. "Vinnie the Oil Man, or maybe Old Man Vitelli, or both."

"Aye," he agreed. "But why would they risk killing a judge? It's dreadful for business."

"That's why they wanted it to look innocent," she said. "This wasn't about sending a statement. This was about removing an obstacle. We thought maybe it was the Tarkov brothers. Sex offenders, good with electronics. But that was before I heard about Carlo."

"You shouldn't set too much stock in that," Carlyle said. "What if it truly was innocuous? You'd wind up barking up the wrong tree."

She nodded. "I don't suppose you know any Mob hitmen who specialize in 'accidental' deaths, do you?"

"Not personally," he said. "Evan's lads tend to be a mite more direct in their approach."

"Bullet in the head from behind?"

"That sort of thing, aye." He considered a moment. "Have you heard of a lad called the Janitor?"

"I don't think so. Who is he?"

"Independent contractor," Carlyle said. "And that makes him a rare breed indeed. Freelance hitmen are few and far between."

"Thank goodness for that," she said. "What's his name?"

"I've no idea. As you might imagine, he values his anonymity."

"Then how do you hire him?"

He frowned. "I've never hired a hitman, Erin. You know that."

"You know what I mean," she said impatiently. "How would Evan hire him?"

"The same way most business is transacted these days. Through the Internet. He has various accounts on the Dark Web. As I understand it, you tell him who you want disposed of. Then he either takes the job or declines. If he accepts, he tells you how much. You deposit half the money into the offshore account he designates. Then he takes care of your wee problem and you pay the balance."

"I don't suppose anybody ever tries to stiff him," she said.

"Short-change a murderous lad who specializes in stealthy assassinations?" Carlyle gave her a wry smile. "I don't imagine he has much difficulty collecting."

"What else do you know about him?"

"Nothing whatever. The lad's a ghost. He's good, but he's expensive."

"How much?"

"It varies by the job. I imagine doing away with a judge would run into six figures."

Erin whistled. "If the Lucarellis have a line on this guy, why didn't they use him to kill Teresa Tommasino? Why'd they come to me?"

"What makes you think they didn't ask him first?"

Erin almost choked on the last bite of her burger. "You think they did?" she croaked, groping for the Guinness and gulping down a mouthful.

"Perhaps. I've no notion what goes through Valentino Vitelli's head."

"So that's your theory? Some goddamn Internet ghost is whacking people for cash?"

"It's a possibility, nothing more. You asked if I knew of any lad who could do that sort of thing. He's the first one who came to mind."

"Can you find out anything more about him? Maybe try to set up a meeting?"

He shook his head. "Not a chance, darling. The Janitor's far too wary to agree to a face-to-face meeting with a copper." He winked. "Even a crooked one."

"Maybe you could hire him yourself," she said. "You've got underworld cred."

"And just who would I want him to kill?"

"Vinnie the Oil Man," she suggested.

Carlyle chuckled. Then he stopped laughing. "You're not serious, darling."

"No," she said. "Well, I don't think so. Maybe. It's not like we'd go through with it."

"Erin, once you employ an assassin, you may not be able to stop him."

"Fine. I'll see what I can find out on my end. Could you at least make some discreet inquiries with your associates?"

"I'll do that," he promised. "Anything else you're needing?"

"I could do with a backrub. And maybe a foot massage."

His smile returned. "Now that's easily managed."

Chapter 9

Erin woke to a hand shaking her shoulder. The touch was gentle but insistent. In the background was a repetitive, obnoxious buzzing sound.

She rolled over and planted her face in her pillow. Maybe, if she stayed there, the hand would go away.

It didn't. "Erin, darling," Carlyle said into her ear.

Erin made a muffled noise into the pillow.

"As you wish," he said. "Desperate measures. Rolf, lad? What's the word? *Hupf!*"

Rolf didn't take orders from just anybody. He was trained and conditioned to obey Erin, and Erin only. However, when he was told to do something he already wanted to do, the Shepherd was willing to be a free agent. He was allowed in bed with Erin, had slept beside her plenty of times, so he knew it was okay. Besides, the alarm was going off, and he knew what that meant: the morning run, breakfast, and work. Rolf *liked* the alarm.

Ninety enthusiastic pounds of K-9 scrambled onto the bed. A paw dug into Erin's back, just above her kidney. She grunted. Then Rolf's nose poked her in the ear. The nose was large, cold, and wet.

"Okay, okay," Erin said, throwing an arm around Rolf and dragging him into an embrace that was half hug and half wrestling hold. "I'm up."

Rolf licked her face.

"Apologies, darling," Carlyle said. "But your alarm's been going these past few minutes. I'd have let you sleep, but…"

"Yeah," she said, keeping her grip on the squirming dog. "You're right, I need to get up. I don't usually sleep through the alarm."

"You looked as though you needed your rest," Carlyle said. "How are you this fine morning?"

"Lousy." Her head felt heavy and her tongue was thick and sticky in her mouth. It was like a hangover, but without the fun of getting drunk.

"Are you ill, darling?"

"No." She sat up, gave Rolf an affectionate shove out of bed, and ran a hand through her hair. "I'm just paying for two straight days on my feet. I'll be fine."

"Coffee?" he suggested.

"Coffee," she agreed.

By the time she came out of the bedroom, wearing her NYPD sweatshirt and matching pants, the smell of fresh coffee was drifting out of the kitchen. Rolf bounced beside her, more than ready to get going. He grabbed his leash from the hanger at the top of the stairs and did a happy dance, crouching low on his front paws and wagging his tail, jumping from side to side.

"In a minute, kiddo," she told him. "Stimulants first."

Rolf kept dancing. He didn't need any stimulants.

Erin took a sip of coffee and shivered at the hot, bitter, delicious flavor. She knew caffeine took time to kick in, but she could've sworn she could feel energy flowing into her as she swallowed. Her head cleared a little. She was starting to feel good. They just had to drill down and identify the Janitor.

Maybe he wasn't their guy, but Erin had a hunch Carlyle knew what he was talking about. Once they had him, they could make their way up the chain to find out who'd hired him. Then...

The buzz of her phone knocked her train of thought right off the rails. She set down her cup on the kitchen counter and pulled the phone out of her fanny pack. Lieutenant Webb's name stared up at her from the screen like a bad weather forecast. Thirty percent chance of thunderstorms and a fifty percent chance of impending doom, she thought.

"O'Reilly," she said into the phone.

"How fast can you get to Sunnyside Café?" Webb asked by way of greeting.

"Where is it?"

"Worth Street, just east of Broadway. Across from the Javits Federal Building."

"I'm at home. I can be there in fifteen. What's up?"

"The Coffee Bandit hit it less than an hour ago. Right after they opened."

Erin blinked. "That doesn't make any sense," she said. "They wouldn't have anything in the register at opening."

"I don't care if it makes sense. It happened. Get over here now."

The coffee was no longer making Erin feel good. Her stomach was suddenly sour. "Sir? What happened?"

"We've got a body," Webb said. "I'm already on scene." He hung up.

Erin stared at the phone. "Shit," she said to no one in particular.

"Bad news, darling?" Carlyle asked.

"Yeah. Nothing to do with you or the judge. I need to change." Erin headed back to the bedroom, peeling off her sweats.

Rolf stopped dancing. One paw hung suspended in midair. He cocked his head, his leash still clamped in his jaws. He couldn't believe it. His perfect morning was falling apart.

* * *

The Sunnyside Café was easy to find. Active crime scenes usually were. Erin just zeroed in on the flashing emergency lights and the Patrol cars out front. She recognized Vic's Taurus among the blue-and-whites. She squeezed her Charger into a space next to a parking garage entrance that wasn't really big enough for it. Then she got out and unloaded Rolf.

The Shepherd hopped down happily. He'd missed out on his run and his morning kibble, but he was wearing his vest, which meant he was working, and that was just as good. Maybe the bad guys were still around. Rolf was an optimist.

Erin flashed her shield to the pair of Patrol officers at the door. Inside, she found the café mostly empty. Two more uniforms were standing around, trying unsuccessfully to look busy. A middle-aged man with a graying goatee stood by the front window, hands in his pockets. Webb and Vic were at the counter, talking to a teenage girl clad in slacks and a white button-down blouse. The girl's hair was tied back in a ponytail and everything about her said "waitress."

"Morning, sir," Erin said, joining the other detectives. "What's the story?"

"Miss, if you wouldn't mind going back to the beginning, please?" Webb said to the girl. It wasn't just out of courtesy to Erin. Eyewitness accounts were notoriously unreliable. He'd be comparing what she said to what she'd already recounted, looking for weaknesses or discrepancies.

"Okay," the waitress said.

"This is Monique Nydell," Webb told Erin. "She was working the first shift today."

"I got here a little before six," Monique said. "Jimmy was already here, getting the grill heated up."

"Who's Jimmy?" Erin asked.

"Jimmy Caps," Monique said. "He's the cook."

"Go on," Webb said.

"I got the chairs down off the tables," Monique continued. "And I did the rest of the opening checklist. Do you want to hear all of it? I checked the till, I wiped down the counter..."

"That's okay," Webb said, holding up a hand. "Thank you. What happened after you opened?"

"I unlocked the front door," the waitress said. "And a man must have been waiting outside, because he shoved right in."

"When you say 'shoved,' what exactly did he do?" Erin asked.

"He pushed me," Monique said, putting a hand up to her opposite shoulder. "Right here, with his hand. Hard. I almost fell over. I said something, and that's when he pulled out the gun."

"What did you say?" Erin asked.

"I think I said, 'Hey! What's your problem?'" Monique said. "But then I saw the gun. He pointed it at me. It looked huge."

"Did you see his face?" Erin asked.

"No. Just his eyes. He had on a mask."

"What color were his eyes?" Vic asked.

Monique thought about it. "Brown," she said. "Or something dark. Not blue."

"What about his skin?" Vic asked.

"He was white," Monique said. "And he had on a hat, I think you call it a watch cap. But he had brown hair."

"You saw his hair?" Erin asked.

"I saw his eyebrows," Monique explained. "And he had a tattoo on his cheek. I saw a little ink under his eye."

"Which eye?" Erin asked eagerly. This was a very important detail, the sort of thing cases hinged on.

"Left," Monique said. "I mean his left, not mine."

"Could you see what it was?" Erin asked.

"No. I only saw the tip of it. It was blue. The ink, I mean."

"Can you remember anything else about this guy?" Webb asked. "What was he wearing?"

"A coat," Monique said. "Black. With a zipper and a couple of pockets. And gloves. And blue jeans."

"Did you get a look at his shoes?" Vic asked.

"No. I was looking at his eyes." She shivered. "And his gun."

"What kind of gun?" Vic asked.

"A pistol. Black."

Erin saw Vic trying not to roll his eyes. Vic was a firearms enthusiast, and to hear a gun described as a "black pistol" was, to him, like a racecar driver hearing someone talk about a fast, red car as if that meant something.

"Was it a revolver or an automatic?" Erin asked.

"A what?" Monique asked.

"Did it look more like my gun, or his?" Erin explained, pointing to the Glock at her hip and the Colt Detective Special Webb was wearing.

"Oh." The young woman looked back and forth between the two weapons. "His," she decided. "It had one of those round pieces."

"A revolver," Webb said.

"I guess. Sorry. I don't know about guns."

"What happened then?" Erin asked.

"He told me to shut up and lie down on the floor," Monique said.

"Do you remember the exact words he used?" Webb asked. Erin knew this was important. It was the sort of question she might be asked on cross-examination at trial, and it would help establish her credibility as a witness for a jury.

Monique shuddered. "He said, 'Shut up, bitch. Get down on the ground or I'm gonna shoot you.' So I got down on my stomach and lay there. I didn't look at him after that."

"Why not?" Vic asked.

"I was scared," the girl said. "I thought he'd shoot me. I closed my eyes."

"What did you hear?" Webb asked.

"Jimmy must have come out of the kitchen," Monique said. "Because he asked what was going on. Then the guy shot him."

Erin and Vic exchanged looks.

"He didn't ask for money?" Erin asked.

"He didn't say anything," Monique said. "Just bang, bang, bang."

"Three shots?" Vic asked. "Are you sure?"

She nodded. "It was really loud. Louder than in the movies."

"Then what?" Erin asked.

"My ears were ringing," Monique said. "But I heard a crash. I guess that was Jimmy falling over. Then the other guy went into the kitchen. And I heard Jimmy. He was breathing, but it was all bubbly and weird."

"What did you do?" Vic asked.

"Nothing." Monique hugged herself. "I was too scared to move. I thought... I thought maybe I'd be next."

"What did the shooter do after that?" Webb asked.

"After a minute or two, he came back. I heard his shoes on the floor. He was standing right next to me. I think he was looking at me. I could... I could feel his eyes. You know what I mean?"

Erin nodded.

"Then Jimmy started to say something. But he couldn't really get the words out. He was choking and coughing. I guess because of the blood. Then the guy shot him again. Three more times. And Jimmy... stopped coughing. Then the guy left."

"Did you see him go?" Erin asked.

Monique shook her head. "I think... maybe I fainted," she said quietly. "The next thing I heard was a man asking if I was okay."

"Is that the guy you mean?" Vic asked, pointing a thumb at the man with the goatee.

"Yes. I told him what had happened, and he took out his phone and called 911. Then he stayed with me until the police got here."

"Were you guys the responding officers?" Erin asked the pair of uniforms.

"That's right," said one of them. "We checked the victim. He was gone when we got here. Multiple GSW, center mass. No pulse, no nothing. Poor schmuck never had a chance."

Erin peered over the counter. Sure enough, a body lay on the floor behind it.

"That's a lot of blood," Vic commented.

"If he didn't die right away, his heart would've kept beating," Erin said quietly. "He would've bled out."

"I don't understand why he kept shooting," Monique said miserably. "Jimmy was already hurt so bad."

"Six shots," Webb said thoughtfully.

"You think...?" Vic said, cocking his head at the waitress.

"Yeah," Erin agreed.

"What?" Monique asked.

"I think you're a very lucky girl," Erin said.

"What my partner means," Vic said, "is that our boy might not have wanted to leave witnesses. But a revolver only holds six shots. So he would've had to reload, and that takes time. And he might not have had any spare ammo on him. Which is why he didn't have any for you."

"Oh God," Monique said. She clutched herself tighter and swayed slightly.

Erin caught the indicators and was quick enough to get there before the girl could fall over. She steered Monique to a nearby chair and helped her sit.

"Real smooth, Vic," Erin growled.

"What'd I say?" Vic said, adopting an air of wounded innocence.

"Do you have a security camera?" Webb asked.

"No," Monique said. "Maybe we should. I don't make that kind of decision."

The guy with the goatee had hurried across the room when Monique had started to go down. Now he was there, looking around at the detectives.

"Excuse me," he said. "Is there anything I can do to help?"

"What's your name, sir?" Webb asked.

"Warren Palmer," the man said.

"Did you happen to see any of the incident?" Webb asked.

"No," he said. "I was on my way to get my morning coffee. I saw this young lady lying on the floor. I thought she might have slipped and injured herself. I didn't know there had been a crime committed. I didn't see anyone leaving. I just wanted to help."

"Thank you," Erin said, thinking that Warren Palmer was very far from being a typical New Yorker. "If you wouldn't mind giving a statement to one of these officers, that'd be a big help."

Ordinarily, she would have taken his statement herself. But she was pretty sure he didn't have anything useful to add. All they needed from Mr. Palmer was the bits of his story that would corroborate Monique's account. And Erin had other things on her mind.

"This is weird," she said to Vic and Webb. "This doesn't sound like a stickup to me."

"No," Vic agreed. "Sounds more like a hit."

"Monique, how well do you know Jimmy Caps?" Erin asked, turning to the waitress.

"I've known him as long as I've been working here," Monique said. "Four months, I guess. He always seemed nice."

"What's his full name?" Webb asked.

She had to think about that. "James Caporetti," she said after a moment. "I'm pretty sure that's right. I don't remember how to spell it, though."

"James Caporetti," Erin repeated. Vic made eye contact with her and nodded. They were thinking the same thing. The Coffee Bandit's target hadn't been the Sunnyside Café. He'd come in gunning for Jimmy Caps.

Chapter 10

"This might not have been the Coffee Bandit," Webb said.

"I hope it wasn't," Erin said.

"How come?" Vic asked.

"Because then it wouldn't be our fault."

Vic chewed on that thought for a few moments. They were watching the CSU team work their way through the café. Monique Nydell and Warren Palmer had given their written statements and gone. A crowd of New Yorkers was peering through the front window. The cops were ignoring the rubberneckers.

"No way," was Vic's verdict. "This isn't on us."

"You sure?" Erin replied. "Because the way I see it, if we'd served the White warrant early this morning, he might be behind bars right now and our victim would still be breathing."

"You're making some assumptions, O'Reilly," Webb said, holding up three fingers. "First, you're assuming White is our guy. Second, you're assuming he would've been home when we came knocking. Third, you're assuming we would've gotten enough in our search to lock him up. Stop kicking yourself. The

NYPD doesn't care what would've happened. All that matters is what did."

"And that's weird enough," Vic said. "All the previous robberies, our guy just cleaned out the register and booked it out of there. This doesn't fit his MO."

"White has a facial tattoo," Erin said. She'd memorized his face off the departmental database. "It's a blue teardrop. Prison ink. And he's got brown hair and eyes."

"That sounds like him," Vic agreed. "I say we go get him, the sooner the better."

"I still want to know why he hit this place," Webb said. "And why he targeted this Caporetti character."

"It wasn't a robbery," Vic said. "He didn't ask for money. The register is still there, unopened. He hit the place way too early in the day, before they'd done any business. The till would've been practically empty."

"That doesn't mean he didn't steal anything," Erin said. "Our witness said the shooter went into the kitchen."

"So the Coffee Bandit decided to steal actual coffee?" Vic suggested. "What is he, some sort of caffeine junkie?"

"Maybe," Webb said thoughtfully. "And maybe we ought to run James Caporetti through the computer and see what pops up."

"You think this was some sort of gang hit?" Erin asked. "White isn't affiliated."

"I'm just playing a hunch," Webb said. "Doesn't Jimmy Caps sound a little like a Mob nickname to you?"

"You think a mobster runs a downtown café?" Erin asked.

"I think one of them runs an Irish pub a few blocks south of here," Vic said.

She shot him a nasty look, but couldn't deny he had a point.

"Got a weapon back here," one of the CSU techs said from behind the counter.

"Our guy left the murder weapon?" Webb asked. All three detectives moved toward the counter.

"I doubt it," the CSU guy said. "It's strapped under the countertop. Doesn't smell like it's been fired recently."

"What is it?" Vic asked.

"Looks like a .38," the tech said. He carefully extracted it by thrusting a metal rod into the trigger guard, so as not to smudge any fingerprints. He held up a snub-nosed revolver very similar to the backup gun in Erin's ankle holster.

"Interesting," Webb said.

"Why is that interesting?" Vic asked. "With all the press the Bandit's been getting, I bet all sorts of café guys are packing now. Wait and see, somebody's gonna get excited and blow the wrong guy away by mistake. It'll happen any day now."

"Probably," Webb said. "Does the mounting look like it was recently installed?"

"No," the tech said. "I don't see any sawdust, and the screws aren't fresh. I'd say this has been here a while."

"So our guy had a gun under the counter," Webb said. "He was expecting trouble."

"Fat lot of good it did him," Vic said.

Webb wasn't listening to Vic. "After you're done out here, do the kitchen, too," he told the CSU guy. "And if you can get a sniffer dog in here, do it."

The tech looked at Webb. Then he looked at Rolf. Rolf, sitting next to Erin, scratched his ear with his hind leg.

"Not him," Webb said. "You'll need a narcotics dog."

"Still playing a hunch?" Erin asked.

The Lieutenant nodded. "Let's go out to your car," he said to Erin. "And see how my gambling instincts are shaping up today."

*   *   *

"You should go down to Atlantic City and play the slots, sir," Erin said a few minutes later. On her car's computer screen was a mugshot of the late James Caporetti.

"I drink and smoke," Webb said. "If I went to casinos, I'd be hopeless."

"Three narcotics busts," she said, running down Caporetti's list of accomplishments. "Two weapons charges, three aggravated assaults."

"Sounds like the Bandit did the city a favor," Vic said.

"Known associate of the Lucarelli Family," Erin went on.

"How did I know that was coming?" Vic asked no one in particular.

"This place was a front," Erin said. "What do you bet Jimmy Caps was dealing out of it?"

"You think that waitress chick knew anything about this?" Vic asked. "We could haul her in and lean on her."

"It's worth a try," Webb said. "But I'd guess she wasn't involved."

"I think you're right, sir," Erin said. "She seemed surprised by what happened. But she might've seen something unusual."

"*Now* can we go get White?" Vic demanded.

Webb stood back from the car, pulled out a cigarette, and lit up. He gave it a few thoughtful puffs.

"He could be getting rid of the weapon right this minute," Vic pressed. "Or ditching whatever he stole."

"The drug angle suggests this really might not be White," Webb said. "Try this on: we've got a guy who heard about a big score of narcotics. He decides to rip off the stash. But he's not a complete idiot, so he doesn't want the Oil Man to know who did it. He decides to copy a guy who's already been knocking over coffee shops. That way he doesn't take the fall for it; both the Mob and the NYPD end up looking at the wrong guy."

"You've been hanging around Erin too long, sir," Vic said. "It's making you too complicated. I think you're overthinking it."

"No, I agree, we need to bring White in," Webb said. "I'm just not sure we'll find anything tying him to this."

"But we still think he's the Coffee Bandit," Vic pointed out. "Either way, we're taking a scumbag off the street."

"You just want to knock down a door," Erin said.

"You got a problem with that?"

*   *   *

"Don't you guys ever sleep?" Erin asked.

"Right back at you, Detective," Lieutenant Lewis replied.

The ESU squad had met the Major Crimes unit half a block away from White's apartment. White's place was a fourth-floor studio on White Street, only a few blocks from the Sunnyside Café. The squad were fully decked out in their tactical gear. Vic had borrowed a helmet and clamped it on his head.

"I miss working with you guys," he said.

"Another day, another warrant," Parker said with a shrug. "It's a living."

"Been meaning to ask," Vic went on. "Do you know if I got transferred out of ESU because of something I did, or was it just my big mouth?"

"Wasn't my call," Lewis said.

"I know that," Vic said. "You weren't my CO. But I figured you might've heard something."

"Why?" Lewis asked. "Did it hurt your feelings?"

"A little, yeah."

"Somebody got an Aspirin for Neshenko? The man's suffering."

Vic snorted. "Forget I asked."

"Guys, can we get down to business?" Erin suggested. "Before this jerk kills anybody else?"

"We'll get there," Lewis said. "Don't get jumpy before the game starts."

"This isn't a game!" she snapped.

"What's eating you, O'Reilly?" he asked, surprised.

"What's eating me is a man is dead!" she shot back. "Because we were twiddling our thumbs when we could've been busting this scumbag's sorry ass!"

"We were not twiddling our thumbs," Vic retorted. "We were trying to catch a guy who killed one judge and tried to kill another. Keep your priorities straight."

"There's nothing wrong with my priorities," Erin said.

"Take it easy," Lewis said. "We're going to do this smooth and we're going to do it right. Now, we're assuming he's armed?"

"That's right," Erin said, taking a deep breath and trying to focus. "A handgun that we know about. Maybe other weapons. He's former military."

"All right, team," Lewis said, keying his radio. "Twig, you've got fire escape."

"Copy that, boss," Twig said into their earpieces. "Got it covered." The sniper was across the street, on the roof of a nearby building.

"Our boy's on Four," Lewis said. "Everyone get a good look at his mugshot?"

There was a chorus of agreement.

"By the numbers, gentlemen," the ESU leader said. "On me."

They moved quickly to the apartment building, keeping close to the wall so their target wouldn't see them if he happened to glance out his window. White had a front-facing apartment and you never knew what might happen.

Parker took the lead through the lobby, the team pausing long enough to bring the elevators to the ground floor. They left one man there to hold the elevators and make sure nothing caught them from behind by surprise. Then they worked their way up the stairwell.

An ESU team on full alert was a scary sight. With their black helmets, visors, and body armor, they looked like a squad of faceless, remorseless killing machines. Erin knew it was mostly an illusion. She knew the men under the armor. She also knew that she, personally, had killed more guys than any of the men with her, with the exception of Vic. But the armor and guns weren't just for show. If Dylan White didn't come quietly, they were prepared to put him down.

The workday had started and the apartment hallways were quiet and empty. The team advanced steadily, rifles held tight against their shoulders, ready for anything.

Nothing happened.

They got to White's door, unit 402. Parker hefted his sledgehammer. The rest of the squad stacked up behind him. Erin was second from the rear, Rolf's leash tight in her hand. Rolf was panting with excitement. He knew all the signs. This looked like a situation where he might have the chance to jump on a bad guy and give him what K-9 officers called a "tooth hug."

Lewis nodded to Parker, who banged on the door with his meaty fist.

"NYPD!" Parker shouted. "We've got a warrant!"

They didn't wait for White to answer. The call was just to let him know they were acting in an official capacity. They didn't want him to have the chance to prepare an ambush. Before Parker's voice had finished echoing down the hall, his sledgehammer was on its way to meet the door.

The apartment door was reasonably solid and triple-locked. It didn't make a bit of difference. The hammer hit it with all of Parker's considerable bulk behind the swing. The door flew open, scattering splinters. The man behind Parker leapfrogged him and charged in, AR-15 at the ready. The other ESU guys were right behind him, several men shouting for anyone inside to show their hands and hold still.

Vic was in front of Erin, hustling in on the tails of the other guys. As she reached the door, Erin heard one of the ESU men yell.

"Drop it! Hands up!"

Erin reached the doorway. She saw the backs of several ESU guys. All of them were pointing guns across the room. A man was standing with his back against the far wall. He had something in one hand, brandishing it like some kind of trophy.

"I can't drop it!" the guy shouted. "Or everybody dies!"

"Grenade!" Lewis called, an instant before Erin recognized the thing in Dylan White's hand. It was olive green, about the size and shape of an apple. He wasn't trying to throw it; he was just holding it. The lever that activated the explosive was clamped under his fingers. The firing pin, Erin saw with awful clarity, was nowhere to be seen.

Everybody was talking and shouting at once. Erin, like the others, had a beat on White, sighting down the barrel of her Glock. There was absolutely no doubt they could kill him. But if they took him down, his hand would relax. Then the lever would pop off the grenade, the fuse would start sputtering, and sometime in the next few seconds, everyone in the room would get a face-full of shrapnel.

Bedlam ensued. Nobody fired, but there was a lot of yelling. White looked wildly around the half-circle of cops, searching for some magical way out. He held the grenade in front of himself, as if it could block bullets.

"Fall back," Lewis ordered. He and his men started stepping slowly away from White.

"That's right," White said hoarsely. His face was very pale. "This baby's got a five-meter fatality radius, and if you're within fifteen, you're gonna have a real bad day."

"Let's just calm down, people," Lewis said. His voice was cool and steady. "Nobody needs to get hurt."

"I'm not going with you," White said. His eyes were bloodshot and his hand was shaking. Erin watched the hand, hoping he wouldn't drop the grenade by accident.

"We can talk about that," Lewis said soothingly.

"You want to talk, we can do it through the door," White replied. "Get out!"

Erin saw a card table next to the window. A folding chair lay on the floor nearby. It looked like White had been sitting there when they'd burst in. On the table were a number of things any cop would find interesting. She saw a pistol, a spoon, a candle, a length of rubber hose, and a bag of something that looked like powdered sugar but almost certainly wasn't. She also saw another two grenades.

"We've got a warrant to search your apartment," Lewis said. "Signed by a judge. You want to see it?"

"I don't give a shit!" White said. "And this is your last warning! Get out!"

"Think about what you're doing, Dylan," Erin said. "If you drop that thing, you're right, you can hurt people. But that won't do you any good. It won't get you out of this room."

"Do you want to die?" White demanded, thrusting the grenade toward her.

"Of course not," she said. "And neither do you. Hell, you haven't even had a chance to use that good shit you've got there."

White glanced at the table. That was the opportunity to take a shot, and if he'd been holding a gun instead of a deadman's trigger bomb, Erin might have taken it. But the moment passed. The ESU team had pulled back to the doorway and most of them had withdrawn, leaving just Lewis, Erin, Vic, Parker, and Rolf. That was sensible. If the grenade went off, they didn't want many people in the room.

"That's China white, isn't it?" Erin went on. "High quality."

"What do you know about that?" White asked.

"I know the Oil Man only gets the good stuff," she said.

Recognition sparked in White's eyes. "How do you know about him?"

Erin briefly considered telling him she was Junkyard O'Reilly, the Mob's NYPD assassin. But that wouldn't help the current situation. In fact, telling him that would probably make him think he had nothing to lose, that she'd kill him the moment she had the chance.

"We've been building a case against Vinnie," she said. "If you can give us something we can use, you might be able to make a deal with the DA."

"No way," he said. "You're coming after me for Murder One. I can't get a deal where I won't do time."

"You'll do some time," she agreed. "But you've done time before. You came out again."

It was important in negotiations to make the other guy believe you were telling the truth and to feel like he had a way out, something to live for. Erin tried not to think about what a fragmentation grenade would do to her and Rolf if it went off.

"Listen to me," she went on. "I want to help you, but you have to let me do that."

"Yeah? How you gonna do that?" There was a heavy layer of sarcasm in White's voice, but under it, Erin thought she caught just a glimmer of desperate hope.

"You were in the Sandbox," she said, using the military nickname for Iraq. "I know other guys who were in the shit. I know you went through some stuff there. And I respect that."

"You know some guys, huh? Like who?"

"A former Marine. Scout sniper."

"What's he to you?"

Out of the corner of her eye, Erin saw Lewis give her a slight nod. The Lieutenant knew that the main thing was to keep the man talking. A guy who was talking was a guy who wasn't acting, and as long as they were negotiating, there was the possibility nobody would get killed.

"A friend," Erin said truthfully. "He saved my life, more than once."

"Were you over there, too?" White asked.

Erin thought about lying, but you didn't want to do that if you didn't have to. "No," she said. "I met him after he came back."

"He bring back any of these?" White hefted the grenade.

"I don't know," she said truthfully. "He probably knows where to get them if he needs them."

"You ever see what they do to a guy?"

"I've seen a couple of car bombs," she said. "A bomb's a bad way to go, Dylan."

"Nah," he said. "Just a second and it's all over."

"Maybe," she said. "But sometimes people survive. Suppose you set that thing off and it doesn't kill you. Maybe it blows your legs off, leaves you paralyzed, eating through a tube. You like the sound of that? Think about some of those guys who set off IEDs over in Iraq. You don't want to end up like them, do you?"

She was looking for the fear on his face and she wasn't disappointed. He licked his lips.

Erin risked a slow, easy step toward him. "*Platz*," she murmured, letting go of Rolf's leash. Every part of her wanted to run the other way, but she had to close the distance. The K-9 settled onto his belly obediently, but his head and ears remained fully upright and alert, waiting for further orders.

"It doesn't have to go that way, Dylan," Erin said. "Jimmy Caps wasn't a civilian. The DA's going to know he was a player. This was all in the game, right?"

White swallowed. "Don't mess with me, lady," he said. "You think I won't kill you?"

"You're plenty tough," she said soothingly, taking another step forward. "You don't have to prove anything to me. Hell, the last time you were locked up, I bet it wasn't nothing to you."

"That's right," he said, conjuring up a little pride. "Did my time like a man."

"I bet you could do it again if you had to," she said. Five walking steps would get her close enough to take the grenade, two or three if she had to lunge for it.

"Hell yes," he said.

"You can plead down to second-degree," she said. "Hell, maybe even manslaughter. You could be back on the street in a year if you play your cards right."

That was almost certainly not true. White's best bet was more like five to ten for the shooting, not even counting the drug and weapons charges he'd also be facing, together with the other robberies, but Erin figured this was a time and place to soft-pedal the estimate. Hope was her best currency right now. She took another slow, easy step. She lowered her Glock and slipped it into her holster, trusting Vic and the ESU guys to cover her. She held up her hands, palms out and open.

"It's going to be okay, Dylan," she said. "You can handle this."

"Course I can," he said, thrusting out his chin.

Erin took another step. Three to go. "Why don't you hand me that?" she suggested. "You've still got the pin, right?"

He uncurled the fingers of his free hand. The grenade's pin was looped around his index finger. "Careful, lady," he warned.

"It's all cool," she said. "Your hand must be getting tired. Why don't you put the pin back in it and rest your fingers, if you don't want to give it to me? Otherwise you might lose your grip without meaning to, and wouldn't that be silly?"

That won her a startled but genuine smile. He looked a little sheepish. "Yeah," he agreed. "Wouldn't want to drop this bad boy, would we?"

"Of course not," she said, sliding another step nearer. She could reach out and touch him now if she wanted to.

White slowly moved his hands together. He fumbled the pin a little, and his fingers slipped. Erin's heart stopped. For a second the grenade shifted against the man's sweaty palm. Then he recovered his grip. The little metal pin made a faint scraping sound as it slid home.

"All right," Erin said. "That's good."

"Okay," White said. "Now why don't you—"

Erin's hands shot out. She clamped her left hand over the top of the grenade, holding the pin in. She grabbed his wrist with her right, holding on for dear life.

"*Fass!*" she snapped.

"Huh?" White replied. He didn't understand the word, but then, Erin hadn't been talking to him.

Rolf was up and on the man less than two seconds later, hurling himself across the intervening space and into White. He'd been trained to go for the right arm, but his partner had that arm, so Rolf went for the other one. White slammed into the wall, Rolf's jaws around his left forearm, Erin holding his right. She twisted and pulled. The grenade popped loose from his hand. It was slick with sweat, squirting through Erin's grasp like a wet bar of soap.

The grenade hit the floor, bounced, and started rolling. "Grenade!" Vic yelled, unnecessarily. Erin heard the thump of a falling body behind her. Then Lewis and Parker were there, lending their strength to hold White in place. The three cops and one K-9 easily subdued the man, tossing him to the ground and cuffing him.

"Clear!" Lewis shouted.

Heart hammering, Erin rocked back onto her heels and drew in a slow, deep breath. The other ESU guys poured back into the room. Vic was lying on the floor a few feet away, curled into a fetal ball.

"Vic?" she said. "You okay? What the hell are you doing?"

Vic didn't move for a couple of seconds. Then he slowly uncurled, revealing a small, olive-colored ball under his massive chest.

"Holy shit," she breathed. "You dove on the goddamn *grenade*?!"

Vic got up on his knees. He looked sourly down at the little sphere, as if it might blow up if he turned his attention elsewhere.

"Thought my vest might take most of the blast," he muttered. "Dumbass thing to do. Wasn't thinking."

"The pin was in it," she reminded him. "It wasn't going to explode."

"Slipped my mind," he said.

Two of the ESU guys clapped Vic on the shoulder. One gave a low, appreciative whistle.

"Shut up," Vic said. He picked up the grenade, holding it gingerly.

"You're a hero," Erin said.

"I said, shut up."

"I'm going to tell Piekarski," she promised.

"No you're not," he said. "If she knew I face-planted on a grenade, I'd never hear the end of it. I got a kid on the way, Erin. I'm not supposed to do crazy shit like this. Not a word. Promise me."

She held up her hands. "Okay, okay. I promise."

"You tricked me!" White protested.

"Yeah, sorry about that," she said. "Oh, and by the way, you're under arrest. Obviously."

Chapter 11

"Grenades?" Webb asked. He was leaning against his desk, arms crossed, frowning.

"Three of them," Erin said.

"Military-issue, M67s," Vic added.

"I know this is America," Webb said, "but where in God's name did he get grenades?"

"He's former military," Erin reminded him. "And you may recall, he got his discharge—"

"—for stealing military equipment and selling it on the black market," Webb finished. "Right. I guess he kept a few souvenirs for himself."

"Looks that way," she agreed.

"He's our guy?" Webb asked.

"Absolutely," Vic said. "Everything matches. He's got powder residue on his hands and clothes. That .38 on his table had been fired recently and I'll bet my left nut the bullets they pull out of Jimmy Caps are .38s. Plus, there's the drugs."

Webb nodded. "Did he confess yet?"

"We haven't asked him anything since we arrested him," Erin said.

"Didn't want him to lawyer up," Vic said. "But he probably will anyway. This guy's been through the system a few times."

"He's a lone operator," Webb said. "What do you think he can give us?"

"Someone tipped him off about the Sunnyside being a drug front," Erin said. "I want to take a run at him and see how he tumbled to that."

"I'll come too," Vic said. "He almost blew me up. I want in on this."

"Fine," Webb said. "Have your fun. I'll observe. With the dog."

Rolf gave him a doubtful look.

*   *   *

"I did what you asked," White said the moment Erin and Vic walked into the interrogation room.

"Yeah, and you tried to blow us up," Vic said, slipping easily into his half of their good cop/bad cop routine. "That doesn't buy you a whole lot of goodwill around here."

"I wasn't gonna set it off," White said. "She's the one that knocked it out of my hand!"

Erin slid into a seat on the opposite side of the table from the prisoner. Vic remained standing, leaning his six-foot-three frame over the table. He towered over White, who was five-foot nine and handcuffed in his chair.

"I get it," Erin said soothingly. "You were scared. Why don't you just tell me what happened?"

"You broke my door down and pointed guns at me!" White said.

"I mean at the Sunnyside Café," she said.

"I don't know what you're talking about," was his predictable reply.

"Dylan," she said patiently. "We've got your gun. We've got the drugs. We've got an eyewitness. We know you were there. This is the time to be smart."

"I never wanted anybody to get hurt," he muttered, looking down at his manacled hands. "This wasn't how it was supposed to go."

Erin decided not to mention the cop White had shot during the earlier robbery. "How did you know Jimmy Caps?" she asked instead.

"Heard he was moving some good shit," White said.

"Dealing on the street?"

"No. He was shifting product to some dealers."

"Which ones?"

White swallowed. "The kind you don't want to screw around with."

"Lucarellis?" she asked.

He nodded.

"And you knew he had a fresh shipment." That wasn't a question. They'd found more than four kilos of high-quality heroin in White's apartment.

"You don't know what it's like," White said quietly.

"What do you mean?" Erin asked.

"Needing to get well," he said. "Get your fix. It's the worst thing in the world, lady. You need it so bad it hurts."

He was staring at his arms. Even from across the table, Erin could see the needle tracks inside his elbows.

"How'd you get on the stuff?" she asked.

"Came back from the war," he said. "Saw some shit. Didn't want to remember it. Going on the nod made it better, for a while."

"Oh come on," Vic growled. "We gotta listen to this crap? He feeding us this wounded warrior bullshit?"

"Take it easy, Vic," Erin said, putting out a hand. "We haven't been in combat."

"Like hell we haven't!" Vic snapped. "I've been shot at. With assault rifles! If that isn't combat, tell me what the hell is!"

"My partner's never been hooked," Erin said to White. "He doesn't get it. I've been around addicts. I understand. That's why you were knocking over cafés in the first place, isn't it? To get money for your habit?"

"Yeah," he said. "That's all it was. I needed cash, see? These guys, they don't take Mastercard."

"But then you got a tip on where you could get the real stuff, without going through the middleman," she prompted. "You weren't going to deal it, were you?"

He looked at her like she was crazy. "For what?" he asked. "Money? Lady, I've been paying good money for this shit for a long time. I'm not gonna sell it."

"You were going to use it yourself," she said. "Four kilos pure, that'd keep you happy a long time."

"Yeah," he said. "I figured I could stop with the stickups. That last one with the cop, I never wanted that to happen. He drew on me, lady! I never would've shot otherwise. It was the training, it came back to me, like a reflex. I saw the gun so I shot. You gotta believe me, I didn't want to hurt him. I'm glad he's gonna be okay. Can you tell him that? Tell him I said that?"

"Of course," Erin said, ignoring Vic, who was rolling his eyes so hard he was practically staring at the inside of his own skull. "But I need you to tell me something."

"What do you want to know?" White shivered slightly. Erin figured he was feeling the first pangs of withdrawal. They'd moved a little too fast; he hadn't shot up yet when they'd knocked down his door.

"Who told you about the drugs?"

"A guy I know," White said, his eyes sliding away from hers.

"What guy?"

"Another vet. Like me. But in a wheelchair."

Erin blinked. "This guy wouldn't happen to be called Benny Silvers, would he?"

It was a shot in the dark, but Erin had met a man on her last case who fit White's description. Benito Argent, AKA Benny Silvers, had informed on the Lucarellis before. He'd probably do it again, especially if the price was right.

"How'd you know?" White blurted out.

"Don't worry about that," she said. "What'd he charge you for that information?"

"Nothing!"

Erin shook her head sadly. "Dylan, I can't help you if you won't tell me the truth," she said. "I know how it goes on the street. Nobody gives anything for nothing. Come on, what's the harm in telling me?"

"I'm serious!" he said. "He didn't want a dime! I was talking to him about finding a dealer and he told me about Jimmy Caps. Said he was helping out a buddy, since we'd both been in the Army. Said Jimmy was sitting on a real good stash and I could get my hands on it. But he said I better come heavy, because Jimmy wasn't nobody to mess with, and he'd be packing. He also said Jimmy screwed him over on some product a while back."

"It all makes sense now," Vic said. "Payback's a bitch."

"Benny told me where and when," White said. "I was gonna give him, like, a percentage, but he didn't ask for it."

"Because you were such a good friend," Vic deadpanned. "Because junkies are so generous with their smack."

"Benny's good people," White said sullenly. "He told me to go in early, so nobody else would be there. I wasn't expecting that waitress. I didn't hurt her! You know I didn't!"

"Because you ran out of bullets," Vic said.

"I didn't want to shoot anybody! But Jimmy started making a move. He was going for his gun. I didn't have a choice. It was him or me!"

"Then what?" Erin asked.

White shrugged. "Then I went in the kitchen and there the stuff was, just like Benny said it'd be. I grabbed it and got out."

Erin stood up. "I think that's all we need, Dylan," she said. "We'll need your written statement, of course. Thanks for your cooperation."

"So you'll tell the DA?" he asked. "That I cooperated?"

"Of course," she said. "He may have some more questions about the Lucarellis, but as long as you play straight with him, it'll help you. I promise."

He nodded. "Could you maybe give me a hit?" he asked. "Just one? A little one? I'm suffering here."

Vic's snort was clearly audible.

"I'll do better than that," Erin said. "I'll see you get the best rehab care the State can provide."

"Along with three meals a day and a roof over your head," Vic added. "You've got nothing to worry about for the next ten to twenty years."

*　　*　　*

"Good work," Webb said to Erin when she and Vic joined him in the observation room.

Rolf wagged his tail and nosed Erin's hand. He always thought she did good work.

"What about me?" Vic asked.

"What you were doing wasn't work," Webb said. "It was recreation."

Vic started to give a snappy answer. Then he just grinned. "Fair enough, sir."

"Now we can close the file on this one and get back to the important case," Webb said.

Erin was startled. "Excuse me, sir?"

"You got his confession," Webb said. "Not just for the Sunnyside job, but for the police shooting, too. It should be pretty easy to tie him to the rest of the café robberies. Between the confession and all the physical evidence, we're handing him to the DA with whipped cream and a cherry on top."

"Didn't know the DA was into that kinky stuff," Vic commented.

"I want to go get Benny Silvers," Erin said.

"Why?" Webb asked. "He doesn't matter."

"Of course he matters," she said. "You heard White. Silvers tipped him off to the drugs."

"So?" Webb replied. "He didn't plan the robbery. He didn't break any laws, O'Reilly."

"Are you still pissed at him about that other thing, with Janovich?" Vic asked.

"Yeah," she said. "Aren't you?"

"Well, yeah," Vic said. "But you gotta compartmentalize, Erin. Benny didn't know how things were gonna go down when he tipped SNEU about that deal. I think he's a lowlife junkie asshole, but Janovich wasn't his fault."

"I know," she said. "I just think there's more to this. White said Benny didn't want anything in exchange for his info. I want to know why not."

"Payback," Vic said. "Just like White told us."

She shook her head. "I don't buy it. White was lying in there."

"Now you think he isn't our guy?" Vic's eyebrows tried to climb right off his forehead.

"Oh no, he's definitely our guy," Erin said. "And he told us some of the truth, but not all of it."

"He left out the part where he shot Caporetti again on the way out," Webb said, nodding. "And I still think he would've shot the other witness, if he'd saved a couple of bullets. You have to work around the lies, Neshenko. You've been a detective long enough to know that."

Vic snorted. "Everybody lies to us," he said. "Even innocent bystanders. Why do they have to do that?"

"Guilty consciences," Erin said. "Back when I was in high school, my dad had this way of looking at me. I called it the 'cop stare.' He didn't know I'd done anything bad, but he thought maybe I might've, so he did a sort of open-ended silent interrogation. And every little thing I'd done would come back to me. I'd lie to him as a reflex. And the worst part was, he knew when I did it. Dad dealt with hardcore criminals. His teenage daughter could never put one over on him. He just let me think I was getting away with it."

"Your point, O'Reilly?" Webb asked.

"My point is, Vic's right," she said. "Everybody lies, all the time. Particularly criminals. It's possible White was telling the truth about what Benny told him, but if so, then Benny was lying to him. And if that's true, I want Benny's angle."

"Why?" Webb asked. "What's it got to do with the NYPD?"

"Call it a hunch," she said.

Webb rubbed the back of his neck. "Every time you get a hunch, I get heartburn," he said.

"She's usually right," Vic said.

"I know that," Webb said. "If she was wrong, it wouldn't cause nearly as many problems. Okay, fine. Go track down this Silvers mope and lean on him. But I want you back on the Rodriguez murder as soon as possible. Our killer is still out there."

"Yes, sir."

"I don't suppose you know where to find Benny Silvers," Webb said, sitting down behind his desk with a sigh.

"No," Erin said. "But I know a guy who does."

Chapter 12

"Check it out, Piekarski!" Officer Firelli said. "It's your booty call!"

"You got it all wrong," Vic said. "We came for you, Firelli. My boot, your booty. I got a bet with Erin. She doesn't think I can fit my size fourteen up that tight ass of yours. I'm thinking I can."

They were outside the Street Narcotics Enforcement Unit's office. That wasn't technically true. SNEU had an actual office in Precinct 5, but Sergeant Logan's team preferred to meet on the street. The squad's motor pool was their impromptu office. Erin and Vic had caught up with them on the edge of Little Italy. Now they were standing on the sidewalk next to Firelli's beloved black T-Bird.

Roberto Firelli, Bobby the Blade to his old gangland associates, took his time staring at Vic's feet. He stroked his thin pencil mustache. "He really a size fourteen, Piekarski?" he finally asked, keeping a poker face.

"None of your damn business," Zofia Piekarski said. She winked at Vic. Most people would've missed the slight bulge on the blonde's midsection, but Erin was looking for it. Piekarski's pregnancy was starting to show a little. Pretty soon it would be obvious.

"You got a new face," Erin said to Logan. The man on Logan's left was short and stocky, sporting a spiky haircut and an impressive assortment of rings on all his fingers.

"This is Officer Landa," Logan said. "Marek Landa. He's been with us since last Tuesday. Landa, this is Vic Neshenko and Erin O'Reilly. They're with Major Crimes. You can tell by their swollen egos."

"Landa's got some big shoes to fill," Piekarski said, the smile falling off her face. There was a moment of silence. Janovich had been everybody's friend. His death had hit the SNEU team hard.

"We were hoping for another Polack," Firelli said, trying to lighten the mood. "The best we could do was a Czech. We figure it's all eastern Europe, so what does it matter?"

"It matters," Landa said. "We got all this ethnic baggage in the old country, goes back hundreds of years. Czechs, Slovaks, Poles, Ukranians, Magyars, you name it."

"Aren't those some kind of bird?" Firelli asked.

"You're thinking of magpies," Logan said.

"Magyars," Landa repeated. "Hungarians, you'd call them." For all his talk of ethnic groups and the old country, Landa's accent was pure Brooklyn.

"Where'd you transfer from?" Erin asked him.

"Vice," Landa said. "Got sick of busting pimps, thought I'd upgrade to drug pushers."

"Best choice you ever made," Piekarski said.

"You guys came looking for me?" Firelli asked, turning his attention back to the Major Crimes detectives. "You're lucky you caught us on duty. We're only working days through the end of the week. Then we go back on nights. What's up?"

"I need to talk to Benny Silvers," Erin said.

Firelli scowled. "What for?" he asked.

"We heard he fed a tip to a street hood," Erin said. "Drug rip that went bad. The pusher ended up dead."

"Yeah, that sounds like Benny," Firelli said. "I have to say, I'm not too keen on talking to him. But I know where he hangs."

"Just point us the right direction," she said. "You don't have to be there."

"Like hell I'll sit this out," Firelli growled. "You may need me along, in case somebody needs to kick the crap out of him."

"Saddle up, team," Logan said. "You don't get to have all the fun by yourself. Where are we going?"

"Just a couple blocks," Firelli said. "We might as well hoof it."

"Beats finding a parking spot in this crazy town," Vic said.

"So you're O'Reilly and Neshenko, huh?" Landa said, falling in step beside them. He looked almost comical next to Vic. Both men clearly worked out a lot, and had impressive arms and shoulders, but Vic was almost a foot taller than Landa. Even Erin had an inch on him in bare feet, and her shoes cheated an extra two inches.

"That's us," Vic said.

"And this is Rolf," Erin added, twitching the K-9's leash. Rolf glanced up at her, but when no instructions were forthcoming, he went back to sniffing the sidewalk.

"I've heard of you," Landa said. "Did you do all the crazy shit they say you did?"

"All of it," Vic said. "Except the one about bungee jumping off the Verrazano Narrows. That wasn't us."

Landa smiled good-naturedly. He had a square-jawed, pleasant face. "Looking forward to working with you," he said. "Heard you were the one who took out Mickey Connor."

"Yeah," Erin said.

"He as tough as they say?"

"Yeah."

"And that guy who tried to blow up One PP?"

"Him, too."

Landa whistled. "I guess this is what it feels like when a guy gets called up from triple-A to play for the Yankees," he said.

"So we're the New York Yankees in your analogy?" Vic asked.

Erin shook her head. "Logan and his team are pros, too," she said. "Firelli saved my life not too long ago. We're all on the same team."

"Oh yeah," Landa said. "Absolutely. Look, I don't mean to go all mushy on you. It's just the first time I've worked with a celebrity."

"I am *not* a celebrity," Erin said sharply. She could already see the twinkle in Vic's eye and wanted to get in ahead of whatever he was planning to say. "I work for a living."

"But if it's not too much trouble, can you take a picture of the two of us?" Vic asked Landa, grinning nastily. "I want to send it to my mom. She'll never believe it. Erin O'Reilly! In person!"

"Shut up, Vic," she said.

Firelli led them onto Bayard Street, along the northern edge of Columbus Park. On their right was a long row of Citibike stalls with the cheap blue bicycles New York had recently poured into the city. To the left were battered brick storefronts with old apartment units perched on top of them. It was like seeing the city's past and future on opposite sides of the same street. They passed a graffiti-plastered parking lot and a convenience store.

"Hey, Erin," Vic said, pointing up. "That sign says 'Convenient Store.' What's the difference between that and a convenience store?"

"I have no idea," she said. "Looks like they've got lotto tickets. Feel lucky?"

"I never feel lucky," Vic said gloomily. "I'd rather try that massage parlor next door."

Piekarski shot him a look. "Oh no you don't," she said.

"What?" Vic said. "They're not all fronts for prostitution. Some of them just give you a backrub. Happy endings are for fairy tales. Landa, you worked Vice. Am I right?"

"It's possible," Landa said. "I've never personally been to a massage parlor that wasn't a front, but there might be a few out there."

"Hey, guys," Firelli said. He cocked his head. "Three o'clock. Guy in the wheelchair."

Erin glanced that way. She saw the long-haired, tattered man sitting near the park entrance. "I got him," she said.

Benny saw them when they were halfway across the street. He made eye contact with Erin and his own eyes went really wide. He grabbed the rims on his wheelchair, spun it with remarkable agility, and started rolling south, putting as much distance between them as possible.

"Benny!" Firelli shouted. "Stop! We just want to talk!"

Benny threw a frightened glance over his shoulder, but he didn't slow down. A pair of pedestrians cried out in surprise as the wheelchair hurtled toward them. They dove to one side, narrowly escaping a collision.

Erin broke into a run. Rolf loped easily at her side, not even trying hard. But Benny was really rolling now. The man might be a broken-down junkie with no legs, but after a couple years pushing his wheelchair, he had arms from hell. On a straightaway, it was going to be a long chase.

At least, it would be a long chase for someone on two legs. "Benny!" Erin yelled. "Stop, or I'm sending my dog!"

The fleeing man kept going another few seconds. Erin sucked in a breath to order Rolf to bite, hoping nobody would catch the incident on camera. If they did, the evening news would have a headline along the lines of NYPD SICS DOG ON CRIPPLED VETERAN.

But then Benny eased down, slowing his chair to a walking pace. Then he stopped and spun it around, a look of resignation on his face.

"What's the matter with you?" Erin burst out, skidding to a halt in front of him. "Why'd you run?"

"Why'd you chase me?" he replied. "I didn't do anything."

"Then why'd you run?" she repeated.

"Everybody runs from the cops," he said. "You *are* here as a cop, right?"

"As opposed to what?" she retorted.

"Who sent you?" Benny asked.

"Nobody," she said. "I just need to talk to you about something."

The rest of the cops arrived. Landa was fully psyched for action, ready for anything. Vic just looked annoyed. Rolf, his tongue hanging out, was happy. He loved running, even if his partner was a slowpoke by canine standards.

"You're not from the Oil Man?" Benny asked.

"No!" she snapped.

Benny gave what he clearly hoped was an ingratiating smile. "So, you came to see me? Been thinking about me? Listen, babe, I may not have legs, but everything else works just fine."

"I'll keep that in mind," she said dryly. "But that's not why I'm here. I want information."

He spread his hands. "What can I do for you?"

"You can tell me whose idea it was to send Dylan White to the Sunnyside Café."

Sometimes it was best to just clobber a suspect with an accusation right at the start and see what his eyes told you. Benny's eyes told Erin plenty. He wasn't surprised; the fact that he'd tried to run had already told her he suspected the reason for their visit. What she saw on his face was a blend of fear and resignation.

"Dylan talked, Benny," she said, almost gently. "How did you think we knew to come find you?"

"If it's any consolation, he didn't come quietly," Vic said. "Jerk nearly blew me up."

"You're not going to let that go, are you?" Erin said. "Nobody made you jump on that grenade."

"You did *what?!*" Piekarski exclaimed.

"Oops," Erin said quietly.

Benny quietly turned his wheelchair and started rolling away. Without taking his withering glare off Erin, Vic put out a hand and grabbed the back of Benny's chair.

"Talk, numbnuts," Vic growled.

Benny sighed. "Look, I hear stuff," he said. "And this didn't have anything to do with me. I'm just the messenger."

"Messenger?" Erin repeated. "For who?"

"Shouldn't that be, for *whom?*" Benny replied.

"And now we're getting grammar lessons from a crackhead," Vic said. "This day just keeps getting better."

"I'm not a crackhead," Benny said indignantly. "I've never smoked crack. Not once. Meth, sure. Weed. Dropped some acid once. But no crack."

Erin leaned forward, resting her weight on the arms of his wheelchair. This brought her face a lot closer to Benny's than she really wanted it; the man didn't bathe nearly often enough. But she ignored the smell and stared into his muddy brown eyes. Behind him, Vic was still holding the back of the chair, keeping Benny from retreating.

"If you're hoping we'll get tired of listening to your bullshit, congratulations," she said. "We are. But if you think that's going to get you off the hook, you're wrong. Who passed you the word on the Sunnyside?"

Benny squirmed. "I can't tell you that."

"Why not?"

"Telling you why not is the same as telling you!"

"Benny," she said quietly. "Spill."

"You work for them!" he burst out.

"The NYPD is behind this?" Landa asked. His tone suggested he hadn't expected it, but though he was skeptical he was open to the possibility.

"Quiet, kid," Vic said. "The grownups are talking."

"Kid?" Landa said indignantly. "I'm twenty-six!"

"Nobody cares," Vic said, not sparing him a glance.

"Give me a damn name!" Erin snarled into Benny's face.

"Schultz!" Benny said, curling defensively.

"Schultz?" Erin echoed. She'd heard him; she just hadn't believed it.

"King Schultz!"

"Kingston Schultz? The lawyer?"

Benny nodded, eager to put someone else on the hook if it meant getting himself off it. "Yeah! Slipped me two Franklins when he told me!"

"How did he know?" Erin demanded.

"How am I supposed to know that?" Benny whined.

Erin released the chair and stood up. "Thanks, Benny. See how easy that was?"

Vic didn't let go. "That's it?"

"We got what we needed," she said.

"Okay," he said. He reached into his hip pocket and pulled out his cuffs. "You know the drill, buddy? Thanks to Mr. Miranda, I've got some stuff I gotta recite to you."

Erin shook her head. "Don't bother, Vic."

"No, I have to," he said. "Seriously. This is some Supreme Court-type bullshit. If I don't, he walks. Or rolls. Whatever."

"I mean you're not putting cuffs on him."

"Why not? These don't go on the legs. He's still got arms, doesn't he?"

"On what charge, Vic?"

"Oh, I don't know. How about accessory to murder, for starters?"

"Why? Because he told a guy he'd heard some other guy had some drugs?"

"Conspiracy?"

"That's weak and you know it."

"Resisting arrest?"

"He stopped running before we arrested him."

"Uh, excuse me, folks," Benny said. "I'm still sitting right here. Are you done discussing me?"

"Get lost," Erin told him.

"What's this whole thing about?" Landa asked as Benny swiftly wheeled himself into Columbus Park.

"You don't want to know," Piekarski said. "But somebody's got some explaining to do."

"It wasn't as dangerous as it sounds," Vic said. "Tell her, Erin. The pin was in it. It wasn't gonna blow up."

"So you're just playing with grenades with the pins in them?" Piekarski demanded. "Vic, we talked about this. No unnecessary risks! You promised!"

"You did?" Erin asked, surprised. That didn't sound like the Vic Neshenko she knew.

"This was necessary," Vic said sulkily. "Sheesh. I was trying to protect everybody else. Next time I'll just let the asshole blow up the room."

"Thanks for the help," Erin told Firelli, leaving Vic and Piekarski to sort out their relationship psychodrama.

"No problem," Firelli said, shaking her hand. "Where you off to next?"

"I guess we'd better go talk to the lawyer," she said.

Vic heard that. "I don't have to wear a tie, do I?" he asked.

Chapter 13

"Sorry," Erin said as they rode the elevator up to Kingston Schultz's law office.

"Forget about it," Vic said. "She'll get over it."

"You know, some women would be glad their guy was brave. What's this about not taking unnecessary risks?"

Vic studied his feet. "Zofia's got this crazy idea I'm gonna get myself killed before the baby's born," he said. "After that thing at Firelli's house, she's feeling the danger. She says I take too many chances."

"We've got a dangerous job, Vic. The danger comes with the shield."

"Can't have one without the other," he agreed. "But it makes you think. How many times have we been shot at?"

"Beats me."

"Exactly. Suppose one of those bullets comes just a little closer. Next thing you know, bang! Everybody's wearing their dress blues and they're handing my mom a flag. And Zofia's not even sitting with my folks, because I was just the boyfriend, right? Suppose you get popped. Is your buddy Carlyle gonna be at the funeral? You think he'll be right there beside your dad, the gangster hanging out with the ex-cop?"

"Knock it off, Vic. Nothing's going to happen to either of us."

"You telling me it doesn't bother you?"

"All of it bothers me."

"How do you deal with it?"

"I used to drink a whole lot of whiskey."

"And I get a bulk discount on vodka at the liquor store. Doesn't solve the problem, though, does it?"

"No. Vic, if that's what's bothering you, why don't you go ahead and put a ring on her finger? Cut through the suspense, make the two of you official."

"Because I'm scared? Hell no! That's the worst reason I can think of to get hitched. Besides, I don't think I'm gonna make it to retirement."

The elevator eased to a stop at their floor. The doors slid open. Rolf peered into the hallway, ears perked. Erin made no move to exit. She was staring at Vic.

"You don't mean that," she said.

"I'm serious, Erin," he said. "You only get so much luck, and I've used up a ton of it. I should've died when those Russians bushwhacked me down in Little Odessa. Maybe again on the airplane afterward. What about that Neo-Nazi asshole who wanted to blow up Manhattan? He and his guys nearly nailed me two or three times, and that's without even thinking about the bomb. Don't even get me started on that crazy kid who burned down the movie theater, plus that jerk with the attack dogs. I've been shot, beat up, had my face broken a couple times. Sooner or later, something's gonna get me."

Erin planted a foot in the doorway to keep the elevator in place. "Vic, look at me," she said. "You can't go around thinking that way, or you really *are* going to get killed."

"I'm not scared," he said. "I just feel like something's coming. Something bad."

"Shake it off," she said, grabbing his shoulder and giving it a good shake. "And if I hear about you getting your palm read, or having some old Gypsy woman flip cards for you, I'm going to Tase you right in the ear and zap some sense through that thick skull of yours. What's the matter with you?"

He shook his head. "I don't know. I guess I'm freaking out a little."

"Because you're going to be a dad?"

"Yeah. Feels unnatural, like I'm trying to be something I'm not."

She squeezed his shoulder. "If it's any consolation, I'll always think of you as the same big meathead who's always got my back."

He smiled. "I appreciate that. So, we gonna beat the crap out of a lawyer now?"

"Vic..."

"Okay, okay. I won't hit him."

"Good."

"I might dangle him out a window by the feet."

"Vic, you can't do that."

"How much does he weigh?"

"What does that have to do with anything?"

"Answer the question."

She shrugged. "I don't know. One-ninety, maybe two hundred?"

"Then I can absolutely dangle him out a window. Hell, I could do it with one hand, for a couple minutes at least. I could bench-press two of the guy!"

"That wasn't what I meant."

*   *   *

Aayla Schultz, Kingston's daughter, was manning the front desk. She met Erin with a bright, apparently genuine smile.

"Detective O'Reilly," she said. "Such a pleasure to have you visit us again! I didn't see your name on the calendar. I hope I didn't miss an appointment."

"You didn't," Erin said. "This is a drop-in thing. Is your dad around?"

"He may be on a call. Please let me check." Aayla picked up her phone and punched a button. "I have Detective O'Reilly and her partner here. Can you spare them a few moments? All right, thanks."

She hung up and smiled at Erin again. "You're in luck. He has a client coming at one, but that leaves him with a few free minutes. Go on in. You remember where his office is?"

"Yes, thank you," Erin said.

Kingston Schultz came around his desk to greet them, extending a hand.

"Detective O'Reilly," he said, smiling warmly. "And Detective Neshenko, I believe?"

"That's right," Vic said. He grudgingly shook hands with the man. Vic hated criminals, he hated lawyers, and he particularly hated lawyers who represented criminals.

"An unexpected delight," Schultz said. "After our chance meeting at the courthouse, I wasn't expecting to see you again so soon. Would you care for coffee? I have some fine black cake as well, an old family recipe."

"Coffee would be great, thanks," Erin said. "Cream, no sugar, please."

"Coffee, black," Vic said. "I'm not hungry."

Schultz poured coffee for both of them and himself. "Please, have a seat," he said, gesturing to a pair of chairs in front of his desk. He sat down in his own leather swivel chair.

"*Sitz*," Erin told Rolf, who sat on the carpet next to Erin.

"I heard about that terrible business with Judge Rodriguez," Schultz said. "How is your investigation proceeding?"

"The NYPD doesn't comment about ongoing investigations," Vic said.

"Of course," Schultz said. "But I do hope you will let me know if I can be of any assistance."

"Ever heard of a guy called the Janitor?" Erin asked.

Schultz laid a fingertip against his chin. "I believe I have heard rumors of a man with that nickname," he said. "But nothing definite. I certainly have never met him."

"What've you heard?" Erin wasn't there to talk about the Rodriguez case, but she wasn't about to pass up the opportunity to pick up anything that might be useful.

"Just gossip, really," Schultz said. "I heard there was a gentleman operating in certain circles who, for a suitable price, could arrange unfortunate accidents. I wish I knew more, but I have never found the need to engage such a man and would not know where to start."

"What about Benny Silvers?" Erin asked.

"Is that the name the man was born with, or is it a street name?"

"Benito Argent, if you'd rather," she said. "Do you know him?"

"Should I?" Schultz was speaking politely, giving nothing away.

"You tell me," she said. "Because when I talked to him less than half an hour ago, he said you'd had a very interesting conversation."

"Ah," Schultz said. "Mr. Argent did avail himself of my services in the course of one of his brushes with the law, now that you mention it. That was some time ago. Any discussion I had with him would, of course, fall under attorney-client privilege."

"Of course," Vic muttered.

"You fingered Jimmy Caps for Benny," Erin said.

Schultz's teeth gleamed. "Are you accusing me of a crime?"

"No," Erin said.

"Yeah," Vic said at the same time.

"And just what crime might that be?" Schultz inquired, cocking an eyebrow at Vic.

"Conspiracy to commit murder," Vic said.

Schultz's smile vanished. "I beg your pardon, Detective," he said coldly. "That is a very strong statement to make in my office, to my face. I trust you have compelling evidence?"

"Vic," Erin said warningly.

"We've got a guy who told us you gave him two hundred bucks to hire a hitman," Vic pressed on.

The lawyer shook his head. "You have nothing of the kind," he said. "Because that is not true."

"Are you denying you gave Benny two bills when you told him about Sunnyside Café?" Vic asked.

"Is it against the law to give money to a panhandler in this city?" Schultz replied. Without waiting for an answer, he provided his own. "Penal Laws 240.25, 240.20, 165.30, and 120.15 are pertinent here. These laws prohibit so-called 'aggressive begging,' which includes tricking, intimidating, or threatening residents of the city. However, Law 240.35(1), which prohibited begging as a form of illegal loitering, was deemed unconstitutional on June Seventeenth, 1991 by the US District Court for the Southern District. The case in question is Loper vs. the New York Police Department. I can provide the text of the court's opinion, if desired."

"Jesus Christ," Vic muttered. "Don't bother. Friggin' lawyers."

"Mr. Schultz," Erin said. "I don't think you've broken any laws, not technically."

"Either a law is broken or it is not, Detective," Schultz said. "Technicality is precisely the point of having laws. That is what allows us to draw lines between what is acceptable and what is not."

She shook her head. "That's where you're wrong, sir. The spirit of the law matters."

"Not in the courtroom," Schultz replied.

"It matters on the street," Erin shot back. "And the street is what we're talking about here. You knew Jimmy Caps was running drugs out of the Sunnyside. Benny got that info and passed it on to Dylan White, who shot Jimmy Caps and ripped off his heroin stash. I know you told him. And I have a pretty good guess how you knew."

Schultz waited politely, folding his hands on his desktop.

"Matthew Madonna ran the Lucarelli narcotics operations," Erin continued. "Right up until his death. You handled his legal matters. You knew a lot about the Lucarellis and their drugs. You'd have to, so you could protect your client's interests. What I want to know is why you did it. What possible benefit would there be for you?"

"I'm sorry, Detective," Schultz said. "I don't think I can help you in this investigation. I have nothing further to say on the subject. Now, if you will excuse me, I have another appointment in a few minutes."

Vic clearly had several things he wanted to say, but Erin didn't think they'd be useful. She stood up.

"Thank you for your time, sir," she said. "My partner and I will be on our way."

"Always a pleasure, Detective O'Reilly," Schultz said. "Detective Neshenko, it has been an interesting conversation."

Vic scowled.

"Have a wonderful day," Aayla said as they walked out of the law office. Erin gave the younger woman a smile. Vic didn't even look at her.

Erin pushed the button for the elevator and settled back on her heels to wait for it to arrive. Rolf looked up at her and yawned hugely, his jaws cranking open and his tongue stretching out.

"He did it," Vic said in a savage undertone. "And you know he did!"

"Yeah," she agreed. "What's your point?"

"You soft-pedaled in there," he said.

"We didn't have a case," she reminded him. "We couldn't haul him down to the Eightball in cuffs. He would've been out in an hour, and he probably would've sued the city."

"He got a guy killed! We could've gotten something out of him!"

"Like what? We've pulled this thread as hard as we can, Vic. It's a dead end. Maybe Jimmy Caps stiffed Matthew Madonna on a drug deal last year. Maybe these guys just didn't like each other. It's a little weird, though. Schultz doesn't usually get his hands this dirty. He's on the legitimate side of the Lucarellis. I think somebody else was working through Schultz, but I don't know who."

"And you didn't try real hard to find out," Vic said. "You wanna know what I think?"

The elevator's arrival interrupted the conversation, so Erin didn't get to find out what Vic thought. The doors slid open. Erin started in.

She stopped short. The elevator was already occupied. A young man was on his way out, walking straight toward her. He looked to be about twenty. He was wearing a suit coat and tie, but somehow managed to make them look like street clothes. And his face was one Erin recognized.

"Alfie?" she exclaimed.

Chapter 14

The last time Erin had seen Alfredo Madonna, the Mob kid had been disappearing into a subway tunnel, on the run from Lucarelli assassins. He'd been scared, tired, dirty, and angry. He'd cleaned up some in the meantime, and he no longer looked scared. His eyes had dark bags under them, but there was a burning intensity in his stare that Erin had only seen in truly dangerous men.

Vic saw it too. He reflexively took two steps sideways, opening an angle between him and Erin. His hand dropped to the Sig-Sauer at his belt.

Alfie clearly hadn't expected to run into them. He stepped away, back into the elevator, and his own hand twitched. But recognition dawned and he stopped moving. His face lost a little of its grim set, but his jaw remained clenched.

"O'Reilly," he said, and his voice was relatively calm. "Looking for me?"

"Not exactly," she said. "I came to see King, but I'm glad I ran into you."

"What do you want?"

"Your sentencing date is just around the corner," she said. "The Oil Man and Vitelli are looking for you."

"Tell me something I don't know." He stepped out of the elevator, which closed behind him. Neither he nor the detectives took any notice of it.

"I heard about Carlo Peralta," she went on.

Alfie shrugged. "Shit happens."

"That doesn't bother you?"

"That son of a bitch killed my dad," Alfie snapped. "You want me to cry because he's dead?"

"No, I want you to think about it," Erin said. "Unless that air embolism was an accident—"

Alfie's derisive snort interrupted her.

"Unless it was an accident," she said again, "it means the Lucarellis have a guy who can get to his target in a prison infirmary. You're not safe."

"Look, lady," Alfie said. "You got anything to tell me I might not already know? Because this is old news. I've got work to do."

"What work is that?" Vic asked. He was studying the kid with unfriendly eyes.

"Lawyer stuff," Alfie said, gesturing toward Schultz's office.

"Lawyer stuff," Erin repeated. "And would any of this lawyer stuff involve talking to King about a certain recently-deceased drug pusher at the Sunnyside Café?"

Alfie covered it well, but he was young and didn't have enough practice concealing his reactions. Erin, a veteran of dozens of interrogations, saw the way his eyes widened ever so slightly.

"You must've known Jimmy Caps," she said. "He wasn't that much older than you. He was working in your dad's business."

"What, you think we have company picnics, bring your kid to work day, shit like that? That ain't how we do in the Life."

"No, it isn't," Erin said. "But your world runs on favors and networking. Your dad would've made sure you knew everybody."

He shrugged again. "I'm already getting violated for my parole," he said. "You trying to get me to admit to hanging around felons? Waste of time."

She shook her head. "I'm saying you already knew him." Her eyes narrowed as the half-formed thought that had been dancing around her head finally came together. "Just like you know everybody in the Lucarelli narcotics operation."

"You trying to get me to snitch? My dad taught me better than that. We've had this conversation. I ain't no goddamn rat."

"I know you're not going to spill anything to me," she said. "But that wouldn't be your play anyway. You told me a while ago, you couldn't pin anything major on Vinnie Moreno or old man Vitelli. You could nail a bunch of the little fish, but what would be the point of that?"

"About as much point as the words coming out of your mouth," Alfie said. "Look, are you arresting me, or what? Get in line. Because I got news for you. I'm already arrested. I'm going back to jail."

Erin didn't give an inch. "You're fighting a war," she said softly. "All by yourself, against the Lucarellis. You don't have an organization, so you're working your contacts, hitting them indirectly, at street level."

Vic whistled. "You're crazy, kid," he said to Alfie. "But I gotta admit, you got a pair of balls you could take to the bowling alley."

"You're right," Alfie told him. "That'd be crazy. I'd have to be nuts to do something like that. They'd kill me."

"They're already trying to kill you," Erin said. "You've got nothing to lose. You know Judge Barberis only let you out because he's in Vinnie's pocket, and they had a guy waiting outside the courthouse to take you down. When you go back in front of him, he's going to throw your ass back behind bars, and once that happens, you're dead meat. Some Lucarelli lifer will come up behind you in the shower with a sharpened toothbrush, and that'll be it for you."

"King's working on that," Alfie said. "Don't worry about me. I can take care of myself."

"No you can't," Vic said. "You're not Batman. You don't know kung fu. You're gonna get your ass killed."

"You want to know if I can fight?" Alfie shot back. "Come and get it, asshole."

One corner of Vic's mouth quirked up in a slight smile. He rolled his neck and flexed his shoulders, loosening them. "Ready when you are, punk," he said. "I could use a little exercise."

"Knock it off, both of you," Erin said. "The way I figure it, Alfie, you've only got a few days left on the outside, and you've got to make them count. You're trying to hurt Vinnie as much as possible. Why? Revenge?"

"I told you what I'd do to him," Alfie said defiantly. "And that's what I'm gonna do."

"You'll never get a shot at him," Erin said. "He's got bodyguards. You wouldn't get within twenty yards."

"What do you care?" he retorted. "This hasn't got shit to do with you."

"I promised your dad I'd look after you," she reminded him. "I don't want you getting yourself killed."

"Then why don't you do your job and get rid of Vinnie?" Alfie demanded. "What's stopping you?"

"I can't just waste anybody I don't like," she said. "Cops don't work that way."

"Then I got no use for you," he said. "If you're not gonna help, I only want one thing from you, lady. Don't get in my way."

He walked past her into the law office without looking back. Erin, Vic, and Rolf watched him go.

"That's a dead man walking," Vic said. "You think he knows it?"

"I don't think he cares," Erin said.

"What do you think he's gonna do?"

"I think he's going to try to kill Vinnie the Oil Man."

It was Vic's turn to snort. "Good luck with that," he said.

"Don't underestimate him," she said quietly. "He loved his dad and he hates Vinnie."

"We all hate Vinnie. I know I do. Don't you?"

"You bet your ass," Erin growled. She stabbed the elevator button with an angry finger. The car was still on their floor, so the doors opened immediately. She got in, Rolf and Vic beside her, and hit the button for the lobby.

"Well, I don't see Vinnie losing any sleep over us," Vic said. "It takes more than hate, Erin. That's just motive. The kid needs means and opportunity."

"He's got the means," she said. "He was carrying."

"Yeah, I know," Vic said sourly. He hadn't missed the way Alfie's hand had strayed toward the inside of his coat. "This punk's already violating his parole. Can you give me one good reason we didn't frisk him and throw his ass back behind bars?"

"Because Vinnie's people are waiting for that to happen. They'll kill him the second he's in genpop."

"Then don't put him in genpop! They've got protective custody for a reason!"

"Vinnie got Carlo Peralta in the infirmary," Erin said. "He wasn't in general population. And Vinnie *liked* Carlo."

"Then why'd he whack him?"

"Because he was a security risk. Don't you get it, Vic? Vinnie will kill anybody, no matter what they've done for him, the second he thinks they're a liability. Why do you think all those guys went down back when he clipped Acerbo and took over the Family? Not all of them would've betrayed him, but he thought one of them might, so they all had to go. Nina Bianchi, too."

Vic leaned against the elevator wall. "Jesus," he muttered. "Why the hell doesn't somebody put two in this asshole's brain and do the world a favor?"

"I thought about it," Erin said.

"Why didn't you?"

"Because I'm not a murderer!" she snapped. "No matter what they say about me!"

"Whoa, Erin," Vic said, holding up his hands. "Take it easy. I didn't mean that."

"I know."

The elevator came to a halt at the lobby. Vic was staring at Erin with a look she'd come to know. It meant he was thinking like a detective, not a musclebound goon who liked to kick down doors. "Holy shit," he said. "You really were thinking about taking him out."

"Forget about it, Vic," she said, stepping out of the elevator and starting across the lobby. "Nothing happened."

"Yeah, I know," he said. "Because Vinnie's still breathing. If you wanted to take that guy out, I think you'd get him."

"I can't do it," she said. "I've already killed more people than I should."

"Those were people who needed killing," Vic said. "You're no murderer, Erin. You're right. All you've done is what you had to. Why is this bugging you so much?"

"Because I'm worried about my soul."

"Your what?" Vic blinked. "Didn't copy."

"My soul," she repeated. It sounded silly out loud. She shifted uncomfortably.

"You talking about religious bullshit?"

"Yeah, and it's not bullshit. Don't you believe in God?"

It was Vic's turn to look uncomfortable. "Well, yeah, I guess so," he said. "I mean, we're not exactly on a first-name basis. I don't bother Him and I hope He extends me the same courtesy. You really think Vinnie's putting your soul in danger?"

She nodded.

"So he's what, the Devil? I guess it would explain some stuff."

"No, Vic, he's not," she said. "He's just a murderous thug with too much power. Listen, this isn't about him. It's about me. Do I want him dead? Hell yes. Would the city be better off without him? Yeah, it would. Is he going to Hell when he dies? If I had to bet on it, he's taking the down elevator. But you talk all the time about how much you hate everything. If I let myself hate him so much that I stop seeing him as a human being, I lose."

"What do you lose?" Vic asked. He was looking at her with a very odd expression on his face, but he wasn't smiling. He was taking her seriously.

"Everything. I talked to a priest about this, you know?"

"Sounds like a good Catholic thing to do. What'd he say?"

"He assigned me a few Hail Marys and Our Fathers and said it was good to talk about it. He said it got it out of my system in a healthy way."

"Wait a second." Vic held up a hand. "You told a priest you were planning on taking out a Mafia boss?"

"Pretty much, yeah."

"Please tell me this wasn't an Italian priest."

Erin cracked a smile. "No," she said. "It wasn't."

"That's all right then. I guess Vinnie's safe from you, but not from our buddy Alfredo Fettucini, or whatever his name is. I wouldn't be too worried if I was him. That kid upstairs isn't you. He's just a punk with a chip on his shoulder."

"Maybe," she said. "But that punk has had a couple months to plan this out, and I don't think he's been thinking about very much else. If I were Vinnie, I'd be sleeping with one eye open."

"You think he closes his eyes? I bet he props 'em open, like Malcom McDowell in *A Clockwork Orange*. Besides, he's got guys all over him. Somebody'll get him, but ten bucks says it's not the kid."

"Ten bucks? You're on." Erin turned in the doorway and offered her hand. Vic, surprised, shook it.

"You got a bet," he said. "What now?"

"Now we go back to the Eightball," she said. "We're done with this. The Café Bandit case is closed."

"You're kidding. First you want to chase it down, now you want to give up? A second ago you thought the kid was masterminding this whole thing, which I still think is nuts. He's about as much of a criminal mastermind as Alex Petrovitch."

"Who's that?"

"A kid who sat behind me in the fourth grade. He used to drink Elmer's glue."

"Drink it?"

"Straight out of the bottle."

Erin made a face. "That's nasty."

"It's non-toxic," Vic said. "Says so right on the label. Probably safer than booze."

Erin's phone buzzed. "Thank God," she said, pulling it out of her pocket. "I don't want to hear another word about your school days. O'Reilly."

"Get to the courthouse," Webb said with no preamble. "We've got a problem."

Cold fingers reached into Erin's guts and started twisting them into a cat's cradle. "What happened?" she asked.

"They made another try for Judge Ferris."

"Is he okay?"

"For the moment," Webb said.

Chapter 15

Erin and Vic saw the flashing lights well before they got to the courthouse. Traffic had backed up badly, and Erin saw at once that her own lights and sirens would do no good at all. Even if all the New York drivers tried to get out of her way, they had nowhere to go.

"Two blocks," Vic said as Erin hopelessly scanned the gridlock for some way through.

"Looks like it," she said.

"Quicker to pound pavement?" he suggested.

"Yeah," she agreed. By alternating between her horn and short bursts on her siren, she managed to convince the cars in front of her to move just enough that she was able to squeeze the Charger into a police spot on the nearest corner.

Vic was out of the car almost before it stopped moving. Erin paused just long enough to pop Rolf's compartment. Then all three of them were running toward the lights.

Erin couldn't see any smoke, which was good as far as it went. But as she got closer, she recognized the big blue and white van of the Bomb Squad. Half a dozen Patrol cars completely blocked the street in front of the courthouse. A fire truck, an ambulance, and an ESU BearCat rounded out the emergency motor pool. She saw uniformed cops, firefighters, ESU guys, and a bunch of courthouse staff milling around outside. She also saw a couple of news vans, camera crews jockeying for the best position to shoot the scene.

"What is this, World War Three?" Vic wondered aloud as they reached the edge of the crowd.

Erin just shook her head. She didn't know enough to even make a guess.

A Patrol officer intercepted them on the courthouse steps. "Hold it!" he said. "You can't go in there!"

"Watch us," Vic said, holding up his gold shield.

The uniform was unimpressed. "We got a bomb threat," he said, not budging. "Until I get the all-clear, nobody goes in."

"This is an explosives-detection K-9," Erin said, twitching Rolf's leash. "We've got orders to be here. Did anything blow up?"

"Not yet," the cop said. "The bomb guys are in there right now. I've got no idea what's going on."

"Then maybe you should get out of the way and let us figure it out," Vic suggested.

Erin decided not to force the issue. She held up a hand to Vic while she fished out her phone and called Webb.

"We're here," she announced when he answered. "What's going on?"

"Come on in," Webb said. "Taylor says it should be safe enough. We're in one of the maintenance corridors, one floor down from the judge's chambers. We've got a custodian here. I'll ask him to show you the way."

"One of our boys in blue is guarding the door," Erin said. "What should I tell him?"

"Give him your phone."

"Here," Erin said, holding the phone out to the cop.

She didn't hear what Webb said to the man, but the officer's face flushed. He tried to say something, got interrupted, tried to say something else, then gave up. "Yes, sir," he finally said. He handed the phone back to Erin. "Sorry," he muttered.

"Thanks," she said. She, Vic, and Rolf jogged up the stairs and inside.

The courthouse was eerily deserted. Even the security checkpoint was empty. Their footfalls echoed hollowly on the marble floor. They paused just inside, trying to figure out where to go.

"Creepy," Vic said. "But it could be worse. You ever been in an abandoned hospital? Those are the worst."

"I've been in the morgue after dark," Erin said.

"Alone?"

"Levine was there."

He made a face. "That's even worse."

"She's not that bad."

"I'm serious. I think I've seen that horror movie."

They heard someone coming down the stairs. A moment later, a middle-aged man in gray coveralls came into view, accompanied by an ESU guy in full tactical gear.

"You the guy who's going to take us up?" Erin asked the custodian.

"I guess so," the man said.

"O'Reilly, Major Crimes," she said. "This is Neshenko."

"Barney Kustosz," the man said, offering his hand. "Pleasure."

She shook his hand. He had a good, firm grip and the leathery, callused hands of a man who worked for a living.

"Follow me," he said.

"What've you got to do with this?" Vic asked as they hurried upstairs.

"We have a leak in one of the hot-water pipes," Kustosz said. "But I found something weird while I was looking at it."

"Define weird," Erin said.

"It looked like a bomb," he said.

"How did you know?" Vic asked. "Bombs don't always look like bombs. Was this a big bunch of dynamite strapped together with one of those digital timers, or what?"

"I was in the Army," Kustosz said. "I know what plastic explosives look like."

Erin shivered. The use of plastic explosives suggested a technically proficient bomber. "I hope you didn't touch it," she said.

"I'm not nuts, ma'am," he replied. "I got the hell out of there and called for help. Through this door, if you'll just come with me."

"You seem pretty calm for a guy who just found a bomb," Vic observed.

"I handled that stuff in the Service," Kustosz said. "It's pretty safe as long as you don't set it off with a detonator. Hell, you can set fire to it and it won't go off."

He led them through a doorway into a cramped corridor, the ceiling a cluster of pipes. It was lit by bare bulbs. The air was heavy and humid. A murmur of voices was muffled by the thick air.

"Feels like the goddamn rainforest in here," Vic said, unzipping his jacket.

"Radiator leak," Kustosz reminded him.

They rounded a corner and saw Skip Taylor with a pair of ESU guys and Lieutenant Webb. The bomb tech was standing on a low stepladder, working on something that was stuck to the overhead pipes by a whole lot of duct tape. A few feet to one side of him, water was flowing steadily out of a gash in one of the pipes. The water was obviously close to boiling. A cloud of steam surrounded the men.

"We're here," Erin announced.

Webb had taken off his ever-present fedora. Sweat and condensation shone on his bald forehead. He wiped his brow with the back of his sleeve and walked toward them. Skip didn't so much as turn his head. He was completely focused on the task at hand.

"We got lucky," Webb said. "People don't come back here too often."

"How bad is it?" Erin asked.

"Pretty bad. If it'd gone off, we would've had a lot of casualties."

"Where are we right now?" she asked Kustosz, though she already suspected the answer.

"Right under Judge Ferris's chambers," the man said. "If I had to guess, I'd say his desk is right about there." He pointed directly at Skip.

"I guess our guy isn't interested in making it look like an accident anymore," Vic said. "And he doesn't care about collateral damage, either."

Erin carefully approached the stepladder. "How's it going, Skip?" she asked.

"Oh, hey, Erin," Skip said, still without looking. "It figures you'd be here. Don't worry, I'm almost done. I think we're okay. No anti-tampering countermeasures, no remote detonator. Just your standard time bomb. I've already disconnected the timer, with a good seven minutes to spare, so it ought to be safe."

"Ought to be?" she echoed. Those weren't words she wanted to hear in reference to a powerful explosive.

"Ninety-five percent," he said. "I just want to make sure. Just a sec." His hands were busy around the bomb.

Erin watched and waited. It wasn't a good idea to rush a bomb-disposal technician.

"Whew, it's wet in here," he said. "Don't want to slip. C4 doesn't go off if you drop it, but if I start chucking bombs around, it'll upset your boss. I think he's still pissed about that grenade in the sewers."

"I remember that," Erin said, smiling at the memory. "You could've warned him you were going to set it off."

"And he could've stood back and let me do my job," Skip replied, throwing Webb a sidelong glance. "Everybody's a football expert on Monday nights. Okay... there! We're clear. Hold up your hand."

Erin did as he asked, and found herself holding a gray lump that reminded her of modeling clay. Skip hopped down from the ladder.

"We're good, sir," he announced to Webb.

"There might be more bombs," Webb said doubtfully.

"Then it's a good thing we've got Rolf," Erin said. "We'll do a sweep, just in case. What should I do with this?"

"I'll take it back and log it into Evidence," Skip said. "Relax. It's perfectly safe now, as long as you don't eat it."

Erin nodded, but she was still glad to get rid of the lump. "How much damage would this have done?" she couldn't resist asking.

"A block of C4 this size would've taken out everybody in the rooms above and below," Skip said. "It would've wiped out that wall and anyone within three or four meters of it. It would've turned the pipes into shrapnel, which would've increased casualties. Might've caused structural damage, but I doubt it. This place is pretty sturdy. Casualties would've depended on who was nearby when it went. Our guy knew what he was doing, that's for sure. The Lieutenant's right; we lucked out."

"Copy that," Erin said. She turned to her dog. "Rolf. *Such!*"

Rolf eagerly began snuffling his way along the corridor. Erin steered him around the leak from the pipe, which was near scalding. They thoroughly checked the maintenance hallway in both directions, finding nothing.

"Looks like we're good, sir," she said to Webb.

"Can I get back to fixing the pipe?" Kustosz asked.

"I don't see why not," Webb said. "And I think the rest of us can go somewhere dry. We've got another K-9 team downstairs, checking the rest of the building. O'Reilly, I want you and your dog to help out. Make sure this is the only device on the premises. Neshenko, you're with me."

"Where are we going?" Vic asked.

"Security station," Webb said. "I think our clever assassin slipped up. Every inch of this building is covered by cameras. With any luck, we're about to have a face to put on our suspect."

"Great," Vic said, loading the word with as much sarcasm as it could take. "I love looking at security footage."

*　　*　　*

Searching a government building for bombs was nothing new for Erin and Rolf; back in their Patrol days, they'd done this sort of thing all the time. They linked up with the other K-9, a Belgian Malinois named Jax, and a pair of courthouse cops. Erin had met Jax's handler at a training seminar a couple of years ago. The handler, a stocky officer called Kruger, gave her a wide grin and a handshake.

"Decided to hang up the gold shield and do some honest police work?" he asked.

"I'm keeping the shield," she said. "But I figured you uniformed types could make use of my superior knowledge and experience."

Jax and Rolf sniffed one another, tails wagging. Then they ignored each other. They were on the clock and didn't have time to socialize.

Kruger was sweeping the ground floor. Erin and one of the courthouse officers started on the second story. There was a lot of ground to cover, but Rolf and Jax were quick and knew their business. Despite the dogs' efficiency, however, it still took almost two hours of methodical sniffing before Erin and Kruger agreed the building was clear.

Courthouse staff poured back in. After fielding complaints from a few irritable clerks and lawyers, all of whom wanted to know why they couldn't have moved faster, Erin took Rolf and went looking for her colleagues.

She found them in front of a security monitor, staring at grainy black-and-white footage. Vic had found a bottle of Mountain Dew somewhere. It hadn't improved his mood. He and Webb were tired and grumpy.

"No more bombs?" Vic asked when he saw them.

"Nothing," Erin confirmed. "Have you got anything?"

"Not a damn thing. We've got that maintenance guy, Custard or whatever his name is—"

"Kustosz," Webb said without taking his eyes off the screen.

"Yeah, that guy," Vic said. "He goes in with his bag of tools. A few minutes later he comes out. He goes straight to the nearest guard and flags him down, just like he told us. Then nobody goes in or out until our guys show up."

"I don't suppose we have cameras in the maintenance corridor itself?"

"Nope," Vic said.

"How far back have you checked the tapes?" Erin asked.

"Forty-eight hours," Webb said.

"That's more than enough," she said.

"We don't know how long that bomb was there," Vic said. "Hell, it could've been there for a week."

"I don't think so," she said. "Our guy didn't plant the bomb until after his first try failed."

"That's a good point," Webb said. "What were you able to find out about this Janitor mope?"

"I've got people looking into it," she said.

Vic snapped his fingers. "Hey, you don't think the Janitor actually is a janitor?"

"It's a metaphor, Neshenko," Webb said wearily. "He's a cleaner."

"I still think I should run down this Customs guy," Vic said. "Just in case."

"Customs?" Erin asked.

"Kustosz," Webb corrected. "With a 'K.' But I don't see the point. He's the one who told us about the bomb in the first place. Without him, Ferris would be in a thousand pieces right about now."

"Oh. Right. That doesn't make sense." Vic's face fell. "And besides, the Janitor is all about clean kills, right? He wouldn't use a friggin' gigantic bomb."

"Right," Erin said. "Where's Judge Ferris right now?"

"On his way back to his chambers, I'd imagine," Webb said. "With his security detail."

"How many guys has he got watching him?" she asked.

"Two," Vic said. "Remember Five Cent and Chunky?"

"Your old ESU buddies? Nichols and Campbell?"

"Yeah. No two-bit rent-a-cops watching Ferris. They've got AR-15s, vests, and everything. Anybody who tries to get by them is gonna have a real bad day."

Erin didn't like it. Her street instincts were clamoring. But she wasn't sure why. "Okay," was what she said. "Now what?"

"Back to the Eightball," Webb sighed. "And we try to find out something about this damned Janitor. Maybe they ought to rename him Ghost."

"You're sure Ferris is okay?" she pressed.

"The man's eighty-two years old," Webb said. "And he's got a pacemaker. For all I know, he'll keel over from a heart attack thirty seconds from now. But as far as this particular homicide attempt goes, he's in no further danger."

"I've got a thing at five," Vic said.

"What sort of thing?" Webb asked.

Vic shifted uncomfortably. "A health thing."

"Everything okay?" Erin asked.

"I'm fine," he said. "I'm the picture of health. It's not for me."

Erin considered. "Oh!" she said. "Is this for…"

"Yeah," Vic said. "She'll drop by Major Crimes to pick me up."

"What is going on?" Webb asked, glancing from Erin to Vic.

"Nothing pertaining to my job, sir," Vic said.

* * *

"It's no big deal," Vic told Erin, once they were back in her Charger. "Zofia saw this thing online about some special diet, supposed to be good for development, and there's this seminar, and she wants me there so I can give her moral support or something."

"I think that's sweet of you, Vic," Erin said. "You're really taking this whole 'dad' thing seriously."

"Yeah," he said gloomily. "Watch. This is gonna end up with me eating a whole bunch of kale. I hate salad."

"We all make sacrifices for the people we love," she said, grinning.

"I'd rather take a bullet for her than a celery stick."

"Now there's a creative murder weapon. How would you kill someone with a celery stick?"

"By force-feeding it to the poor bastard. You're a girl, help me understand this. Zofia likes steak as much as I do. More, even."

"Sorry, can't help you. I don't like kale either."

Back at the Eightball, they spilled out of Erin's car. Vic headed upstairs. Erin peeled off to visit Skip Taylor in his basement office, affectionately nicknamed the Blast Pit.

Skip opened the door. "Hey, Erin," he said. "I had a feeling you'd drop by. Find any other devices?"

"No," she said. "I was wondering if you'd gotten anything on the one you disarmed."

"C'mon in," he said. "Coffee?"

"Where'd it come from?"

"Instant packet," he said. "Decaf. Caffeine sometimes makes my hands shake. Not good when you're handling bombs."

Erin made a face. "Instant decaf? That's not even coffee in my book. No thanks."

Skip pointed to his work table. "There's your bomb," he said. "No fingerprints in the C4. That stuff's just like Silly Putty. It'll hold an imprint. But our guy must've been wearing gloves."

"Worth checking," she said.

"It's a military explosive," he went on. "I was just tracing the chemical markers. Looks like this particular bomb came from a batch that was last seen getting loaded onto a munitions ship right here in New York."

"I guess it didn't make it wherever it was going," Erin said.

"Somebody skimmed a little," Skip said. "Or a crate got misplaced. That happens sometimes, you know. The brass says it doesn't, but it does. A box gets mislabeled as sleeping bags, next thing you know, some Army surplus store is wondering what they're doing with a bunch of military-grade bang."

"But no theft was reported?" she asked.

He shook his head. "That means it was either an honest mistake, or they've got someone on the inside. And if somebody's dealing C4 under the table, that's probably a Mob thing. I just e-mailed the ordnance guy at the state armory, but I can already tell you what he's going to say."

"Nobody saw nothin,'" Erin guessed.

"Bingo. The military is just like the rest of our government. Their first impulse when something goes wrong is to cover their ears and pretend nothing happened. Now, about the mechanics of the device. The timer and detonator are simple enough. The detonator's a blasting cap, standard mining equipment. No way we can trace that; those things are a dime a dozen. The timer's a re-wired digital clock. You know what's weird?"

"What?"

"All these years doing EOD work, I never actually saw a bomb with numbers counting down until now. It actually had little red numbers. I disconnected the clock at seven minutes and three seconds. That doesn't happen in real life. Terrorists don't do that."

"What're you saying, Skip?"

"I'm saying it's a weird bomb," he said. "Doesn't fit the MO of anybody I can think of. It looks more like a movie prop."

"So it wouldn't have gone off?"

"Oh no, it would've gone off all right." He shrugged. "Maybe your guy just watched too many '90s action movies. It wouldn't be the first time I've heard of an explosive that was a little... um... cinematic."

He actually winked when he said that. Erin scowled. Skip had helped her with a fake bomb not that long ago, but that was top secret. She shook her head.

"Zip it, Skip," she said.

"Anyway," Skip said, having the decency to look a little embarrassed. "That's all I've got. It's a simple device. No shrapnel sleeve, no fancy security measures. Easiest bomb I've disarmed."

"Okay, thanks," she said. "Let me know if you find out anything else."

"Copy that."

Chapter 16

"Let me see if I've got this straight, sir," Vic said. "We're trying to ID a killer whose MO is that his victims die in ways that look like accidents."

"That's right," Webb said.

"So as far as we know, his prior victims may not have been classified as homicides. In fact, they probably weren't."

"Right again."

"Do you have any idea how many accidental deaths there are in this damn city?"

"No," Webb said. "The accidental ones don't land on our desks."

"Kira Jones probably knows," Erin said. "But I bet it's a couple thousand."

"Per year?" Vic asked.

"Yeah," she said.

"Tell you what," Vic said. "How about you give me a needle, I'll drive out into the countryside, find a nice haystack, and hide the needle in it. Then you can find the needle. Oh, and I won't tell you which haystack it's in."

"Something you'd rather be doing, Neshenko?" Webb asked.

"Yes, sir. Police work."

"I'm sorry if we're not serving enough high-risk warrants for your tastes," Webb said. "Maybe you'd like me to contact this city's criminal element and lodge a complaint on your behalf."

"Would you, sir? I'd appreciate that."

"While we're waiting to hear back from them, I'd like you to at least try," Webb said. "And one thing you might try is cross-referencing accidental deaths with members of the judiciary and other people you think might be likely targets."

"Mobsters?" Erin suggested.

"Maybe, but I doubt it," Webb said. "There's not much point making a gangster's death look like an accident. You might as well have a run-of-the-mill hitman put a bullet in the back of his head. That might actually attract less attention than some freak accident. No, I think we're looking at targets peripheral to the underworld, civilians that might cause a stink if they got murdered."

"I don't think the city stats are sorted that way," Vic said.

"If being a detective was easy, everybody on the Force would be doing it," Webb said. "Quit bitching and get to work."

After an afternoon grinding away at her computer, Erin had to admit Vic had a point. A needle might have been easier to find. They didn't even have a good place to start. She tried cross-referencing accidental deaths with defendants in Judge Ferris's courtroom, but it was a hopeless search.

"We need to find the Janitor," she said at last, a few minutes before five. "If he doesn't talk, we've got nothing."

"She's right, sir," Vic said. "God, I hate hitmen. Especially competent ones."

"You've got a lot of hate," Erin said.

"Yup," Vic said. "It's what gets me out of bed in the morning."

"Talking about me?" a woman said from the stairwell. "That's sweet."

"Hey, Zofia," Vic said, and in spite of his earlier complaining, Erin saw the way his eyes lit up when he saw her. "C'mon in. I'm just finishing up here."

"What're you working on?" Piekarski asked, walking across the office to look at the whiteboard. "Oh, the judge thing."

"Yeah," Vic said. "But we're just spinning wheels."

Piekarski studied the board. "Who's the Janitor?" she asked.

"We don't know," Erin said. "It's just a nickname."

"And he's trying to kill Judge Ferris? What a bastard."

"Yeah, he almost got him again this afternoon," Vic said. "Planted a bomb under his office. But a civvie spotted the bomb before it could go off. A for-real janitor, if you can believe it. I think that's what you call ironic. He had a funny name. Custer or something."

"Kustosz," Webb said wearily.

"Cute," Piekarski said.

All three detectives gave her blank looks.

"Kustosz," Piekarski said. "It's Polish for 'custodian.' It'd be like a surgeon being named Doctor, or an artist being named Painter. It's a crazy coincidence. What? Why are you all looking at me like that?"

"Son of a bitch," Vic said quietly.

Webb was already on the phone. "This is Lieutenant Webb, Major Crimes," he said, talking fast. "I need to know if you have a Barney Kustosz on your custodial staff. This is extremely urgent. That's K-U-S-T-O-S-Z."

Erin didn't wait for the answer. One coincidence was one too many as far as she was concerned. She grabbed her own phone. The number for Ferris's office was saved on it. She jabbed the screen and held her breath as it rang once, twice.

"Judge Ferris's chambers," the woman on the other end of the line said. "How may I help you?"

"Ms. Lockhart?"

"Yes?"

"This is Erin O'Reilly, Major Crimes. We met earlier."

"Yes, I remember, Detective. What—"

"Is the judge in?"

"Yes, but—"

"Get him, yourself, and everybody else out of there," Erin said. "*Right now.*"

"Please tell me what's going on, Detective."

"No time. You're in danger. Get out! Move!"

Years of Patrol work, followed by years of K-9 handling, had taught Erin how to put all her authority into her voice. It cut through Julia's uncertainty and confusion. Erin heard the other woman call out to the judge.

"Howard? It's the police. They say there's another threat. We need to vacate the building."

Erin heard Ferris say something in the background. He sounded irritated. Someone else spoke, probably one of his protection detail. Then Julia came back on the line.

"We're on our way out," she said. "Where do you think—"

There was a hollow, metallic bang, followed by a shrieking hiss, like the world's largest tea-kettle. A man started screaming. It was an awful, breathless sound that went on and on.

"Oh my God," the secretary said softly.

"What's going on?" Erin demanded. She was running for the stairs, her phone against her ear. "What's happening?"

"Howard!" Julia screamed. The line went dead.

*   *   *

Vic caught up with Erin in the garage. He slid into the passenger seat as she cranked the key and stomped on the gas. Rolf stuck his head through the porthole between the seats, ears perked, tongue hanging out. The K-9 knew something was up, and he wanted in on it.

While Erin slalomed through traffic, lights and siren engaged, Vic turned on the police-band radio. The airwaves were full of chatter.

"10-13! We need a bus to the courthouse, forthwith!" someone was shouting.

"That's Nichols," Vic said, referring to the ESU officer nicknamed Five Cent.

"Possible bomb explosion at the courthouse!" someone else said. "Upper floors!"

"Officer down!" Nichols shouted.

Then the voices started overlapping, tripping over each other.

"Is anyone claiming responsibility?"

"Is it terrorists?"

"We need to contact Homeland Security!"

"FDNY is en route."

"What's the casualty report?"

"Somebody secure the prisoners at the courthouse! This could be a jailbreak."

"Attention, all officers," a man said, and though he didn't speak loudly, his serious voice cut through the chatter. "This is Captain Holliday at the Eight. We have a situation, but we have procedures to handle it. You've been trained in these procedures and the people of New York expect you to act like it. All of you have jobs, so do them, without panicking. If you need to be on this channel, identify yourself properly, state your business clearly. Otherwise, keep the airwaves clear."

There were a few seconds of embarrassed silence.

"Ah, this is Sergeant Younger, at the courthouse, shield three-three-two-seven," a man said in a calmer tone. "We've had a single explosion. No smoke alarms triggered. We've got one ESU casualty reported, possibly others. Building is secure."

"I'll just bet it is," Erin growled, speeding up. "I can't believe we missed a bomb. We checked Ferris's office! Rolf should've smelled it!"

"I can't believe we were face to face with that asshole!" Vic said. "I should've made him. God damn it, he was right there!"

"We both should've seen it," she said. "A little too convenient. We got played."

"But we've seen his face," Vic said. "I'm not gonna forget it."

"And Rolf knows his smell," she added. "Plus, we've got him on camera. We can run him through facial recognition."

"Oh, goodie," Vic said. "That's about as good as our sketch artists. That program's useless."

"Not if we've got him on file. If we have a mugshot, it'll match him."

"You really think this guy's got a record? When he's been a damn ghost for who knows how long?"

"We should've had him," Erin repeated. "Remember when he hit Ferris's house? He dressed as a telephone repairman. That's what he does. He breaks something, then he dresses as a maintenance guy and people just let him in."

"Every building's only as secure as its custodial staff," Vic agreed. "Sneaky. But how'd he get through the courthouse checkpoints?"

She shook her head. "We'll find out."

* * *

Even more emergency vehicles were clustered around the courthouse than the last time Erin had been there. The 10-13 "officer needs assistance" call had brought all the available Patrol units in the area which, in downtown Manhattan, was an awful lot of cops. They'd put up portable barricades to keep the crowd of curious New Yorkers at bay. Since it was after five, and most workdays had ended, a large number of civilians were looking on.

By the time Erin, Vic, and Rolf worked their way close enough to see what was happening, a pair of EMTs was bringing a stretcher toward their ambulance. A bulky figure lay on it, but they were a little too far out to see any details.

Erin showed her shield to the officers on the perimeter. Two of the cops started moving one of the barricades to let the detectives through.

"Excuse me," a woman said from just behind them. Erin turned to see a familiar platinum-blonde face, pretty under a heavy layer of makeup.

"Not right now," Erin said.

"Holly Gardner," the woman said, undeterred. "Channel Six News. I understand there's been another assassination attempt on a New York judge. I just have a couple of questions."

Erin ignored her. Vic turned and gave the woman his patented angry scowl.

"You want a comment?" he asked.

Holly gave him a brilliant white-toothed smile. "Thank you, Detective," she said. "What can you tell our viewers?"

Vic glanced past her to the cameraman, who was busily filming everything. "Is this live?" he asked.

"Live across the eastern seaboard," Holly said brightly. "Now, my first question is—"

"Lady," he interrupted, speaking slowly but forcefully. "How about you stop hassling us and let us do our job, before I take that microphone and shove it right up your ass? How's that for a comment?"

Holly's smile only faltered for a moment. She turned back toward the camera. "Emotions are running high in the New York Police Department," she said, "as they struggle to work out how this terrible event could have happened. At this moment, details are still sketchy, but at least one police officer has been wounded. A source within the Department says—"

Erin grabbed Vic's arm, tugging him away from the reporter before he could say or do anything else.

One of the EMTs saw them coming out of the corner of his eye. He held up a hand. "We're busy, fellas," he said. "We gotta get this guy to Bellevue, stat."

"These guys are my friends," Vic said. "What the hell happened to him?"

Erin caught sight of the wounded man. She was momentarily frozen in place, staring. She'd seen worse sights, but not for a while. Her last cup of coffee tried to climb up the back of her throat. She gulped the acidic bile back down, leaving sour residue on her tongue.

"Scalded," the paramedic said over his shoulder, loading the stretcher into the back of the vehicle. "Steam burns, bad ones. Plus some shrapnel."

"Steam?" Vic echoed. "I thought it was a bomb."

"Talk to the other cops," the EMT said. "That's your department, not mine. Come on, Joe, let's roll out."

The ambulance's engine roared to life. Its siren sounded and it drove off in the direction of the hospital, parting traffic as it went.

"Shit," Vic said quietly. "That was Campbell."

"How could you tell?" Erin asked. "I didn't recognize his face, all swollen and... and burned like that."

"He's wearing ESU tac gear," Vic said. He looked like he might throw up. "And Nichols was talking on the radio, so I know he's pretty much fine. God, Campbell's got fucking *kids*."

"He'll be okay," she said, hoping it was true. "It's probably not as bad as it looks. Let's find Nichols."

"He'll be with the judge," Vic said. "Doing his job."

They found Officer Nichols with Judge Ferris and Julia Lockhart. Ferris was sitting on the courthouse steps, two steps up from the sidewalk. His secretary was seated next to him. Nichols was standing, rifle in hand, scanning the crowd for potential threats. Ferris had a bandage wrapped around his head. His white hair was streaked with blood, but his eyes were bright and clear. All three were soaking wet. Julia was shivering, though some considerate cop had draped first-aid blankets around her and Ferris.

"Your Honor," Erin said. "Are you okay? Shouldn't you be going to the hospital?"

"I'm quite all right, young lady," Ferris said. "A piece of metal grazed my temple, drawing a shocking but harmless amount of blood."

"You really should have a doctor see you, Howard," Julia agreed.

"Nonsense," Ferris said. "They have their hands full with that poor young man. His condition is far worse than mine."

"What happened, Nichols?" Vic asked the ESU officer. Erin saw that Nichols had a couple of small cuts on his face and the backs of his hands, but he seemed mostly intact.

"We were moving out of the office," Nichols said. "The goddamn radiator blew up. The office had this big metal one against the back wall, next to the judge's hide-a-bed. I was looking the other way, turned around in time to catch a couple pieces of it. Campbell was closest, between the blast and the rest of us, so he took most of the force."

"How'd it explode?" Erin asked.

"Hell if I know," Nichols said. "All I heard was a bang, like a big piece of metal hitting concrete. Next thing I knew, it was like a firehose was spraying the room, except it was hot water, damn near boiling. Poor Chunky caught it right in the face."

"Jesus," Vic said.

"If I'd still been sitting at my desk, I would have been boiled like a lobster," Ferris said. "I owe you thanks, Detective O'Reilly. You saved my life."

"If I'd been quicker, nobody would've been hurt," Erin said. "Where's everyone else who was inside?"

"Over there," Nichols said, indicating a crowd of lawyers and staff. "They evacuated the whole building again."

"Our guy's long gone," Vic predicted, following Erin's stare.

"Maybe," she said. "But he hung around the house after he rigged the bathroom. I think he's watching right now, seeing if his plan worked."

"Then we'd better get you under cover, Your Honor," Nichols said, clearly thinking about snipers.

"That's not this guy's style," Erin said. "But yeah, it's probably a good idea anyway. God only knows what he'll come up with next. He'll drop a construction crane on you or some damn thing."

"We'd better take a look inside," Vic said.

"Maybe we can pick up his trail," Erin said.

"Please catch him, Detectives," Ferris said quietly. "Quite enough people have already suffered on my account."

Chapter 17

Erin, Rolf, and Vic were greeted by water trickling down the stairs outside Ferris's office. A dense cloud of steam filled the air. They stepped carefully on the marble floor. It was dangerously slick with moisture.

"Didn't they drain the pipes?" Erin wondered aloud.

"Yeah, but that takes time for a building this size," Vic said. "A whole lot of water would've come out. You know anything about old plumbing?"

"The house I grew up in had hot-water radiators," she said, peering into the judge's chambers. "Dad handled the everyday maintenance. He had to bleed them in the winter."

The floor was awash. The judge's desk had taken a good hosing from the burst radiator. Sodden lumps of paper were strewn around the room, floating on a couple inches of water. The water was warm, but no longer scalding.

"What do you mean, bleed them?" Vic asked.

"Air builds up in the pipes," she explained. "There's valves on the radiators. You open them up to let the air out. Otherwise the hot water doesn't circulate right and your house gets cold."

"The whole thing's kind of like a nuclear reactor, isn't it?" Vic said. "Like the coolant loop, I mean."

"I guess," she said, picking her way across the room. She could feel the water soaking through her shoes into her socks. "Except for the radiation."

Rolf splashed beside her, happy enough. He didn't mind water one bit. He nosed curiously at a soggy legal brief.

"Maybe that's why they call them radiators," Vic said. "Any idea how you make one of them explode?"

"It must be a pressure thing," Erin said. She'd reached the radiator on the far side of the room. It was a massive old iron device that looked as solid and formidable as a steam locomotive. However, one of its heavy coils had split open, peeling back like a banana. Water dripped from the gash in a steady, monotonous rhythm.

"Interesting thing about water," Vic said. "You can't compress it. You can squash air down, but water has to go somewhere. That's called Pascal's Law."

"You're a physicist now?"

"I do have a college degree, Little Miss Smartass. You think maybe our guy just blocked the outflow from this unit?"

"We'd have to talk to a plumber," she said. "But I'm guessing it was something like that, if he didn't stick an explosive charge in the pipe while he was working on it."

"Would your dog have smelled it in there?"

"Through solid metal and underwater? I don't know."

Rolf cocked his head, apparently perplexed by the idea that he might not be able to sniff something out.

"*Such*," Erin told him, directing him toward the radiator.

Rolf snuffled at the metal for a moment. Then he moved on, sniffing at Ferris's desk and around the rest of the room.

"No explosive residue," she said. "But CSU should be able to make sure."

"What I want to know is, why plant the bomb?" Vic asked. "Obviously it was never supposed to go off."

"It was a decoy," she said. "He needed time to set up his little booby trap. Somebody might've noticed if he just wandered into a maintenance corridor and didn't come out for a long time. He must've gone in and made the leak in the pipe himself. Then he called in the bomb. Of course we trusted him, once we found the device. Then we just let him hang out in there for a couple of hours, unsupervised, while we thought the danger was over, and he nearly got Ferris."

"He did get Campbell," Vic growled. "And I'm gonna get him, the slick bastard. And when I do, I'm gonna force-feed him his toolkit, one socket wrench at a time, until he shits stainless steel."

"We've got to catch him first," she said.

*　*　*

Webb arrived a short while later, along with Skip Taylor and a CSU team. The technicians immediately kicked everyone else out of Ferris's office and started going through it for evidence. Skip went back into the maintenance corridor to see what he could find out from the pipes. Erin, Vic, and Webb headed to the security station to get their hands on the camera footage. Their next stop after that was Erin's Charger, where she loaded the files onto her computer and sent them back to the Eightball. Then she made a phone call.

"Internal Affairs, Detective Jones," were the words which met her ear.

"Hey, Kira," Erin said. "This isn't exactly an IAB problem, but we're really shorthanded, and Major Crimes doesn't have anyone at the house at the moment. I was wondering if you could do us a solid."

"What do you need?" Kira Jones asked. "I do have a day job, you know. You're lucky I'm still at the office."

"Yeah, I know. And I appreciate this. I was hoping you could run a face through the recognition program and see if we get any hits. It's a long shot, but we need a break."

"Okay, fine," Kira sighed. "Any idea who this guy is?"

"Former military, probably," Erin said. "He's a contract killer for the Mob. Poses as a janitor."

"Go ahead and send him to me. I'll see what I can do."

Almost before she'd hung up, Erin texted Kira Kustosz's photo.

"You think we should have your mutt track him?" Vic asked as she hit the Send button.

Erin shook her head. "He had an exit lined up. He's either on the subway or in a car by now. We aren't going to nail this guy by running after him."

"You're right," Webb said. "We need an ID. Then we have something to go on. He knows we saw his face and we got his alias, but he doesn't know we know his Mob nickname and MO. He'll move, but he may not move quite fast enough."

"Absolutely," Vic said. He leaned against the side of the Charger and put his hands in his pockets. "Because we're moving real fast right now. Blinding speed."

Erin didn't have the heart to needle Vic about his sarcasm, because he was right. Being a detective, unfortunately, meant a lot of waiting for other people to get back to you. In the meantime, they had very little to do. She settled back in the driver's seat and closed her eyes. Rolf rested his chin on her shoulder. Webb walked a few feet away and lit a cigarette.

Time passed. Rolf circled in his compartment, curled into a ball, and went to sleep. Vic pulled out a scary-looking survival knife and trimmed a hangnail. Webb smoked two more cigarettes.

Erin's phone buzzed. Kira's name showed on the screen.

"Your guy isn't in the NYPD database," Kira reported.

"Worth a try," Erin said. "Thanks anyway."

Kira wasn't done. "So I decided to cross-check with the military," she said. "I ran it against service photos of soldiers from the Tri-State area."

"Good thinking," Erin said, sitting up. "Did you get a hit?"

"Maybe. It's an old photo, more than twenty years. I'm lucky it was digitized. It's not a perfect match, but it's close."

"Define close."

"Eighty-nine percent."

"That's good enough for me. Who is it?" Erin rolled down her window and waved to get Webb and Vic's attention. They hurried over as she put the phone on speaker.

"Binkowski," Kira said. "Bartosz Binkowski. I have no idea if I'm saying that right. I'm betting he goes by Bart."

"Sounds like a Polack," Vic said, nodding.

"That scans," Webb said. "It fits his alias for this job."

"He was in the Second Armored Division," Kira said. "Logistics and support. He was a mechanic, what they call a T/5. That's a Technician, Fifth Grade."

"So he's got technical skills," Webb said. "I'm liking the sound of this guy. Where is he now? He's not still in the Army, is he?"

"He's forty-six," Kira said. "He was discharged from when the Second Armored was inactivated after Desert Storm. He's not drawing disability or a pension. Looks like he used his GI benefits to enroll in technical school. After that, the Army lost track of him. I could try to run him down a little further, but why should I have all the fun?"

"Translation: you've got work to do and you don't feel like you should have to do any more of ours," Erin said, smiling.

"Thanks, Kira. You've done plenty. Can you send me his Army photo?"

"On the way."

A few seconds later, the face of a young man popped up on Erin's computer screen. All three detectives peered at it.

"Yeah, that's him," Vic said. "Of course, now he looks like his own dad, but I'd bet my pension this is our guy."

"And we've got a name," Webb said. "Let's nail this son of a bitch."

*　　*　　*

Erin could have gone home. Maybe she should have. She'd worked a full day, driving up and down Manhattan. She was tired. Her feet were soaking wet and the late-autumn chill was seeping into her from the ground up. On top of that, Rolf was wet, and the smell of damp dog permeated her car. She hadn't eaten a reasonable meal in far too long.

But the man who'd killed one New York judge and nearly killed another was still out there, planning his next move. And now they had a name, a face, and a history. They were on the home stretch, she could feel it, and this was no time to pause for breath. Now was the time to pour it on.

There was nothing to do at the courthouse. CSU and the Bomb Squad would pass along whatever they found. So the detectives drove back to the Eightball. Erin stopped along the way to pick up some Chinese takeout. Vic dove into his fried rice before they'd even arrived, to Rolf's intense interest.

"Makes you think," Vic said around a mouthful of rice as she parked the Charger and they got out.

"What does?" Erin asked.

"This Janitor mope. Doorknobs, radiators... the guy could probably kill you with half the stuff in your house."

"As if I wasn't paranoid enough already," she said. She reached out to open the door leading into the stairwell. Then she hesitated, her hand hovering an inch from the metal handle.

"See what I mean?" Vic said grimly.

"The sooner we grab this guy the happier I'll be," she said, making herself take hold of the doorknob. Nothing happened, of course.

But grabbing their suspect was easier said than done. Bartosz Binkowski had neither a listed phone number nor an address in New York. They tried New Jersey and Connecticut, in case he commuted in from the Tri-State Area, but came up empty.

They moved on to employment records. They had Binkowski's Social Security number, so if he was using his real identity, they might be able to track him that way. But either he was too careful to leave a digital footprint, or he made enough money as a hitman that he didn't bother with a day job.

The Veterans' Administration was likewise no help. He was drawing no benefits from them and the only address they had was fifteen years old. Lacking better leads, Vic looked into the apartment listing. After a few moments, he sat back from his computer and vented fifteen seconds' worth of quiet expletives.

"No good?" Erin asked.

"The whole damn building got torn down a decade ago," he said. "It was re-zoned for commercial development. Now it's an office building. I don't know where he's sleeping now, but it's sure as hell not there. Maybe he's living in the sewers, like that Eurotrash terrorist."

"Don't remind me," Erin said. "But there's no way he's living down there. He wouldn't be able to keep clean. We would've smelled it on him. It took a week and three baths to get the stink out of Rolf's fur."

"There you go again, thinking with your nose," he said. "What time is it?"

"Late." She hadn't looked at a clock in a while. "How you doing, sir?"

"I was just thinking we should get some teenagers on the Force," Webb said. "They *like* staying up all night. We could give them the data-retrieval jobs and the rest of us could get some sleep."

"Wouldn't work," Vic said. "They'd just plagiarize the files from some website and pretend they did the research."

"Who've we got watching Ferris now?" Erin asked.

"They've detailed a full ESU squad," Webb said. "As I understand it, they're living at his house with him."

"He's staying at home?" Erin was alarmed.

"Relax, O'Reilly. They'll have turned it into a fortress by now."

"Yeah, but it's a fortress Binkowski's been inside," she said. "He knows the layout. He may have some other surprises lying around."

"This guy isn't a super-genius," Webb said. "He doesn't think of everything and he doesn't plan fifteen moves ahead. We've stopped him twice."

"We didn't stop shit," Vic said. "The first time, Ferris only survived because the wrong person went to the bathroom. After that, we got damn lucky with the timing and Campbell still got wasted. We've got to keep getting lucky. He only needs to score once."

"I think I'd better check in with my sources," Erin said. "I had my guy asking around. Maybe he found something we couldn't."

Carlyle picked up his phone on the second ring. Erin could hear the background noise of the Barley Corner, the happy chatter of a busy pub. "Evening, darling," he said.

"Could you find anything out about the Janitor?" she asked.

"Nothing definite. I've done what I could. I can tell you he's unaffiliated, a free agent. Have you any idea how rare those lads are?"

"Hitmen for hire? I have no idea. It's not like they post their resumes. Anything else?"

"I'm near certain he lives in Manhattan."

"How do you know?"

"I spoke with someone who claims to have met him. This Janitor's a light-haired man, going gray, about my age. Brown eyes. Firm jaw, weathered face."

"That fits," Erin said. "I met him earlier today."

"Really?" Carlyle was surprised. "So he's in custody?"

"He slipped us. We didn't know who he was at the time. And we don't know where he's gone. But I've got a name. How good are your contacts?"

"Decent, but I wish Corky was here. He's really the best lad when it comes to finding lads."

"I need to locate Bartosz Binkowski. He's probably working some sort of maintenance job, maybe off the books, if he's working at all. I know you're not Corky, but maybe you know some of his union guys who could help."

"I might, at that. Can you give me a few hours to make some calls?"

"Yeah, but we're on a clock. Every minute gives this jerk more of a chance to throw another plan together."

"Since we're looking for a mechanic, you're familiar with the main rule of engineering, aren't you, darling?"

"What's that?"

"Everyone wants it fast, they want it cheap, and they want it good."

Erin sighed. "Yeah, I know. And you have to pick two. Fine. The info needs to be good and it needs to be fast. I don't care about cheap."

"If I go spreading money around, word may get back to the wrong ears."

"If we're too slow, somebody else dies."

"If you're wanting to remind me we're playing at the high-stakes table, darling, I knew that already."

"Right. Sorry."

Chapter 18

"It's ten o'clock," Webb said. "We should have been done five hours ago. You do know we don't have overtime in the departmental budget, right?"

"I'm compensated by love of my work," Vic said.

"I'm waiting on a phone call," Erin said. "Besides, I used to work nights all the time."

"I've got a squad of masochists," Webb sighed. "I'm too old to be keeping these hours. Do we have any reason to expect a major break in the case tonight?"

"Best case scenario, we find out where the guy works," Erin said.

"And he won't be working until tomorrow," Webb said. "So I'm going home to get reacquainted with my bed. It might've forgotten what I look like. Call me if there's anything I absolutely need to know. Otherwise, please don't."

The Lieutenant shut down his computer and walked out of Major Crimes, taking the elevator. The others watched him go.

"I guess I'll hang around a little longer," Vic said.

"Nothing waiting for you at home?" Erin asked.

"That's the thing," he replied. "There might be someone waiting. I'd just as soon stay here. Remember that thing I was supposed to go to with Zofia?"

"Vic, she's a cop too. She understands. When there's lives on the line, the Job comes first."

"Oh, she understands all right, but she'll still be pissed off. I'll take my chances with you and the hitman. Better odds."

Erin nodded. She was working on her DD-5s, writing up the various incidents she'd been involved in. When you were a detective and you weren't talking to suspects or checking crime scenes, chances were you were doing paperwork. Rolf, being sensible, had curled up next to her desk and gone to sleep. She'd have to remember to give him a late supper. It'd make sense to stock a bag of kibble in her desk in the future. She wondered why she'd never thought to do that before.

Her phone buzzed. She snatched it up. Rolf opened one sleepy, quizzical eye.

"O'Reilly," she said.

"I spoke to a lad I know," Carlyle said. "Another lad, going by Binkowski, has a position at the Lincoln Center. Specifically, he works backstage at the Vivian Beaumont Theater."

"How good is this info?" she asked, grabbing a pen and jotting it down.

"I'm thinking it's solid."

"How'd you get that so fast?"

"There's a union called the IATSE," Carlyle explained. "That stands for the International Alliance of Theatrical Stage Employees, unless I'm mistaken. Corky made some connections with them year before last, broadening his influence."

"I wouldn't think that was the sort of thing the Mob would be interested in."

"Because we're all a lot of Philistines with no appreciation for the Arts?" Carlyle chuckled. "Nay, darling, Corky's interested in all the unions. Organized labor's a grand source of illicit income. I just had the thought that this lad likes to pretend he's something he's not, so I wondered if he might be involved in the theater. From that it was a short jump to thinking of stagehands, as his skills would fit with that manner of job."

"It's too bad you didn't become a cop," she said. "You'd have made a top-notch detective."

"I played a hunch and got lucky. But he may not be the one you're looking for. There's more than one Binkowski in New York."

"We'll look into it. Thanks."

"Don't mention it, darling. Will you be coming home soon?"

"Probably. I'm going to see what else I can run down on this guy first."

"I'll keep the fires burning for you."

When Erin hung up, Vic was looking at her. "Sounds like you've got something," he said.

She went to the whiteboard and wrote out the name of the theater. By the time she finished, Vic's fingers were already busy at his keyboard.

"The theater's on West 65th," he reported. "Just north of Hell's Kitchen. Half an hour away, maybe less this time of night. I think my mom took me there once, when I was a kid."

"Your mom took you to the theater? I had no idea."

"*Swan Lake.* Russians have a thing about ballet. Hey, looks like they're putting on a production of *The King and I*. Isn't that the one about King Arthur?"

"You're thinking of *Camelot*," she said. "*The King and I* is about that Englishwoman who goes to Siam. Haven't you seen the movie?"

"Any gunfights in it?"

"Not that I remember."

"Then no."

Erin shrugged it off. "We still don't know where Binkowski is living," she said. "So we'll have to stake out the theater and hope we can snag him there. But if he's still trying for Ferris, he may have called in sick. Lord knows when he'll be back on the job. I just don't see what else we can do."

"Okay, let's go." Vic stood up.

She looked at him blankly. "Go? Where?"

"To the theater."

"Now?"

"Yeah. Weren't you listening? They're showing a play. It's happening right this minute. If we hurry, we can get there before it's over."

"You think he's there now? Tonight?"

"I think it's worth a shot. At least we can show his picture around, see if anybody recognizes him. But if you'd rather wait for tomorrow..."

"No, you're right. No time to waste." Erin got to her feet.

Rolf bounced up immediately, wide awake, tail in motion. This looked promising.

*   *   *

"I can feel myself getting more cultured," Vic said. "Look around. We got libraries, schools, theaters... you sure we're still in New York?"

"New York's got plenty of culture," Erin said. "You and I just see the ugly parts of the city most of the time."

"That's because people don't get whacked in places like this," he said, giving the Vivian Beaumont Theater an appreciative look. "Look at that. There's the friggin' Juilliard School right across the street! Isn't that where they send you if you're some sort of musical prodigy?"

"I think so," she said.

"You ever think of going?"

She gave him a look. "Are you kidding? I carry a tune like a concealed weapon."

"I thought maybe you played the piano or something, back when you were a kid."

"I played soccer." Erin paused on the sidewalk. "I guess this is the place."

The two detectives and one K-9 went up a flight of concrete steps to the plaza level of the theater complex. It was nighttime, but the area was well lit. A few people were hanging around, talking in small groups.

"Maybe we should wait until the show's over," Erin said.

"Yeah, great idea," Vic said. "Then we can try to find this punk in the middle of two hundred other people on their way home."

"I was thinking we didn't want those two hundred people in the line of fire if this goes sideways," she said.

"You thinking about the last theater we were in?" Vic asked. "The one that burned down? Or maybe the one before that, with the magicians throwing knives and blowing shit up. I'm telling you, the NYPD is no friend to the performing arts, leastwise not when we're around."

"Vic, if he's here, it's because he doesn't know we're on to him. He's not going to be armed to the teeth. He may not even be armed at all."

"You forgetting this guy almost killed four people with a radiator? You think he needs weapons?"

"If we see him, we'll call for backup immediately," she promised. "But I think this is probably a wild-goose chase."

"You ever actually chase a wild goose? I bet your mutt could catch one."

"Probably," Erin said. She walked up to a pair of glass doors and went through, Rolf close beside her.

"Good evening," an usher said. He was standing beside the theater entrance, looking very neat and well-groomed in a burgundy vest over a white shirt.

"Evening," Erin said, showing the gold shield on her belt. "We're with the NYPD, Major Crimes. We need to know if one of your employees is working this evening."

"Oh," the guy said, surprised. He was very young, probably a drama student pulling in a little extra income. "Um... I think I'd better get my boss. Can you wait here a second?"

"Sure," Erin said. Faint strains of music drifted through the door. It sounded vaguely familiar, though Erin hadn't seen *The King and I* since she was a little girl.

They waited a few minutes. Then the usher returned with a much older, gray-haired man.

"Mr. Murdock," the usher said. "Here they are. They're looking for one of our people."

"Bartosz Binkowski," Erin said. She held up a printout they'd enlarged from the courthouse security camera. The image was grainy but recognizable.

"Bart?" Murdock said. "Is he in some sort of trouble? We've never had any problem with him."

"Is he here?" Erin asked. "Tonight?"

"Well, I think so," Murdock said. "He's on the schedule. I don't know that I've seen him personally. We've got a lot going on right now. It's opening night, and there's always a few wrinkles to iron out."

"Where would he be?" Erin asked.

"Backstage," Murdock said. "But can't this wait? I'd like to avoid any disruption of the play."

There were times to play your cards close to the chest, and times to lay them on the table.

"Sir, this man is wanted for murder," Erin said. "He's tried to kill other people, too. We need to take him into custody immediately, before anyone else gets hurt."

Murdock blinked. "Really?"

"Yeah," Vic said. "So, are you gonna stand there, or are you gonna help us?"

"Aren't I supposed to see a warrant or something?" Murdock asked.

"We don't need a warrant," Erin said impatiently. "We're not searching the premises. The only thing we're planning on removing is Binkowski himself. The picture I showed you is from a security camera at the courthouse. That footage was taken today when Binkowski, posing as a courthouse custodian, tried to murder someone. Sir, we really don't have time to discuss this."

Murdock cleared his throat and wiped his forehead. "Yes, of course," he said, speaking low and fast. "Please follow me. Right this way."

"Better call it in, Vic," Erin said as they followed the man.

"Dispatch, this is Neshenko," Vic said into his phone. "Shield six-nine-nine-two. Requesting Patrol units to Vivian Beaumont Theater, on West 65th. Possible sighting of suspect Binkowski, wanted in connection with the death of Judge Miranda Rodriguez and attempted murder of Judge Howard Ferris. Suspect is to be considered armed and dangerous."

"My God," Murdock murmured as he fumbled for his keys, unlocking a door which led into a back hallway. "The man's worked here for years. Model employee. Here we are. Employee lockers here, the backstage area is around to the right."

The lockers were gray sheet metal perforated by horizontal slits, a row of them standing along one wall. Erin took a moment to scan them.

"C'mon," Vic said. "He's not here. I thought we were in a hurry."

"Just a minute," she said, finding the one labeled BINKOWSKI. "Can you open this, sir?"

"Why?" Murdock asked. "I thought you needed a warrant to search."

Erin cursed inwardly. He was right. If he didn't give permission, she couldn't legally open the locker without a warrant. And getting a warrant would take time, time she wasn't sure they had.

"What're you looking for?" Vic asked.

"Anything he was wearing," Erin said, cocking her head toward Rolf.

"Gotcha," Vic said. He examined the locker. It was secured with a combination lock. "You know, this thing doesn't look too sturdy. There was a trick I had back in high school. I wonder..."

"Vic..." Erin said warningly.

He wasn't listening. He took hold of the latch, gripped it tightly, and gave a sharp upward tug. At the same time, he kicked the bottom of the locker. There was an echoing clang and the door popped open.

"You can't do that," Murdock protested.

"I didn't unlock it," Vic said, giving the man his trademark fake-innocent wide-eyed stare, the one that always failed to convince his colleagues.

"We're not removing anything," Erin said. "We won't even touch anything." She saw a leather jacket hanging from a peg. The locker was otherwise empty. That was fine; as long as the jacket had been worn by Binkowski, it was all she needed.

"I don't understand," Murdock said.

Erin ignored him. "Rolf," she said, pointing to the jacket. "*Such!*"

Rolf eagerly thrust his muzzle at the jacket. He snuffled at it, committing the scent to memory. Then he cast about with his snout, testing the air. His entire body stiffened, from his nose to the tip of his tail. Wagging vigorously, he lunged forward, heading backstage.

"Thanks, buddy," Vic said to Murdock. "We'll take it from here."

Erin knew the backup was on their way, would be there in a matter of minutes. Maybe they ought to wait. But her blood was up now, her nerves humming with the thrill of the chase.

Rolf weaved his way down dark hallways, hot on the trail of his quarry. He knew the man he was following had been this way, and not long ago. The scent was fresh in his nostrils. The man might be a bad guy, in which case he might get to bite him. Even if not, Rolf knew his partner had his favorite rubber Kong toy in her pocket. That made everything worthwhile. He plunged ahead, throwing his shoulders against the leash, trying to get his two-footed partner to move faster.

Rolf came to a metal stairway. He scrambled up the steps, panting and wagging. Erin hurried behind. Vic was right on her heels. Murdock, still feebly protesting, was left behind. Erin heard him saying something about liability issues, at which point she stopped listening.

They reached a catwalk above the stage. Erin realized the performance was going on some twenty feet below them. The chorus was singing the words "Run, Eliza, run! Run from Simon, run!" She could see, almost directly below, the play-within-a-play, *The Small House of Uncle Thomas*. Music washed over her.

Up ahead, a man was working a system of ropes and pulleys, doing something with the backdrop. Another stagehand was handling a spotlight, shining it down on the center of the stage, tracking the movements of one of the actresses.

Rolf, catching sight and scent of his target, barked sharply.

The man at the ropes looked up and Erin saw a face she remembered from the courthouse. His eyes widened for a moment, then narrowed.

"Freeze, Binkowski!" Erin snapped, grabbing her gun with her free hand.

"NYPD, asshole!" Vic said over her shoulder.

Binkowski was holding a rope with both hands. With no expression at all on his face, he made a circular motion, almost too quick to follow. The rope looped around the chest of the other stagehand, under his arms. Binkowski let go.

"Don't!" Erin shouted, but it was too late. On the other end of the rope, a heavy canvas background painting began to fall. With a startled cry, the stagehand was yanked off his feet and over the side of the catwalk into space.

Erin's eyes followed the unfortunate man, just as Binkowski wanted. She couldn't help it. Vic dropped his gun and made a desperate lunge. His pistol clattered on the catwalk as he vaulted the railing, holding on with one hand as he snatched at the falling man with the other. More by luck than judgment, he snagged the guy's ankle.

"Don't move or I'll shoot!" Erin yelled at Binkowski, taking aim.

"Your buddy's in trouble," Binkowski said calmly. "Better reel him in before he falls."

"I will kill you!" Erin promised him.

"Oh my God!" the stagehand wailed.

The music faltered. Somebody in the audience screamed. People were running around on the stage, two stories below.

"Don't worry about me," Vic grated out. "I'm just friggin' fine." He was suspended in midair, arms stretched wide, holding not only his own weight but the poor stagehand as well. The backdrop was providing some counterweight on the pulley, but not enough for Vic to reel him in.

It was a momentary stalemate. Erin knew she had to take Binkowski, but she wasn't willing to trade Vic's life for the assassin. She hesitated. Her eyes slid toward Vic.

Binkowski's left hand dropped to the railing. He grabbed the handle on the spotlight, swinging it up to point directly in Erin's face. The light was blindingly bright. She closed her eyes reflexively, seeing giant purple sunbursts on the inside of her eyelids.

"*Fass!*" Erin shouted, letting go of the leash.

That was all Rolf had been waiting for. He sprang at Binkowski. Erin heard a short exclamation from the man. There was a scuffling sound, the click of Rolf's claws on the catwalk, and the dog's deep-throated snarl. She blinked frantically, trying to clear her vision.

Through streaming eyes, Erin saw a blurry image of a man and dog struggling on the narrow catwalk. Binkowski was poised on the railing, trying to jump clear, but Rolf had his right arm in his jaws and no intention of letting go.

Erin took a step toward them. Binkowski's foot slipped. He pitched sideways. Then he tumbled over the railing, his arm wrenched into a grotesque angle by the weight of the dog. Rolf planted his paws and strained, but the man was too heavy. However, the K-9 had been ordered to bite. When he got the "bite" command, he wasn't supposed to let go, not for anything.

"*Pust!*" Erin shouted, Rolf's "release" command.

It was too late. Binkowski's full weight dragged at the dog, yanking him over the railing. Man and dog plummeted into space.

Chapter 19

Erin wasn't a screamer. She always rolled her eyes at women in movies who wasted their energy screaming their heads off when they ought to be running, or fighting, or doing something useful. So not a sound passed her lips as she watched Rolf fall from the catwalk, separated from her by ten feet that might as well have been ten miles. But inside her heart, her soul was screaming itself raw.

She was frozen in place for two seconds; two endless, horrible seconds. Then her training and experience asserted themselves, fueled by helpless anger. She couldn't do a thing for Rolf at that moment, but she had another partner who needed her. She shoved her Glock back into its holster, turned, and grabbed Vic's arm.

"I got you," she said.

"Never doubted it," Vic said. His voice was tight with strain. Erin could feel the muscles and tendons in his arm. The limb was quivering with exertion.

"Oh Jesus!" the stagehand babbled. "I'm gonna fall! I'm slipping!"

"Quit squirming, idiot," Vic growled. "Or I really will drop you."

Pure chaos had erupted in the theater below. Dozens of voices were shouting, screaming, talking over one another. Erin, her hands fully occupied holding onto Vic, risked a very quick downward glance. She saw Binkowski on the stage, flat on his back, one leg crumpled under him, Rolf lying on top.

The Shepherd moved. Erin's heart leaped. Rolf wriggled onto his belly. The Shepherd stood up. He still had Binkowski's right arm in his jaws. His tail started wagging.

"Rolf's alive!" Erin gasped. Tears were running down her cheeks. She told herself it was probably the aftereffect of the spotlight shining in her eyes.

"That's great," Vic said, teeth gritted. "Now how about getting us out of this?"

"I can't lift you, Vic," she said. "Not along with him. You weigh a ton."

"Right," he muttered. "Okay. Can you just hold on? And get ready to catch him?"

She shifted her grip, wrapping her hands around his wrist. She braced her feet and locked her arms. Then she nodded.

She knew Vic spent a lot of time at the gym. Where she concentrated on general fitness and running, Vic loved lifting weights. He had the arms and shoulders to prove it, but Erin had always assumed it was mostly for show, to display his masculinity for the world. Now she found out she'd been wrong.

He sucked in a deep breath. His muscles flexed. He gave a growl of effort that turned into something that was almost a roar. And he pulled.

Without the pulley taking some of the stagehand's weight, he never could have managed it. Even with its assistance, it was a near thing. The hapless man slowly rose, Vic hauling him up one-handed by the ankle. The big Russian pulled in one steady, continuous motion, bringing the other guy level with the catwalk.

"Get... him..." Vic said.

Erin let go of Vic's hand and seized the whimpering stagehand's other leg. She managed to thread him under the railing and onto the catwalk. As she did so, the rope that Binkowski had thrown around him slid loose. The heavy canvas backdrop thumped to the stage.

She turned back to Vic, who was heaving himself toward her. She got his free hand in hers and guided him to safety. He rolled heavily over the railing and landed on his hands and knees on the catwalk, paying no attention to the way the metal grille bit into his palms and kneecaps.

"Shit," he gasped. "Goddamn Mel Gibson *Lethal Weapon* bullshit. Never had a problem with heights before. Not going up in a rollercoaster. Never again. No skiing, no skydiving, no bungee jumping. No way. Feet on the ground. Christ on crutches."

"You okay?" Erin asked.

He waved a hand at her without looking up. His face was very pale. "No problem. Go. Take care of Rolf. Make the arrest. Don't let that bastard get away."

"I don't think he's going anywhere," she said. Leaving Vic and the whimpering fetal ball that was the stagehand, she ran for the stairs.

The actors and audience had no idea what was going on. They'd seen a man come down like a meteor into the middle of a Rogers and Hammerstein musical, a pissed-off German Shepherd riding him all the way. Now the dog, growling vigorously, was biting the man, who was obviously seriously injured. Rolf's vest identified him as a police K-9, but some of the bystanders still thought they ought to do something. One of the more adventurous cast members began to cautiously approach the Shepherd, patting the air and making soothing noises.

"Good doggie," he said. "Good, good doggie."

Rolf growled deep in his chest. He didn't need a stranger to tell him he was a good boy; he knew that already. But while he agreed with the actor's assessment, he didn't trust the guy one bit.

"Back off!" Erin snapped at the actor, running to her dog. "NYPD! Give me some room!"

"What's going on?" a man called from further back in the theater. "NYPD!" A pair of Patrol officers were pushing through the crowd, but they were having trouble. Everyone was on their feet, milling around, trying to see what was going on.

"Call a bus!" Erin yelled back. "We got one wounded. Serious fall, probable broken bones."

Rolf, hearing her, wagged his tail harder, but he didn't let go. He hadn't heard, or hadn't registered, her release command. He'd been given one specific job and he intended to keep right on doing it.

"Easy, kiddo," she said, kneeling beside him. "*Pust.*"

Rolf immediately let go. He pranced back and cocked his head, waiting to be told what a good boy he was by the only voice that really mattered.

"*Sei brav,*" she said, getting the words out through a sudden lump in her throat. He'd very nearly jumped to his death just because she'd told him to, and all he was asking in return was a cheap rubber chew-toy and a few kind words. She could hardly believe he wasn't dead or crippled.

She yanked the Kong ball out of her pocket and tossed it to him. He grabbed it in midair with a joyful leap, plopped down, curled his front paws around it, and started making wet squeaky sounds of delight.

Erin knew she had to check him for injuries. The Shepherd was as tough as they came, and might not even know he'd been hurt. But Binkowski was obviously badly wounded. The man hadn't moved since hitting the stage. Blood was pooling under the back of his head, and that was never a good sign. His eyes were open, but she couldn't tell if he was conscious.

"Bart, can you hear me?" she said, carefully looking him over. He'd landed badly, striking the ground with his shoulders and head first. It was incredible his skull hadn't cracked like an egg. She couldn't move him, not when he almost certainly had head and neck injuries.

Binkowski blinked. His eyes focused on her face. He licked his lips. There was blood on his mouth and staining his teeth. He'd probably bitten his tongue.

"Hell of a thing," he murmured. His voice was barely audible.

"Why'd you jump?" Erin asked, bending close to him. "For God's sake, we were just going to arrest you."

"Wouldn't have lasted," Binkowski said. "Not in prison. Know too much. Too many bodies... where they're buried."

The Patrol cops clambered up onto the stage. "Bus is on the way, Detective," one of them said. "Should be here in ten."

"Hear that, Bart?" Erin said. "The ambulance is coming. We'll get you fixed up. Don't try to move."

Binkowski's lips curled in something that might have been a smile. "Won't be a problem," he said. "Don't think I can. Can't feel anything... past my neck. Don't have to worry... about me... anymore. Think maybe... I'll clock out early."

"Oh no you don't," she said. "You don't get to die on me."

"Why not? Want to know about... bodies?" He was still smiling. "Too many. Haven't got time... to tell you about... all of them."

"Why'd you do it?" she asked.

"Why not? Money was good."

That wasn't a good enough answer, but Erin knew it was the only one she'd get. She found his pulse in his wrist. It was erratic. His skin was cool to the touch. He was in serious shock.

"Bart," she said. "Who hired you? To kill the judge?"

"That old man?" Binkowski said, and he actually laughed. It was a weak, halting sound, more like a coughing fit. "Easy job... wouldn't you think? Over eighty, got a bad heart. Old bastard just won't... go down. Never saw a guy... harder to kill."

Binkowski stopped laughing. He closed his eyes and drew in a weak, shuddering breath.

"Who?" Erin demanded. "Give me a name!" She was gripping his hand tightly, even though she knew he couldn't feel it.

"Oil Man," Binkowski murmured. "Who else?"

"Why?"

"Favor, I think." Binkowski was having more trouble getting the words out. "One of his guys... has a son. On trial. Wanted... better judge. Make sure... he gets off."

"Vitelli?" Erin asked. "Valentino Vitelli?"

"That's him," Binkowski said.

"Was Valentino in on the plan?"

"Had to be."

"Can you prove Vinnie Moreno gave you the order?" Erin pressed.

"Of course not. Nothing written down. Didn't talk to him direct."

Erin swore silently. She felt the Oil Man slithering out of her grasp yet again.

"Not your problem," Binkowski whispered. "Got one more trick... up my sleeve."

Erin felt a chill run through her own body, like a jet of ice water. "What are you talking about?" she asked.

"Didn't mean to get the lady," Binkowski said. "Sorry. But doorknob's just one trick. Got backup plan..."

"At Ferris's house?"

"Yeah. In case I missed. Got another toy..."

"What is it?" she demanded. "Where?"

"Won't get anybody but him." Binkowski smiled again, faintly. "Good trick. Last laugh's... on me."

"Tell me!" she shouted, putting her face just inches from his.

"Say goodnight, Your Honor..." Binkowski whispered. His lips parted again, as if he was going to laugh one last time. His eyes rolled back. His chest rose once more. It sagged back as the breath left his shattered body.

"He's had it," one of the Patrol cops said. "Broken neck. Skull fracture too, I'll bet. Surprised he lasted that long."

The other Patrol officer wasn't so ready to give up. "Starting compressions," he said, dropping down beside Binkowski and beginning CPR. He'd keep at it until the paramedics arrived to either take over or call a time of death.

Erin stood back. She was thinking hard. What had Binkowski meant, *"Say goodnight?"* She looked at her watch. It was a little before eleven. That was definitely time for sensible people to be saying goodnight and going to bed.

Going to bed...

With fingers that suddenly felt slow and clumsy, she fumbled for her phone. She punched Ferris's name on her contact list, praying she wasn't too late.

Chapter 20

The phone rang. Erin held her breath.

Vic hurried onto the stage. He looked at Binkowski and frowned.

"So that's how it is, huh?" he said.

Erin held up a hand for him to be quiet. The phone rang again.

"And you," Vic said to Rolf. "That's the craziest shit I've ever seen. You're a goddamn credit to the Force."

Rolf, still busy with his chew-toy, didn't bother to respond. The phone rang a third time.

"Come on," Erin muttered. "Come on, come on, *come on.*"

"Yes?"

Erin closed her eyes and silently thanked God. "Your Honor?" she said.

"Speaking," Ferris said. "And if my old ears aren't mistaken, you would be Detective O'Reilly. How are you, young lady?"

"I'm glad you're okay," she said. "Where are you right now?"

"I am sitting in my study with a volume of Emerson and my beloved Roy Bean at my feet, sipping a glass of my personal white lightning as a nightcap. Roy is quite recovered and none the worse for wear. I suspect he may have received a mild sedative, nothing worse."

"Does your drink taste funny? Anything off about it?"

"No, it tastes exactly as it ought. Though the taste is not precisely the point when it comes to moonshine. What is the matter? Are you afraid someone might have poisoned my victuals?"

"Yeah, I am. Listen. Don't touch *anything*. Stay right where you are. Actually, no. Get out of the house. Get your protection detail and go somewhere else. Anywhere else. I'm on my way."

"What do you know, Detective?" Ferris's voice sharpened. He no longer sounded grandfatherly. Now he sounded like the judge who had sentenced mobsters to die behind bars.

"We've got a credible threat," she said. "It's in your house. I don't know more than that yet. I'll call you when I get there."

"You know your business," Ferris said. "I will so inform my guardians. Is it likely a sharpshooter is lying in wait outside my home?"

"No. We got the guy."

"In custody?"

She glanced at Binkowski. The Patrol officer was still doing CPR, but it was a formality.

"Dead," she said.

"I see." Ferris sounded neither particularly upset nor relieved. "Thank you for keeping me apprised, Detective O'Reilly."

"What'd that jerk tell you?" Vic asked. "Binkowski, I mean. Not Ferris."

"Tell you in a minute." Erin was already calling Dispatch. The call went through. "This is O'Reilly, shield four-six-four-oh. I need the Bomb Squad to Judge Ferris's residence, Staten Island, forthwith. We have a credible threat of a device on the premises. The building's being evacuated right now. Device is probably located in the master bedroom."

"Copy that, O'Reilly. Bomb Squad has been notified and is en route. ETA thirty minutes."

Erin hung up. Now, finally, she could tend to her partner. She went to her knees beside Rolf.

"How's it going, kiddo?" she asked, running her hands up and down his legs, looking for heat, swelling, or tenderness.

Rolf continued happily chomping on his toy, his tail swishing back and forth. Things were great. They couldn't be better.

"Did you see what he did?" Vic commented. "That's the most badass thing I think I've ever seen."

"I didn't tell him to release fast enough," Erin said, shaking her head. "I never thought... Jesus. I feel terrible."

"How come? He got the bad guy and it looks like he's fine. That loser must've cushioned his fall."

Erin turned a haunted look on him. "Vic, don't you get it? I basically told him to kill himself and *he did it*. For me."

"You told him to risk his life, not throw it away, and that's not on you," he said, laying a hand on her shoulder. "Shit, I just practically suicided for a complete stranger. That's the Job for you. You think he didn't know it was a long way down? That was a *choice*. He did it because he loves you and he trusts you."

"I know." She closed her eyes. "That's one hell of a weight to carry sometimes."

"I hear you. But what now? Sounds like we've got somewhere else we need to be."

"We have to get to Staten Island. Binkowski left a little surprise in Ferris's house."

Vic slapped his forehead. "Another one? When did he have time? How'd we miss it the first time around?"

"I don't know. We'll sort it out. Skip's team is on the way, but we'd better get there too."

"Think we ought to wake up the Lieutenant?"

"I think we have to."

"He's gonna love this. Five bucks says he finally got to sleep, like, ten minutes ago."

"No bet."

*　　*　　*

"Here we are again," Webb said.

"You're not mad, sir?" Erin asked. They were standing in front of Ferris's house, illuminated by the red-and-blue flashers of four squad cars. The Bomb Squad's big blue and white van was parked front and center. Skip had cut the power to the judge's house again, so they were able to track the squad's progress through the building by the beams of their flashlights through the windows. The techs had been working for a while. Erin didn't even want to think about how late it was.

"Mad?" Webb said. "I'm not even surprised. I knew something like this was bound to happen. I don't know why I even bothered going to bed. Your suspect's officially deceased, by the way. He got to the hospital a few minutes ago. DOA. Fractured skull and shattered spine."

Erin nodded. "He hit the floor pretty hard."

"How exactly did he fall?" Webb asked.

Erin hesitated.

"Rolf got him," Vic said. "Bum-rushed the bastard clean off the catwalk. Grabbed hold and rode him down. Friggin' awesome. Sir."

"I guess I'd better fill out a use-of-force report," Erin said. She needed to do that every time Rolf bit someone. K-9s occupied a curious position in the NYPD, somewhere between that of sworn officers and deadly weapons.

"That's his first kill, isn't it?" Vic said.

She hadn't thought of it that way. "I guess so," she said. "But Binkowski was on his way down anyway. Not sure Rolf killed him. He might've died anyway if he'd landed wrong."

"And we're sure that was the Janitor?" Webb asked.

"Absolutely," Erin said. "He confessed right before he died. Two Patrolmen were close enough to hear. They can confirm."

"Thank God for that," Webb said. "Do you have any idea what was going on?"

"This whole thing was about the Vitelli trial," she said. "Valentino Vitelli didn't want Ferris presiding. Removing him would put Judge Barberis in charge instead."

"And Barberis belongs to the Lucarellis," Vic said.

"Allegedly," Webb said wearily.

"Allegedly," Vic agreed, rolling his eyes.

"Vinnie the Oil Man agreed to take care of things for his *capo*," Erin said. "He decided to use the Janitor because he wanted it to look like an accident."

"Because otherwise we might look a little closer at Barberis," Webb said. "And if he is in the Lucarellis' pocket, they want us far away from him."

"But Ferris kept getting lucky," Erin said. "And by now, even if he gets struck by lightning, we're unlikely to believe it was an accident."

"'If he should be struck by a bolt of lightning, I'm going to blame some of the people in this room,'" Vic quoted, putting a raspy hoarseness in his voice.

"Is that supposed to be a Marlon Brando impression?" Webb asked.

"Binkowski had already set up a final fallback plan," Erin said, ignoring the interruption. "That was the last thing he told me before he kicked off. He must've done it when he was in the judge's house the first time."

"Thorough," Webb said. "Any idea what it is?"

"He said it would only get the judge, nobody else," she said. "And he made a crack about saying goodnight."

"So that's why we're assuming the bedroom," Webb said. "I spoke to Ferris on the way here. He hasn't been in his bedroom since the Rodriguez killing. He was at the hospital most of that night. Then he went to the courthouse. He keeps a bed and a change of clothes there, in case of emergencies. He was about to hit the sack tonight when O'Reilly called him."

"Something's happening," Erin said, pointing to the house. One of Skip's guys was standing in the doorway, waving them over.

"You gotta see this," the man said as they approached. "This is unbelievable. Never seen anything like it."

*　　*　　*

"It's perfectly safe," Skip said from the bedroom. "You need to come inside to see it."

"You're sure?" Webb asked.

"This thing needs electricity and we turned off the juice," Skip replied. "And it'd only be dangerous if you had some extra hardware in your chest. But you'd want to leave your phones outside if we still had power."

Mystified, the three detectives filed into the judge's bedroom. In the dancing flashlight beams, Erin saw what looked like pieces of the doorframe lying on the floor. Skip pointed to the door.

"You see it?" he asked.

The flashlights reflected from something metallic that ran around the door. It looked to Erin like a spring of some sort.

"What are we looking at?" Webb asked.

"Copper coil," Skip said. "Our boy pried off the doorframe and laid the coil all around the door. Then he nailed it back in place. There's a wire across the floor, too. He cut a slit in the carpet and laid it in there. You can see it if you shine your light just right, but it's easy to miss. Ordinary overhead lights wouldn't make it show up too bright. This guy's one clever son of a bitch."

"I don't understand," Erin said. "Is it another electrical trap?"

"Sort of," Skip said. "Do you know if the judge has a heart condition?"

"Yeah," Erin said. "He's got a pacemaker. He had a heart attack a few years back."

Skip nodded. "What we've got here is a homemade electromagnet," he said. "Our guy plugged it into that outlet over there. When the house has current, there's a strong magnetic field in this doorway. It'll screw up any magnetic data storage, like a computer hard drive, and it'll wipe a Smartphone. You or I wouldn't even notice it, but if the judge had gone through here..."

"His pacemaker would've been knocked out," Webb said. "And he really would've had a heart attack."

Vic whistled. "That might've worked even better than the doorknob trick," he said. "No contact burns, no sign of any outside influence. He would've just keeled over on his own bedroom floor. That sneaky bastard."

"How come your guys didn't find this on their last sweep?" Webb asked.

"Sorry about that," Skip said, uncharacteristically abashed. "The problem was, we'd cut the power. So there wasn't any juice running through the coil while we were searching the house.

The perp did a good job hiding it. If I hadn't spotted the wire in the carpet, we would've missed it this time, too."

Vic shook his head in silent, reluctant admiration.

"What do you want me to do with it?" Skip asked.

"Disable it," Webb said. "But leave it in place for the CSU guys. They'll want pictures. This one's going in a textbook."

"That's easy enough," Skip said. He took a pair of wire cutters out of his bag and snipped the coil in two places. "There. No circuit, no magnet, no problem."

"So we can tell Ferris it's okay to go to bed?" Vic asked.

Skip paused and cleared his throat.

"I think we'd better keep Ferris out for now," Webb said. "We've found two very dangerous booby-traps. We've got only the word of a dying hitman that those are the only ones. I think we'll all sleep easier under a different roof."

"You think the Oil Man's gonna try for Ferris again?" Vic asked. "With someone else?"

"I think he'll cut his losses," Erin said. "Sending more hitmen would just attract more attention. Besides, it's not his kid on trial. He doesn't really give a crap about Vitelli's family. He can tell Valentino he gave it his best shot. Then he just goes on with business as usual. That's Vinnie for you. Loyalty only runs one way with him. Everybody else is expendable."

"But we're not pulling Ferris's protection," Vic said.

"No way," she agreed. "I think we need to leave it in place until the Vitelli trial is over."

"Good work, O'Reilly," Webb said. "You saved a good man's life tonight."

"I'm not the only one," she said. "Vic saved a civilian at the theater."

"Oh? I haven't heard that part."

"I'm sure it'll be in his report," she said. "And it'll definitely be in mine."

"Could we leave it out?" Vic asked. "Please?"

"Why?" Webb asked. "Don't you think a commendation would help balance out all your insubordination rips?"

"Well, yeah," Vic said, looking at his shoes. "But Zofia's already pissed at me for that damn stupid stunt with the grenade. If she hears I've been doing acrobatics without a safety net, I'll never hear the end of it."

"Falsifying a DD-5 to keep your girlfriend in the dark is definitely against NYPD policy," Webb said. "But I'll tell you what. Fill out the paperwork. We'll file it and nobody here will breathe a word to Officer Piekarski. The only way she'll know about it is if she dives into the archives to read your old Fives. And honestly, how many cops do you know who do that?"

"None of them," Vic said. He glared at Erin. "He means you. Not a word this time."

"I promise not to tell Zofia about your brave and selfless act," she said. "I'll just keep telling her you're a violent thug."

"I knew I could count on you," Vic said, perking up.

Chapter 21

Erin was almost home. She could even see the Barley Corner, less than a block away. When her phone buzzed, she was tempted to ignore it. She was utterly exhausted. All she wanted was what Carlyle would call "a wee nip" and then bed.

But an NYPD detective was never completely off duty. With a sigh, she pulled over, put on her flashers to avoid getting rear-ended, and swiped her screen.

"O'Reilly," she said, trying to sound more awake than she felt.

"I hope I didn't wake you," said a familiar voice. It was an older man, a guy with a thick Long Island accent.

It took her a second to place him. "Mr. Vitelli," she said, getting it before the pause had become too awkward. "Sorry. You caught me at the end of a really long day."

"Yeah, I heard about that," Valentino Vitelli said. "You been running all over town. I respect that, but we've got a saying in the old country. 'If I sleep, I sleep for myself. If I work, I don't know for whom.' You know what I mean?"

"Not really," she confessed.

"It means you gotta make time for yourself to rest, in the middle of all your working. And that's why I'm calling you. You may remember, a little while ago I extended an invitation."

Erin was too tired and he'd come at her sideways, unexpectedly. She had no idea what he was talking about. "Come again?" she said.

"Dinner, at my place," he said. "You and your good friend Cars."

"Oh, right," she said. "That's very generous of you to offer."

"Forget about it. I want you to come. It'd be an honor. How about tomorrow? Or today, I suppose, seeing as it's after midnight. What do you say? Eight o'clock?"

"Mr. Vitelli…" she began, having no idea what she was going to say. Did she want to refuse? Accept? What would Phil Stachowski tell her to do?

"Valentino, please," he said. "You can even call me Rudy if you want, like my friends do. Eight o'clock. Milly's making lasagna. You'll love it. You have a good night, now."

He hung up before she could get another word in. Erin stared at the phone.

"What the hell?" she asked the world in general.

Rolf, the only other occupant of the car, nosed her ear to let her know he was listening. She absently stroked his head. After a minute, she turned off her flashers and put the Charger back in gear for the last hundred yards of her drive.

Her day was ending, but the Barley Corner was still awake and busy. The place was bursting with patrons. A wave of sound, mingled cheers and groans, washed over her as she opened the door. Hardly anyone even noticed her arrival. Their attention was fixed on Carlyle's biggest TV screen, where the bottom of the display announced that Wales was playing Ireland in a rugby match.

Erin squeezed through the crowd, Rolf trailing a step behind. She found Carlyle at the bar, a half-finished glass of Guinness in front of him.

"Evening, darling," he said, standing to greet her. "Are you done for the night?"

"More or less," she said, barely able to hear him. "It's busy in here. Can we talk upstairs?"

"My pleasure," he said, extending a hand toward his apartment door.

The heavy, soundproofed door cut off all but the loudest cheers, leaving a very faint murmur. Erin leaned against the door with a sigh.

"Big game?" she asked.

"European Cup," he said. "Sad to say, the Irish appear to be doing what we do best."

"And that is?"

"Losing valiantly. Is everything all right, darling? You look like you've been through the wars."

"Get me a drink," she said. "Then I'll explain."

"Fair trade," he said with a smile.

Once they were settled on Carlyle's couch, a glass of Glen D for each of them, she told him what had happened. He listened closely, raising his eyebrows when she recounted how Rolf hadn't let go of Binkowski even as he was dragged over the edge. He nodded as she described the Janitor's final trap.

"Devious," he said. "Would it have worked, do you think?"

She shrugged. "Maybe. If a pacemaker goes on the fritz, it doesn't mean the guy will have a heart attack right there on the spot. Ferris might've lived. I think that's why it was a backup plan. Binkowski was counting on the doorknob or the radiator."

"I can't say I'm sorry the Janitor has cleaned up his last mess," Carlyle said. "A lad like that can make you nervous."

"I've got plenty to get on my nerves without him," she said. "I haven't even told you about Vitelli."

"What about him?"

"Apparently you and I are invited to supper with him at eight."

"Grand."

"No, it's not grand. Think about the timing. This has to have something to do with his hitman going down and his son being on trial."

"Not necessarily. It's not widely known that Binkowski was the Janitor. Perhaps Mr. Vitelli is merely networking with his friend in the Department."

"Maybe. But I don't like it."

"Oh, he'll want something, have no doubt of that," Carlyle said pleasantly. "But that's no reason not to be gracious. I'll fetch a good bottle out of the cellar to bring with us. I don't doubt it'll be an interesting evening."

Erin reminded herself that Carlyle hung out with dangerous Mob bosses all the time. This was just another social engagement for him. She forced a smile.

"You're probably right," she said. "But there's a limit to how gracious I'm prepared to be. I'll be wearing a wire."

"Of course, darling. As will I. Graciousness and prudence aren't mutually exclusive."

"I'd better get some sleep," she said. "I've been running on all cylinders. Things are blowing up, people are dying, and I'm wiped out. Are you going back downstairs?"

"Aye. There's work yet to be done. My night's far from over. But you needn't wait up for me. I'll be an hour or two, I'm thinking."

"Okay. Good night."

He kissed her. "Pleasant dreams, darling."

*   *   *

Rolf was fighting Binkowski. The K-9's teeth clamped onto the Janitor's arm, tearing flesh and cracking bone. Binkowski grabbed Rolf around the neck as he stumbled backward. They tumbled over the catwalk railing, but this time, instead of a twenty-foot fall onto a wooden stage, it was a literally bottomless pit. Erin watched helplessly as her dog spun into endless blackness.

She woke with a breathless gasp, soaked in sweat from the nightmare. When you worked dangerous cases, your subconscious didn't have to dig deep to find good, juicy material. Rolf was there when she sat up, sleeping at the foot of the bed, a reassuringly warm and solid presence. But there was no chance of getting back to sleep.

Carlyle had come in sometime during the wee hours. He lay beside her, eyes closed, breathing slowly and evenly. Erin envied him.

She tried to shrug off the bad dream. Her morning routine calmed her a little. She put on her sweatpants and NYPD sweatshirt, made a cup of coffee, and headed for Central Park for her daily run.

She was a little early. The park was quiet and mostly deserted, the sun not yet up. Some people might have hesitated to go running along the dim paths, but Erin had two friends with her: a ninety-pound German Shepherd and a snub-nosed .38 revolver. She also knew that most street criminals were in bed by five in the morning, sleeping off their drugs of choice.

By the time she finished her first lap, she was feeling pretty good. Rolf loped easily beside her, tongue flopping of his mouth. As she passed the park entrance, another jogger fell in step with her. He also had a dog; a shaggy, disreputable thing about half Rolf's size.

"Morning," she said.

"Morning," Ian replied.

"How's Miri?"

"Outstanding." Miri, Ian's rescue dog, was a shy creature of no particular breed. She adored him. As they ran, she stuck so close to his hip that her snout brushed his leg with every stride.

"Cassie and Ben?"

"They're good. You?"

"I'm fine."

"Mr. Carlyle says you're meeting Mr. Vitelli tonight."

"That's right."

"Expecting trouble?"

"Not especially. Should I?" She gave him a sidelong glance.

"Always."

"Will you be there?"

"I'll drive you. Be in support distance."

"You think Vitelli will try something? At supper?"

"These guys will hit you anywhere," he said. "Best bet is when you're not expecting it."

*   *   *

The work waiting for Erin at the office was the stuff detectives didn't like to do. The courthouse incident and the fight at the theater had left a massive heap of paperwork in their wake. Erin reluctantly waded in. Vic and Webb showed up a little later and joined in the fun.

"You oughta make the mutt write up some of these," Vic said. "He's the one who took out Binkowski."

"He has trouble with keyboards," Erin said. "No thumbs."

"Hey, Lieutenant," Vic said. "Shouldn't Rolf be on modified assignment?"

"No," Webb said. "But you and O'Reilly maybe ought to be. You know, police K-9s almost never actually kill anybody. I don't even know what the NYPD's procedure is in this case. O'Reilly ought to know."

"I don't, sir," Erin said. "I never thought it'd happen. Rolf doesn't go for the throat. This was a crazy fluke."

"IAB will let us know if there's anything we ought to be doing," Webb sighed. "In the meantime, it looks like we're all on desk duty anyway, so I don't suppose it matters much."

"Where's Ferris right now?" Erin asked.

"Last I heard, he was at a safe house on Staten Island," Webb said. "Don't worry about him, I'm sure he's fine."

"Me too," she said. "Binkowski said Ferris was the toughest contract he'd ever had."

Vic snickered. "A hitman loses to a guy twice his age. That's one for the record books."

"It's not that funny," Webb said. "We lost a judge, remember. And one of our own is in the hospital. Hot-water burns are nothing to sneeze at."

That sobered Vic up. "Would it be okay if I went over there at noon?" he asked. "I feel like I oughta check up on Campbell."

"Of course," Webb said. "Maybe we should all chip in and get him a get-well present."

"How about a hot water bottle?" Vic suggested.

Webb shook his head. "I've been wearing a shield more than twenty years and I still can't believe what passes for humor in this job."

* * *

The rest of the workday dragged by without much incident. Vic made his trip to Bellevue and returned a couple of hours later, reporting that Officer Campbell was doing as well as could be expected.

"He's conscious," Vic said. "The docs hope the scarring won't be too bad, but we'll have to see. Campbell says he understands now why narcotics are illegal on the street. Anything that makes you feel that good has to be against the rules."

A short while after Vic got back, Holly Gardner showed up with her inevitable camera crew. She had a whole array of questions about the death at the theater. Webb and Erin declined to comment. Vic commented, colorfully and at length, until the reporter exited Major Crimes.

"Was that really necessary?" Webb asked once Holly had gone.

"I actually learned some new swear words there," Erin said. "That was impressive."

"I figured she can't use a soundbite on the news if it's full of profanity," Vic explained.

"I hate to admit it, but that's a good point," Webb said. "But don't do that again, particularly within earshot of the Captain's office."

Captain Holliday poked his head out of the corner office. "What was that, Lieutenant?" he inquired politely. "I didn't quite catch any of that."

At five, Erin shut down her computer and collected Rolf, feeling like she'd worked a normal nine-to-five job for once. She was surprised it didn't bother her more. She said her goodbyes to the other detectives and went down to her car. Once she was behind the wheel, she called Phil Stachowski.

"Everything's okay," she said. "But I thought you should know, I'm having dinner with Valentino Vitelli at eight. Carlyle's going to be there too."

"Business or social?" Phil asked.

"With these guys, it's usually both," she said.

"Will you have your wire?"

"Yeah."

"Be careful."

"I'm glad you told me that, Phil. Because if you hadn't, I was planning on getting plastered and telling Vitelli all about our little undercover operation."

"You say that like it's a joke, Erin, but some undercovers have actually done things like that. You know what happened to them?"

"Nothing good."

"Exactly. Let me know if anything major comes up."

"Copy that."

Erin hung up. She had time to get home, walk and feed Rolf, and rest for a little while before changing for dinner. Maybe she could actually spend a little time with her boyfriend, too. That would be a nice change of pace. She wondered, not for the first time, what Vitelli wanted to discuss with her. Because she'd told Phil the truth. Dinner with a mob boss was never a purely social occasion. He'd want something from her.

Chapter 22

Valentino Vitelli was a murderous Mafia goon, a street hood who'd climbed the Lucarelli ladder over the backs of less fortunate and less ruthless thugs. But he considered himself a gentleman, so Erin and Carlyle prepared themselves accordingly. Erin dressed conservatively in a dark blue blouse and black skirt. She didn't like wearing nylons, but she wore a black pair for this occasion. Her makeup was muted; no scarlet lipstick on this night. Carlyle wore his gray Armani suit, accented by a blue silk necktie and pocket square chosen to match Erin's ensemble.

Erin carried a handbag which contained her .38 revolver. Carlyle was armed only with a bottle of wine, stowed carefully in a gift box and held under one arm. Ian was packing his customary Beretta nine-millimeter under his jacket, and Erin wouldn't have been at all surprised if he had some heavier hardware in the trunk of Carlyle's Mercedes.

"What's to drink?" she asked as Ian steered them south toward Long Island.

"Chateau Lafite Rothschild," Carlyle said. "2010 vintage."

"Sounds expensive."

"Expensive's a relative term, darling. Some would call a five-dollar coffee expensive, but those of us in Manhattan know better."

"Something tells me that wine cost a little more than five bucks."

"Are you really wanting to know?"

"How bad could it be?"

"Eleven."

"Eleven hundred dollars?!" She almost choked on the words.

Carlyle nodded. "It's best not to skimp when paying tribute to a gangster. Not to worry. I didn't purchase it specially for this occasion. The bloody bottle's been gathering dust in my cellar practically since it came over from France. Nobody at the Corner's ever likely to drink it. I don't know what I was thinking when I purchased it."

"Not many French wine connoisseurs down at the Irish pub, huh?"

"I fear not. And I've no illusions about Mr. Vitelli's appreciation for Bordeaux vineyards, but he's Italian, and he certainly likes wine more than your average Irishman. At least it's being sacrificed in a good cause."

The Vitelli family owned a brownstone near Carroll Park. It was a nice neighborhood, fronting on a park. Pedestrians were out for an evening stroll, some of them with their dogs. Everything was safe and ordinary on the surface, but the hairs on Erin's neck prickled as Ian pulled over to let them out.

"You know who lives just down the block?" she said.

"Vincenzo Moreno," Carlyle said. "We're in Lucarelli territory, sure enough."

"I wish I'd brought Rolf," she muttered.

"We're not going into battle, darling," he replied.

"Like hell we're not," she said. "Talking to gangsters without him is like leaving my gun unloaded. I know I probably won't need it, but if I do, I'll be sorry."

"It's another fine New York evening," Carlyle said. "Just the two of us, out to a dinner party together." He gave her the smile that still made her go a little wobbly in the knees, even after all their time together.

Erin glanced back at the Mercedes. Ian would wait right there in the car. He wouldn't fall asleep. He'd stand guard. Scout Sniper school had taught him to be very patient.

They climbed the stairs to the brownstone's front door. Carlyle rang the bell. Only a few seconds later, a beefy Italian opened the door. He looked more like a bar bouncer than a butler, in spite of his well-tailored suit.

"Evening," he said.

"Hey, Enzo," Erin said, recognizing Vitelli's bodyguard. "How's it going?"

"Can't complain," Enzo said. He stepped back to let them in, shutting the door immediately behind them.

New York brownstones had a certain similarity to them. Erin was reminded of her brother's house, though the Vitelli residence was decorated much more expensively. The entryway floor looked to be real marble, the bannister was coated with gold leaf, and at the foot of the stairs was an honest-to-God classical Greek statue of some ancient goddess or other. It felt more like a movie set than a home. Erin had the feeling if she poked her head into the kitchen, she wouldn't find grade-school watercolors stuck to the fridge with magnets.

Enzo took their coats and ushered them into the living room. Then he withdrew. Valentino Vitelli was waiting for them, standing in the middle of a pair of open French doors which led to the dining room. He was clad in a pinstripe suit that screamed old-school Mafia, from his fresh-shined black shoes to the red carnation in his lapel and his slicked-back gray hair.

"Welcome," Vitelli said. "Cars Carlyle. Last time I saw you, it was in your place downtown. You was very hospitable there. I only hope I can return the favor."

Carlyle shook hands with the other man. "I don't doubt it, Mr. Vitelli. The pleasure's mine."

"Why don't you call me Rudy?" Vitelli said.

"As you please," Carlyle said. "And of course you know Erin O'Reilly."

"Absolutely," Vitelli said. He took Erin's hand, bent over it, and kissed the back of it. "I never forget a face, but couldn't nobody forget yours. I am honored to be your host this evening. Milly's in the kitchen finishing up supper, but she's just dying to meet you. What can I get you to drink?"

"I'm a whiskey girl," Erin said.

"Of course you are," Vitelli said. "I can't claim my whiskey's as good as what Cars keeps behind his bar, but I'll do what I can. And you?"

"The same," Carlyle said. He held out the box. "Here's a wee something for you and Mrs. Vitelli."

"It's not gonna blow up when I open it, is it?" Vitelli asked. He paused just long enough for Erin to blink. Then he laughed and opened the box. "Oh, this is real nice. Thanks, Cars. I appreciate it. And I appreciate you making time in your busy schedule to come all the way down to Brooklyn."

Behind Vitelli, on the other side of the dining room, the kitchen door swung open. A heavyset brunette, obviously Italian, came out.

"Oh, here she is," Vitelli said. "The lady of the house. Milly, this is my good friend Morton Carlyle, but don't nobody call him that. He goes by Cars. And this here is the one and only Erin O'Reilly, finest of New York's Finest. Cars, Miss O'Reilly, this is

Milena. She's the jewel of my heart, the apple in the sticky caramel of my life."

"Haven't heard that one before, you big softie," Milly said, her voice showing her own Brooklyn origins. "Go on now, have a seat. Supper's gonna be on the table in a minute."

The couple traded affectionate glances. Erin was surprised, amused, and even a little touched. Carlyle pulled out a chair for Erin before taking his own place at Vitelli's right. Milly disappeared back into the kitchen, emerging a moment later with a very large bowl of Caesar salad and a basket of garlic bread. Then she brought out a steaming tray of fresh-baked lasagna.

"Wow," Erin said. "This looks terrific and it smells amazing."

Milly beamed. "Aw, it ain't nothing," she said. "Just an old family recipe. But it's Valentino's favorite."

"I'm afraid so," Vitelli said, patting his belly. "She spoils me rotten. Now, if you'd all bow your heads a minute?"

He proceeded to say grace. At least, Erin assumed that was what he was doing, but he did it in Italian, which Erin didn't speak.

The meal was served family-style, with the food in the middle of the table. It was delicious. Milena Vitelli certainly knew her way around a kitchen. Erin had seconds and was sorely tempted to take more.

Conversation was completely innocuous. Plainly, Vitelli didn't talk business in front of his wife. Erin reflected that Phil Stachowski would be wasting an hour going through the tape that her hidden microphone was dutifully recording. Anyone listening would think it was an ordinary dinner party with two couples who were, if not close friends, at least amiable.

Dessert was tiramisu, accompanied by cups of excellent coffee. Then, after dinner, Milly took the dishes and started cleaning up. Erin offered to help.

"Aw, that's sweet of you, honey," Milly said. "But you're a guest. I got this. You gotta keep an eye on the boys, make sure they don't get into no trouble. You know how boys get without no supervision."

Vitelli, Carlyle, and Erin retreated to the upstairs parlor, a room furnished with a strong emphasis on leather upholstery. Vitelli opened one of his desk drawers. He took out a cigar box and extended it toward them.

"No thanks," Erin said. "I don't smoke."

"Nor I," Carlyle said. "Explosives and open flames don't mix well."

Vitelli laughed. He selected a cigar for himself, snipped off the end, and lit it. "Brandy, then?" he asked.

"Now that I'll gladly take," Carlyle said. Erin also accepted a glass. The liquid was dark reddish-brown. Holding it, she felt again like she'd stepped onto a movie set.

"It's too bad my boy couldn't join us tonight," Vitelli said. "He sends his regrets. His mama's going out of her head about him. A terrible thing, what's happened to him."

"I'm sorry for your troubles," Carlyle said diplomatically.

Erin said nothing. Gabriel Vitelli was awaiting trial because he'd murdered his pregnant fiancée. He had nobody to blame but himself, but she didn't think it would be wise to mention this.

"I'm grateful for all you've done for my family," Vitelli went on. "It wasn't an easy thing, and I appreciate it."

"Forget about it," Erin said.

"But now we've got this ugly business with that judge," Vitelli said. "This isn't how I wanted things to go at all. Now we've got two people dead, and my boy's still gonna be standing in front of that tough old bastard."

Erin fought the urge to give Carlyle a sidelong look. Vitelli knew who Binkowski was. That was the only possible explanation for him to mention two deaths.

"I didn't know the Janitor was doing your cleanup," she said. "All I knew was he'd knocked off a judge and was trying for another. Nobody knew why. We had to move on him."

Vitelli made a dismissive wave with his hand. "Nobody's blaming you," he said. "It was just one of those things. One hand don't know what the other's doing. That's what happens when you got all these buffers. It usually keeps people safe, but sometimes you get guys running into each other, nobody knows what's happening, and somebody gets hurt."

"I know what that's like," Erin said, remembering a recent incident involving two squads of plainclothes cops. That screw-up had left one of her friends dead.

"What course of action are you suggesting, Rudy?" Carlyle asked.

"I can't suggest no course of action," Vitelli said. "You can't put the toothpaste back in the tube. Can't nobody touch the judge now. Everybody would know it was a hit. The whole thing was a waste. What we gotta do now is think about what's happening at the courthouse."

"What do you mean?" Erin asked.

"We got two things going down," Vitelli said, holding up the first two fingers of his right hand, the smoldering cigar wedged between them. "First, I wanna talk about my boy, and how we're gonna get him outta trouble."

"I thought the trial wasn't going to be a problem," Erin said. "Since we took care of the star witness."

That was for the benefit of her wire. Every time she got Vitelli to admit he'd been involved in the car bombing that had apparently killed Teresa Tommasino, she hammered another nail into the legal coffin she intended to bury him in.

"Maybe," Vitelli said. "But there's that damn engagement ring, and there's other stuff, too. The DA thinks he's got enough, or he would've dropped the charges by now. You gotta find out why he's so confident, and then you gotta make some of that evidence go away."

"I'll see what I can do," Erin said. "But it'll be hard to get access. That stuff's under lock and key. Detectives have to sign for evidence, and that leaves a paper trail a mile wide. I can't just walk into Evidence and walk out with everything we've got on Gabriel."

"You're a clever girl," Vitelli said. "Figure it out. We got a little while yet before the trial, you got time."

"If I do that for you, I'm going to need to see something in return," Erin said.

"Yeah, don't worry about none of that," Vitelli said with another dismissive wave. "Haven't we always taken good care of you, Vinnie and me?"

"You've been more than generous," Carlyle said.

"And that brings me to the second little matter," Vitelli said. "You might've forgot about it, but that little weasel Alfie Madonna is gonna be in court tomorrow."

"I can't get him off," Erin said. "He already pled out. He's going back to prison."

"I don't want you to get him off," Vitelli said. "We tried that once, it didn't work. He's a little piece of shit, but he's a lucky one. We lost a bunch of guys trying to take care of him on the outside. We'll wait till he's inside now, where he can't run and hide."

"It's been arranged?" Erin asked.

"Yeah, it's all taken care of. We got good, solid guys inside."

"So what's the problem?"

Vitelli shook his head sadly. "My boy hasn't said nothing about the Family," he said. "I brought him up right, to show proper respect and to keep his mouth shut. But Mattie Madonna's kid, he don't respect nothing. What I hear, he's gonna give a statement before he gets sentenced."

"So?" Erin asked. A defendant had the right to address the court before sentence was passed. Most guys used it as an opportunity to express remorse in the hope of leniency.

"The way I hear it, he's gonna name names," Vitelli said grimly. "He's gonna drag the Oil Man himself into the middle of everything. He's gonna spill everything he knows."

"Surely the lad doesn't know much," Carlyle said.

"It ain't clear how much the kid knows," Vitelli said. "You heard about that café that got knocked over, and Jimmy Caps getting clipped?"

"Yeah," Erin said, perplexed. "My squad had that case. We got the guy, don't worry. It's handled."

"That ain't the point," Vitelli said. "The point is, Jimmy Caps was one of ours, and Alfie Madonna fingered him. Alfie wasn't supposed to know about Jimmy! And Jimmy ain't the only one. We've had four guys get ripped off this past week. There ain't nothing wrong with our security. Somebody's a rat and I know who. The Madonna brat knows more than he should. He told the judge he's got valuable information he's gonna reveal, and he's gonna do it in front of the courtroom, and TV cameras, and God only knows who!"

"He told Barberis that?" Erin asked.

"His lawyer said it to the judge," Vitelli said. "But that's the same as him saying it. We can keep the cameras out of the room, but not the reporters. It'll be in all the papers."

"Why's he doing this?" Carlyle asked. "Is he hoping for some sort of bargain, a reduced sentence?"

"Nah," Vitelli said. "If that was the case, it'd be between his lawyer and the prosecutor. They'd hash something out behind closed doors. This ain't that. This is the kid throwing bombs. He don't care what happens to him, he's just trying to do damage."

"That's a problem, all right," Erin said. "What do you mean to do about it?"

"Can you get to Alfie before he sets foot in court?"

Erin felt a surge of nausea. There was only one reason Vitelli would ask that. "I don't even know where he is," she said, truthfully enough. "Ever since that botched hit drove him out of WitSec, he's been laying low."

"Can you take care of him in the courthouse?"

"Are you out of your mind?" Erin snapped. "That place is crawling with Marshals, it's full of security cameras, and you can't bring in guns. They've got sniffer dogs at the entrance, so explosives are a no-go, even if we wanted to do that. And I'm not going to set off a goddamn bomb in a New York courthouse! Anyway, with the Janitor trying to blow up Ferris, security's going to be tight like you wouldn't believe. It's impossible to hit anyone in the courthouse right now. It can't be done."

Vitelli nodded. "I was afraid you'd say that," he said. "What do you say, Cars?"

"Erin's got the right of it," Carlyle said. "Given a month or two to plan, I might be able to come up with something, but not overnight. It would take time and preparation."

"Then we'll just have to see what the kid says," Vitelli said heavily. "At least I can guarantee he won't be testifying at no other trials. That dirty rat won't last a week inside."

Erin stared at the glass in her hand. The rusty color of the brandy now reminded her of old blood. Her stomach lurched.

"Maybe you oughta be there," Vitelli said. "I will be, and so will the boss."

"Vinnie's going to be there?" Erin exclaimed. "In court?"

"Of course," Vitelli said. "You think he's gonna take this thing on hearsay? No way. He's gotta hear what this punk knows. Otherwise how are we gonna know what we gotta protect?"

Chapter 23

"That went rather well, I thought," Carlyle said.

Erin looked over her shoulder, watching the Vitellis' brownstone disappear around the corner. Ian drove the way he did everything, with calm, smooth competence. The tires on the Mercedes hummed softly on the blacktop.

"You thought it went well," she echoed. Shaking her head, she squeezed the hidden button in her underwire, stopping the recording.

"Aye," Carlyle said. "We ate an excellent meal, learned a fair few things worth knowing, and parted on good terms. Nobody tried to do away with us. In the Life, darling, that's the sort of thing that makes a dinner a great success."

"He wanted us to murder Alfie Madonna! In the middle of the damn courthouse!"

"Isn't this the purpose of your undercover work?" he asked mildly. "He said a great many incriminating things which both of us recorded."

"Alfie's going to die," she said bleakly. "You heard Vitelli. The kid is dead meat. Do you think Alfie knows that?"

"I rather think the lad doesn't care," Carlyle said. "As our host said, he's throwing bombs. All he cares about is harming Mr. Moreno. If he can't harm him directly, the lad will settle for damaging his interests."

"What do you think he's going to say tomorrow?" Erin asked.

"Who can tell?" Carlyle answered. "But if he wanted to attract the Oil Man's attention, he's certainly succeeded. This may be one of those cautionary tales about being careful what one wishes for."

"I wouldn't want Vinnie to notice me," she said. "Everything that man touches dies. But at least Judge Ferris is safe."

"As safe as a lad of his years can be," Carlyle said. "And you've done away with his colleague's slayer. You ought to feel you've done well."

"I don't," Erin said. "Vitelli and Vinnie were behind the whole thing, and we've got nothing to tie them to it. Oh, sure, there's Binkowski's dying declaration, but that's not even enough for an indictment. We'll burn Vitelli one of these days for ordering the hit on Teresa, but what about the Oil Man?"

"They don't call him that for nothing," Carlyle said. "He's a slippery one. But he'll not wriggle free forever. Sooner or later, lads like him always go down."

"Yeah," she said morosely. "If the NYPD can't get him, maybe a heart attack will."

"Perhaps," he said. "But I'd be surprised if natural causes were the end of him."

"I didn't thank you," she said.

"Thank me? For what?" He seemed surprised.

"If it hadn't been for you, we wouldn't have found Binkowski," she said. "Not before Ferris went into his bedroom, and maybe didn't come out again. You helped catch a hitman, but you also helped save Ferris's life."

"I wonder what he'd say to that," Carlyle said, smiling. "Being saved by a career criminal."

"You're not a career criminal. You're just a guy who ended up working as a criminal for a while. It's not who you are."

"That's sweet of you to say, darling. And speaking of career criminals, are you planning on visiting court tomorrow?"

"I think I'd better," she said. "I need to hear what Alfie's got to say. I have the feeling it'll be a show worth watching."

*   *   *

"This is the first time I've heard of a detective who *wanted* to hang around with a bunch of lawyers," Webb said.

"It's just a sentencing hearing," Erin said. "It won't take long."

"Are you worried Alfie's gonna get whacked?" Vic asked. He took a long pull from his customary early-morning bottle of Mountain Dew.

"Not really," she said. "Kingston Schultz is pretty cagey. I'm sure he's figured a way to get his client into the building without anyone taking a shot at him."

"I'll come too," Vic said.

"You don't have to do that."

"I know I don't have to. I'm offering. You're taking the mutt."

"I'm taking the mutt, as you call him, on the off-chance somebody manages to smuggle another bomb into the courthouse. He's useful."

"And I'm not?" Vic gave her a wounded look.

"Okay, fine," she said. "You can come. I may need a piece of mobile cover if mobsters start shooting. You can be my personal bullet sponge."

"That's more like it."

"Are either of you planning on doing any actual police work today?" Webb asked.

"What are you talking about, sir?" Vic replied. "We closed the Binkowski case."

"And I'm sure you've properly filled out and filed all the paperwork pertaining to that case," Webb said.

Vic cleared his throat and looked away.

"We'll take care of it, sir," Erin said.

"I'm sure you will," Webb said. "Just try not to kill anybody else while you're out there."

"We didn't kill Binkowski," Erin said.

"Nope," Vic agreed. "All she did was sic her dog on him. Fangs and the fall killed him."

"Rolf's fangs didn't kill him," she snapped.

"Anyway, they take our guns away in there," Vic said. "Erin couldn't kill anybody if she tried. Now me, I've got my own built-in guns."

He flexed his biceps expressively. Erin looked at Webb. The Lieutenant held his poker face, but only barely.

"98% lean, homegrown American beefcake right here," Vic said.

"Why do I have the sudden urge to go vegan?" Erin replied.

* * *

The courthouse looked the same on the outside as it had before all the excitement. The emergency vehicles were gone, as were the temporary barricades. But three Marshals were stationed on the courthouse steps, one holding a rifle, all of them stony-faced and alert. Inside, Erin counted twice as many guards as usual.

"How come extra security always makes me twitchy?" Vic asked as he, Erin, and Rolf approached the metal detector. "It ought to make me feel safe."

"Guilty conscience?" she guessed.

"Could be," he said. "I was thinking maybe it had something to do with repression."

"What do you mean?"

"I have no idea. I just remember that term from an intro-psychology class I took freshman year. I should've hung around that class we investigated a little while ago. You know, the one about psychopaths? I might've learned something useful."

"Being a street cop will teach you plenty about violent nutjobs," she said. She unbuckled her holster and gave her Glock to the guard at the checkpoint. Then she knelt down and took out her ankle piece, which she also handed over. Vic surrendered his Sig-Sauer and his own backup gun, a snub-nosed automatic that looked like a toy in his big hand.

"Which theater is this show gonna be in?" Vic asked. "I checked my ticket stub, but it didn't say."

Erin took a moment to examine the posted schedule. "That one, I think," she said, pointing.

"Okay, let's get in there before all the good seats are taken."

"This isn't entertainment, Vic."

"Well, it sure isn't work, so I don't know what else to call it."

"Detectives!" a woman called.

"Oh, Jesus," Erin said without turning around. "You've got to be kidding me."

"I just have a few questions," Holly Gardner said, hurrying up to them.

"And I've got a few answers," Vic said. "Four-letter ones. Want me to spell 'em?"

The reporter smiled brightly, refusing to be provoked. "Who was Bartosz Binkowski?" she asked Erin.

"The NYPD doesn't comment on ongoing investigations," Erin said.

"According to my sources, that investigation is now closed," Holly said triumphantly. "So it isn't exactly ongoing, is it? Viewers will want to know why the New York Police Department killed a theatrical stagehand last night."

"I'm sure there'll be a press release shortly," Erin said. She started walking away from the other woman, hoping Holly would take the hint and go away.

"Is it true, Detective, that this is the dog that killed Mr. Binkowski?" Holly asked, refusing the hint. She trotted alongside. At least she didn't have her cameraman with her this time.

"Mr. Binkowski was killed because he fell twenty feet onto a hard surface and broke his damn neck," Vic growled. "Maybe you want to do a piece on workplace safety instead of hassling cops?"

"What connection does Mr. Binkowski have to the death of Miranda Rodriguez?" Holly pressed.

Erin stopped. She had her hand on the door that led to the courtroom. "Look, Ms. Gardner," she said, her patience exhausted. "Binkowski wasn't a stagehand. He was a contract killer who murdered Judge Rodriguez and tried to kill Judge Ferris at least three times. We were there to take him in and find out who he was working for. I'm sorry he's dead, but I'm only sorry because we needed information from him. He was a lousy human being who lived a violent life and got what he had coming. But if I could've taken him in alive, I would've done it. I don't like killing people and I try pretty hard not to. There's your soundbite. Are you happy now?"

Holly beamed. "Thank you, Detective," she said. "Don't worry, I'll cite you as an anonymous source in the Department. Now, if I could just ask what you're doing here this morning? Are you following up on additional threats to the city's judiciary?"

"We're just observing a sentencing hearing," Erin said. "Pretty boring stuff."

"Oh, I'll just sit in, too," Holly said cheerfully. "You won't even know I'm here."

"Want to bet?" Vic muttered.

The courtroom was sparsely populated. A hearing for a small-time hood like Alfie Madonna wasn't exactly front-page news, in spite of Vitelli's fears. Erin saw the bailiff, the prosecutor, the stenographer, a pair of Marshals, and a handful of spectators. The spectators fit into three categories: reporters, bored New Yorkers, and scary-looking guys with Mediterranean complexions. Two of the scary guys were sitting on either side of Valentino Vitelli, who gave Erin a bland look and then ignored her.

Erin and Vic picked seats about a third of the way from the front, on the aisle. Rolf lay down at Erin's feet and curled his tail around his snout. Holly Gardner, to Erin's annoyance, sat directly behind them.

"What do you know about Alfredo Madonna?" Holly asked.

"What are you even doing here?" Erin shot back. "Shouldn't you be eavesdropping on your police scanner and chasing squad cars?"

"Detective O'Reilly, I'm doing my job," Holly said. "I'm a crime reporter. We aren't that different, you and I. Both of us try to understand why a crime happens, who is responsible, and what effect it has."

"Yeah," Vic said. "Except then you go and sex it up for your viewers to get ratings, while we're actually doing something useful, putting bad guys behind bars."

"We don't have to be adversarial about this," Holly said. "I can make you look good, and between us, the NYPD could use as much good press as it can get."

Erin rolled her eyes. "I don't give a damn about how I look on the evening news," she said. "If you're in the market for wannabe celebrities, shop somewhere else."

"Detective and second-generation NYPD cop Erin O'Reilly doesn't want to be famous," Holly said with a twinkle in her eye. "She has no interest in celebrity or in being the next big thing. All she wants is what she learned from her father; to serve and protect her community. See how easy that is?"

Vic snorted so loudly that several people looked at him.

"Don't do me any favors," Erin said. "And leave my dad out of this."

"I got a tip about this hearing," Holly said, her tone becoming more businesslike. "The defendant is expected to make some sort of dramatic statement. That's why you're here, too, isn't it? You were with his father, Matthew Madonna, when he died."

"You know a lot about this," Erin said.

Holly shrugged. "You're not the only woman who knows her job, Detective. And that's why we have several representatives of, shall we say, one of New York's clandestine business interests in this room."

"You mean the Mob guys?" Vic said. "I hadn't noticed."

One of the aforementioned goons raised a phone to his ear and said something into it. A moment later, the door swung open and Vincenzo Moreno walked in.

He looked like he always did; a slickly handsome Italian man in his fifties, not a single gray hair on his well-oiled head.

His pinstripe suit and fresh-shined shoes were more expensive than anything Erin owned. He was flanked by a pair of stone-faced Mafia bruisers. The bodyguards scanned the room. Then one of them took up position three rows from the front of the courtroom. Vinnie walked down the aisle, the other guard trailing him.

When he reached the detectives, he paused. He, Vic, and Erin eyeballed one another. Vic glared with undisguised hostility. Erin tried to keep emotion out of her face. She hated Vinnie more than anyone she could think of, but she couldn't let him see it.

"This is a surprise," Vinnie said. "Two representatives of New York's Finest. Detectives O'Reilly and Neshenko, if I'm not mistaken."

"And I count six representatives of New York's sewer system," Vic said, glancing from Vinnie to his bodyguards and back.

"You keep one of your dogs on a leash," Vinnie said to Erin. "Are you sure it's the right one?"

Erin played it cool. Vinnie thought she was a hired killer for the Mob. She needed to balance that image against that of an upstanding policewoman, in front of a TV news reporter. This was going to be delicate.

"I wouldn't expect you to be in court, Mr. Moreno," she said. "Not unless you were the defendant."

"Life has a way of surprising us," Vinnie said, smiling. It was the sort of smile an alligator might make while it floated close to an unsuspecting swimmer.

"Think we'll have any surprises today?" Erin asked.

"I suppose we'll find out," Vinnie said.

"Mr. Moreno," Holly said, standing up and extending a hand.

Vinnie's bodyguard stepped between them.

"Relax, Dario," Vinnie said. He motioned the guard to one side and took Holly's hand. "And who might you be, young lady?"

"Holly Gardner, Channel Six News," Holly said. "Let me say what an honor it is to meet you in person, Mr. Moreno. I've heard so much about you, and I'd love to get to know you better. Would you care to answer a few quick questions?"

"Perhaps at a later time," Vinnie said. "I don't normally give interviews, but for so lovely a member of the press, I might make an exception. Are you doing anything for dinner tonight?"

Holly gave him her very best wide, white-toothed smile. "I'd be delighted," she said.

"If you'll just give your contact information to Dario here," Vinnie said, "I'll get in touch."

Holly, all aflutter, handed a business card to the expressionless guard. Vinnie smiled with a warmth that might have convinced Erin if she didn't know him better. Then he went to his seat, sandwiched between Dario and the other guard, one row behind Vitelli.

"Wow," Holly breathed. "That's Vincenzo Moreno himself! Vinnie the Oil Man!"

"Yeah," Vic said. "Too bad you don't have your cameraman here. He could've caught you drooling all over him."

"Judge Barberis banned cameras in court today," Holly said. "And I was not drooling over him."

"If he was a hot dog, you'd have had him in your—"

"Vic!" Erin snapped. "That's enough!"

"Sheesh," he said. "What's got you in a twist? I thought you hated reporters."

"I do," she said. "But I hate sexist pigs even more."

Chapter 24

The door opened again. Erin swung around to look. Kingston Schultz and Alfie Madonna came in. Alfie was wearing a brand-new suit, which made him look like what he was; a kid just out of his teens playing dress-up. He would never look totally respectable, no matter what he had on. His hair was slicked back, but a patch of it behind his right ear was sticking up. He had rings on three of his fingers, one of which was a truly tasteless pinkie ring with an enormous gemstone. He also had on a bracelet made of some sort of thin wire, wrapped several times around his arm. His tattoos peeked out of his cuffs and over his starched collar.

One of the Marshals at the door left his post and walked down the aisle beside the kid and his lawyer. Alfie seemed calm on the outside, but Erin saw the tension in his neck and shoulders.

"Careful," Vic murmured as Alfie and his little entourage got close to Vinnie and his goons.

"Is it true?" Holly murmured in Erin's ear. "Did Vinnie Moreno kill Alfredo's father?"

"Not personally," Erin said without thinking. She was watching Alfie, wondering what he'd do.

It was anticlimactic. Alfie walked past Vinnie's row without saying a word, hardly even glancing at him. He took up his place at one of the front tables. Schultz detoured to the prosecution's table, exchanged a few quiet words with the prosecutor, shook hands with him, and returned to his client's side.

"I've been to a few of these," Holly said. "What sort of sentence do you think the prosecutor will ask for?"

Erin shrugged. "It's clear-cut parole violation," she said. "They charged him with Murder Two, but that got dropped, so they're not playing hardball. The weapons violation and aggravated assault are the most serious things. Nobody cares he was associating with a felon, since that felon was his own dad. I'm guessing he'll get three to five, tops."

"There won't be any victim-impact statement," Holly said thoughtfully. "Just the defendant and his lawyer."

"Yeah, it won't take long," Vic said. "You'll still have plenty of time to do your hair and nails in time for your date."

"You do such a good job pretending to be a hard-ass, I'll bet you almost believe it yourself," Holly said to Vic with a sweet smile. "But I don't think you're as hard as you act."

"I'm plenty hard, I'll have you know," Vic said.

It was Erin's turn to snort.

"That wasn't... shut up!" Vic growled. "This is why I don't talk to reporters."

"All rise," the bailiff said, saving Vic from any further embarrassment. The detectives got to their feet, along with everyone else in the room.

Judge Pasquale Barberis entered the courtroom, magisterial in his black robe and carefully-combed silver hair. He took up his place behind the lectern, gave it the obligatory smack with his gavel, and said, "Court is now in session."

The proceedings droned past Erin's ear as the court was reminded of the purpose behind the day's proceedings. The defendant, Alfredo Madonna, had pleaded *nolo contendere* to violation of his parole, including aggravated assault and felony weapons possession. Accordingly, the court would now hear the prosecution's statement.

The prosecutor didn't look much older than Alfie himself. This was obviously an open-and-shut case that had been given to him because he was new in the DA's office, needed the experience, and probably wouldn't screw this one up too badly. He gave a short, uninteresting statement about the need to be firm in enforcement of parole conditions, asked the court to impose the maximum allowable penalties, and sat down again.

Then it was Kingston Schultz's turn. The lawyer gave the judge a warm smile. He turned the same smile on the rest of the court, talking to everybody present, though Barberis was the only audience whose opinion really mattered.

Alfredo was a good boy, Schultz said, a boy who had made a few foolish decisions and fallen in with bad company. He'd made mistakes, but he'd paid for those mistakes with several years of his life. He'd been released from prison only a couple of months before his father had been murdered right in front of his face. Hadn't the poor boy suffered enough? Yes, he had kept a pistol in his possession, but that was because of a genuine fear for his own life and that of his father. Events had proved this fear to be regrettably well-founded.

The boy acknowledged his wrongdoing, Schultz said, and was prepared to pay society's price. But surely that price should not be exorbitant. Alfredo was ready and willing to contribute to society, to work hard and move on from his youthful indiscretions. Punish the boy, Schultz finished, but do not destroy him.

"Not bad," Vic muttered. "I almost feel sorry for the little punk."

"I understand the defendant wishes to exercise his right of allocution," Barberis said.

"Elocution?" Vic said.

"Allocution," Holly corrected him. "Federal rules require the defendant be allowed to speak on his own behalf before sentencing. This is what we've been waiting for."

She sounded excited. Erin wondered what Holly was expecting; some sort of courtroom monologue straight out of the movies, probably. *You can't handle the truth*, she thought with a smile.

But Holly wasn't the only one. Vinnie and Vitelli sat up a little straighter and leaned forward. The court was utterly silent as Alfie got to his feet.

He cleared his throat and looked down at his hands, as if he had cue cards. He opened his mouth and worked his jaw to loosen it.

"My father..." he began. Then emotion choked him up and he trailed off. Schultz laid a hand on his arm. Alfie cleared his throat again and started over.

"My father didn't want me to be nothing like him," Alfie said. "He wasn't a bad guy, but lots of people thought he was. He was in a tough business with tough guys, a business you could get hurt in. He wanted me to make something of myself. But I wasn't no good at school. I didn't make good grades, didn't know nothing about college.

"All I ever wanted was to measure up to my dad. Ever since I was a kid, I looked up to him. He had respect. He had honor. He had his code, he taught me how to act, what to say, what to do.

My mom, we lost her when I was a little boy, so Dad did the best he could. I loved my father."

Erin saw Valentino Vitelli nod slightly, a reluctant show of respect.

"I did some bad stuff," Alfie went on. "And I fell down for it. But I stood up and did my time. I didn't complain, just like my father taught me. I got out. But some other stuff was going on. Some guys my father was working with, they decided they could run things better without him, and they got rid of him. One of his best friends tried to take him out, and my father killed him. Self-defense. But there was more of them, and Dad wouldn't run away."

Alfie paused, blinking and wiping at his eyes. "Excuse me, Your Honor. I begged him to run. I knew they'd just keep sending guys until they got him. But my father had his honor. He wasn't gonna run, no way. So he fought, and I was right there beside him when they killed him. I couldn't protect him. I let him down.

"After that, I was pretty mad. I had all these thoughts of revenge, of what I wanted to do to the guys that killed him. But I've been doing some thinking, and I know better now."

"What the hell?" Vic whispered.

Erin didn't understand either, nor did the Lucarellis. Vitelli leaned back in his chair and whispered something to Vinnie.

"Revenge don't solve nothing," Alfie said. "And that's what I wanna say here, in front of everybody. I loved my father, but my father's gone, and nothing's gonna bring him back. I'm a reformed character, I'm a good citizen, at least I'm gonna try to be. And if I could meet the man who killed my father face to face, if he was in this courtroom today, I'd shake his hand and forgive him. Because I'm trying to do the right thing for once in my life. I'm trying to do what my dad would want me to do. I know I'm going back to prison for a while, and that's okay. I just hope when I get out again, I'll be a man Mattie Madonna would be proud of. That's all I got to say."

Alfie sat down again. A murmur of conversation ran through the courtroom. Barberis picked up his gavel and banged it down.

"Order!" Barberis said. The murmur died away. The judge gave the defendant a long, searching stare.

"The court sentences Alfredo Madonna to thirty-six months' imprisonment," Barberis said. "Prisoner to be remanded into custody. These proceedings are adjourned."

He swung his gavel one more time. Alfie stood up. The bailiff moved toward him, pulling out his handcuffs.

"I guess we came all this way for nothing," Vic said.

"Strange," Holly said, clearly disappointed. "I guess we can do a little segment on it, a human-interest bit at the end of the broadcast. Something about redemption and forgiveness, warm people's hearts a little."

Alfie shook hands with Schultz. Vinnie and his goons stood up to go. Vitelli remained seated. Alfie looked Vinnie's way.

"Excuse me," he said. "Mr. Moreno?"

Vinnie paused. Erin saw the wariness in his face. Vinnie was a survivor. He didn't trust anybody, not even in a courtroom full of cops. But Alfie wasn't armed, the Marshals had seen to that, and Vinnie had a pair of beefy thugs to protect him. This was the safest ground they could be standing on. He wasn't scared. And he'd won. Erin saw the smile, almost a smirk, as the Oil Man turned toward his dead enemy's son.

"You have something to say to me, Mr. Madonna?" Vinnie asked politely.

"I just wanted to thank you for everything you've done for my family," Alfie said. The bailiff was nearby now, jingling the cuffs, but the man hesitated. Alfie wasn't going anywhere. There was no harm in observing a few courtesies.

"You're very welcome, young man," Vinnie said.

"Will you shake hands with me?" Alfie asked.

"Of course," Vinnie said, still smiling. He stepped toward Alfie.

Erin didn't like it. She couldn't have explained why, but it felt all wrong. Everything Alfie had done, leading up to this moment, made no sense at all. Why would he have gone to all that trouble just to get eyeball to eyeball with Vinnie Moreno and shake his hand? Not to forgive and forget, that was for damn sure.

She grabbed the back of the chair in front of her and shot to her feet. "Wait!" she exclaimed.

Vinnie was already reaching for Alfie's hand, that false smile of reconciliation on his smooth, handsome, ruthless face. He froze, starting to turn reflexively toward the sound of Erin's voice.

Dario was a well-trained bodyguard. He reacted instantly to the unexpected shout, moving to cut off his employer from the nearest potential threat—in this case, Alfie. He moved fast for such a big guy, sidestepping between the two men.

Alfie was moving too. He punched Dario in the face.

Dario weighed well over two hundred pounds. He was built like a minivan. Alfie was about one-sixty and skinny. His fist should have bounced off Dario's thick skull. To Erin's astonishment, the big man went down screaming, clutching at his face.

Everyone else, Erin included, lost half a second wondering what the hell had just happened. But Alfie had been expecting it and was still in motion. He grabbed at his own wrist. His bracelet was held together with a magnetic clasp. It popped open and unspooled in his hand, leaving a single loop around his opposite wrist. Quickly, efficiently, he whipped the wire around Vinnie's neck. He stepped in close, pressing against Vinnie's back, and pulled the wire tight.

The entire courtroom froze. Erin was standing in the aisle, ten feet from Alfie and Vinnie. Rolf and Vic had both reacted to her and were also up. Holly was staring wide-eyed at the scene. Dario was rolling on the floor, hands over his eyes. The bailiff's handcuffs dangled from his hand, empty manacles swinging to and fro. He pulled his sidearm with his free hand and leveled it at Alfie.

Vinnie held very still. The wire pressed into his neck, almost disappearing from view.

"Drop the weapon! Hands in the air!" one of the Marshals shouted. The other Marshal started moving to the side to widen the angle and get a clean shot. Their guns were drawn and aimed.

"Nobody move," Alfie said. His voice was tight with emotion. "This is piano wire. I pull, his head comes off."

"Take it easy, Alfie," Erin said. "Think about what you're doing."

Alfie actually laughed. "I've been doing nothing but think about this," he said. "This moment right here. I've been waiting for it."

"Listen to Miss O'Reilly, kid," Vinnie said. "Don't throw your life away."

"Like you care about my life!" Alfie said. "As if I didn't know. You got guys waiting to take me out the second I go into genpop. You're just mad I got to you first."

"You're a bright kid," Vinnie said. "I can see that. You can be useful. I've underestimated you, that's obvious. Why don't we talk about this like businessmen, make a deal?"

"Alfie, this isn't what your dad would want," Erin said, holding out a calming hand. She wondered how she could get close enough to grab his arm.

"I don't know what Dad would want, because this son of a bitch killed him!" Alfie retorted. "He throws people away, people who never did nothing but what he told them to, like they was nothing! And he don't even get his own hands dirty!"

"But you were right," Erin said. "Revenge doesn't solve anything. This guy's not worth it."

The Marshals were closing in, one coming down the aisle, the other circling around to flank Alfie. Rolf was poised and ready. The K-9 could be on Alfie less than a second after Erin told him to, but that would be too slow. Erin had never seen a piano-wire garrote in action, but she'd heard stories. The fine wire could cut flesh like a knife. If Alfie pulled it tight, he very well might be able to take Vinnie's head clean off.

"You made your point," Vinnie said. "You've still got options, kid. But if you use that, you've got none. No future. Nothing."

Alfie laughed again. "That's where you're wrong," he said. "See, that's your problem, Vinnie. You're predictable. I knew you'd be here today, just like I know you'd never let me live, not after I've got you like this. And there ain't nothing you can say to tell me otherwise."

"I'm telling you again, drop it!" the Marshal snapped. "I will shoot!"

Alfie looked past Vinnie, straight into Erin's eyes. He quirked a slight, apologetic smile.

"I never had no choice," he said.

"No!" Erin shouted. But Alfie's hands tightened suddenly. He flexed his wrists. The wire noose drew in.

Vinnie tried to say something, but his throat opened and blood poured down in a sudden sheet, soaking his expensive Italian suit. His hands flew up to his neck, but there was no strength in his fingers and he scrabbled uselessly. His knees buckled. Alfie let go of him and spread his hands wide, stepping back from the stricken man.

The bailiff got to Alfie first, tackling him to the floor beside Vinnie. He planted a knee in Alfie's back and snapped the cuffs on him. Vinnie's other bodyguard stood transfixed, an expression of shocked disbelief stamped on his face. Then Erin and Vic were there. Vic was on his phone, calling Dispatch. One of the Marshals spun on his heel and ran out of the room to fetch reinforcements and medical assistance. The other raced into the mix of people, gun still in hand.

Erin knelt beside Vinnie. Bubbles of blood were forming at the front of his throat, where his windpipe had been laid open. More blood pulsed out with every frantic beat of the man's heart. Alfie had cut at least one of his carotids, maybe both, and the jugular vein for good measure.

Vinnie stared up at Erin, his eyes a mute, desperate appeal. He continued to fumble at his neck with fingers gone pale and cold from shock and blood loss.

Erin took his hand and held it. His fresh blood was warmer than his skin. "I can't do anything for you, Vinnie," she said quietly. "This is it. You've got minutes, maybe seconds. You want to make peace with God, you'd better do it now."

His breath wheezed and gurgled. He squeezed her hand once. Then his legs jerked spasmodically, his eyes rolled back, and Vincenzo Moreno went still.

Chapter 25

"When I told you not to kill anybody else, I was joking," Webb said. "I didn't mean you should go out and do it."

"We didn't kill him!" Vic protested. "Hell, we didn't even touch him until after his throat got cut! This isn't our fault!"

They'd retreated upstairs to Judge Ferris's chambers while the Marshals tried to sort out the mess in the courtroom. Ferris's office still looked like a bomb had gone off in it, which was pretty much what had happened, but it was a private space that wasn't being used, so it would do for the moment.

Webb had arrived with impressive speed for a man of his age and physical condition. He'd dropped everything and hurried over as soon as he'd gotten the word. Now he was looking at them, hands on his hips, shaking his head.

"We didn't kill Binkowski, either," Erin reminded Webb.

"I'm aware of that," he said. "But you know how this is likely to play in the media. The same two detectives are present at two fatal incidents within twenty-four hours. Is anyone going to buy that as coincidence?"

"Nobody knew Alfie was going to do what he did," Erin said.

"But you wanted to be there," Webb said. "You insisted on it. Why? What did you know? What in God's name happened in that courtroom?"

Erin opened the door to Ferris's outer office, made sure nobody was there, and closed it again. "Alfie played Vinnie," she said. "He's been setting this up ever since he went on the run after the Lucarellis tried to kill him. His plan this whole time was all about getting close enough to nail Vinnie."

"How, exactly, did he manage that?" Webb asked.

"Alfie had to solve a few problems," she said. "Vinnie lived in a fortress. He had armed guards around him twenty-four seven. And he knew Alfie hated him. He'd never let the kid get close enough to take him out.

"Alfie had to get Vinnie where his guards wouldn't be armed, but Alfie could get right up in his face. And he had to do it fast, because he was about to get thrown back in prison. He had a court date. If he didn't show up, he'd become a fugitive, and having to hide from the cops would only make it harder to get Vinnie.

"The first thing he did was make himself a nuisance. He started feeding tips to guys on the street about vulnerable Lucarelli dealers. He did some of it through his lawyer, Schultz. A few drug rip-offs got Vinnie's attention."

"Suicidal of him," Vic commented.

"He had nothing to lose," Erin said. "Vinnie and Vitelli were already going to kill him. Then he had his lawyer tell his judge he was prepared to spill his guts about the Lucarellis in open court."

"Like I said, suicidal," Vic said.

"It was all part of the plan," Erin said. "Alfie had Vinnie worried. He'd already done some minor damage to the organization. Vinnie didn't know how much Alfie's dad told him about the Family's drug operations. For all Vinnie knew, Alfie might be able to bring down the whole thing."

"What was the point of that?" Webb asked.

"To get Vinnie into the courtroom with him," Erin said.

"Where his goons couldn't bring in guns," Vic said. "It leveled the playing field."

"You're saying he deliberately laid an ambush in a courthouse?" Webb asked.

"That's exactly what he did," Erin said. "But that only dealt with his first obstacle. He still had to get near enough to Vinnie to kill him, and he had to have a weapon to do it with. So he pretended to surrender. He didn't spill any Mob secrets. He swore he was a born-again good citizen and he wasn't carrying any grudges."

"And Vinnie bought that?" Webb asked. Skepticism was written all over his face.

"Vinnie was an arrogant prick," Erin said. "He was used to sacrificing the people around him to get what he wanted. He was a powerful man, at the very top of his organization. He thought Alfie was a nobody, a dumb street punk. Alfie told him what he wanted to hear. Vinnie didn't need to believe it. He just needed to let Alfie get within three or four feet of him."

"And then the kid went for him," Webb said. "I understand that. What was the weapon? And how'd he get it into the courtroom?"

"It was a piano-wire garrote," Vic said. "Disguised as a decorative bracelet. Sneaky. The metal detectors would've picked it up, but the courthouse cops thought it was just a piece of jewelry. And speaking of jewelry, he played a pretty neat trick with that pinkie ring."

"What pinkie ring?" Webb asked.

"Alfie knew he might have to get past a bodyguard," Erin said. "He was wearing a bunch of rings. One of them had a stone in it, way too big to be a real gemstone."

"It was hollow," Vic said. "Just thin glass. Wanna guess what was inside?"

"I don't need to guess," Webb said. "Because I have a couple of professional detectives here to tell me."

"Pepper spray," Vic said with a nasty smile. "Concentrated. Not an aerosol. Pure, liquid pain. When he punched that guy, the stone cracked open and the poor son of a bitch got a face-full of riot juice. Right in the eyes. No wonder he went down. So would I."

"He'll probably be okay," Erin said. "He's at the hospital now. He can't see anything out of his left eye, and his right one's pretty blurry, but the doc thinks he'll get his sight back."

"Harsh," Webb said.

"Then he whipped the wire around Vinnie's neck and that was all she wrote," Erin said.

"He's lucky the Marshals didn't blow him away," Webb said.

"He was threatening to kill his hostage," Vic said. "In that situation, the shooters are gonna hold their fire unless they've got a perfect kill-shot lined up, and even then, they'd want their boss to give them the go-ahead. And once Madonna cut Vinnie's throat, nobody else was in danger. The kid wasn't armed anymore. There was no point shooting him."

"Clever," Webb said. "But the kid had to get awfully lucky for all this to line up."

"Psychology, mostly," Erin said. "He was counting on Vinnie to act like Vinnie."

"I don't buy it," Webb said.

"That's what happened, sir," Erin said.

"I believe you, O'Reilly. What I don't buy is that Alfredo Madonna could come up with something like this. It's some Machiavellian stuff we've got here, and Machiavelli may have been Italian, but that kid isn't exactly Machiavelli."

"I'm pretty sure he didn't come up with the whole thing on his own," Erin said.

"Who else are we looking at?" Webb asked.

"Kingston Schultz," Erin said.

"The lawyer?"

"That's him."

"Why would he do that?"

"He's been the family's lawyer forever. He had a lot of respect for Alfie's dad. They trusted each other. He's been looking after Alfie's interests ever since Mattie died."

"How does the kid going down for Murder One count as looking after his interests?" Vic asked.

"This is the Mafia we're talking about," Erin said. "These guys don't forgive, they don't forget, and they always pay back an insult. Schultz's family have been Mob lawyers ever since Prohibition. They're part of that culture. Hell, the whole thing might've been Schultz's plan to take down Vinnie, and Alfie was just a willing sacrificial lamb."

"Some lamb," Vic said. "Did you see the look on his face when he took Vinnie down? Like a guy who's getting laid for the first time and loving it."

"Thank you for that image," Webb said dryly. "Can you prove this about Schultz?"

"Not a bit of it," Erin said, shaking her head. "He's too smart. We know he passed the tip on the café job to the Coffee Bandit, but that didn't break the law. We're never going to tie him to this unless Alfie talks."

"You think he will?" Webb asked.

"No way," Vic said. "That kid thinks he's old-school Mafia. *Omerta* and all that bullshit. He got that from his dad. He's proud of what he did and he'll claim it was all his own idea. Who knows? It might even keep him alive."

"How so?" Erin asked.

"Think about it," Vic said. "Before, he was small-time. A two-bit hood with a price on his head. He would've been lunch meat in prison. Now he's the guy who took out Vinnie the Oil Man in the middle of a courthouse, surrounded by cops! People are gonna respect him. More to the point, they're gonna be scared of him. Watch, he'll be a big man in maximum security."

"Vinnie's got friends who may disagree with you," Webb said.

"Vinnie didn't have a single friend on Earth," Erin said. "Vic's right. This was Alfie's best shot at surviving prison. Sure, he'll be inside for twenty to life now, but his chances of surviving went way up. And he got his revenge. From his perspective, he won."

"I guess none of us are gonna be too broken up about that," Vic said. "The world's a better place without Vinnie in it, and the bastard sure as hell had it coming. What were you thinking, Erin?"

"About what?"

"Holding his hand, whispering sweet nothings to him. If you didn't tell him he was on his way straight to hell, I don't know what you had to say to him."

She shrugged uncomfortably. She'd been asking herself the same thing. "He was dying," she said. "There's no point taunting a guy who's on his way out. I was keeping up appearances."

"Bullshit," Vic said. "You actually felt bad for the guy. I don't believe it. You wanted him dead. Hell, you would've killed him if he'd given you a reason! Now you turn into Mother freaking Teresa?"

"I used to think it was easy to tell the bad guys from the good guys," she said. "Now I think it's easy for good guys to turn into bad ones. We're not as pure as you think, Vic. Firelli over in SNEU used to run with a street gang. They still call him Bobby the Blade, and just a few days ago, he threatened to kill another cop. And he did. Firelli's one of the *good* ones! Homeland Security caught that hacker who brought down the city's power grid, and what did they do? They gave him a damn job! He works for the government now! I've talked to gangsters who'd do anything for their sons, and sons who'd do anything for their fathers. Alfie's a bad guy and so is Vinnie, but Alfie did what he did out of love as much as hate."

"What are you saying, Erin?" Webb asked with unusual gentleness.

"I'm saying I'm a cop, not a judge," she said. "I don't get to pass sentence on these guys, and I don't get to judge them. If they break the law, I take them in. That's my job. The rest is between them, the DA, and God. Vinnie was a vicious, murderous, psychopathic asshole, and I'm not going to lose sleep over him getting killed. But even if I'd shot him myself, it would've been my job to try to patch him back together the second he hit the ground. If I can't do that, I ought to turn in my shield."

"Wow," Vic said. "Ask a question, get a sermon. Next thing you know, you'll be joining the priesthood."

"I'm Catholic and I'm female, dumbass," she said. "I can't be a priest."

"Guess you'll have to go on being a cop, then," he said. "And as long as we're talking about justice, I nearly forgot."

He reached into his pocket and hauled out his wallet. Flipping it open, he extracted a ten-dollar bill and handed it to Erin.

"What's this for?" she asked.

"I bet you ten bucks Alfie wouldn't get Vinnie," Vic said. "I may not be a Mafioso, but I pay my debts."

"I didn't just see that," Webb said. "I did not watch two detectives pay off a wager over a gangland hit. I hope that never gets out. And maybe, if we're really lucky, when this is on the evening news it won't have Major Crimes' fingerprints all over it."

Erin and Vic looked at each other. Neither one said anything.

The door opened. Rolf barked. The three detectives spun around with the guilty expressions of toddlers caught with their hands in the cookie jar. A man in full tactical gear filled the doorway, rifle in hand, face boxed in by a heavy black helmet.

The man looked them over for a second. Then he said, "Clear," and got out of the way, revealing a white-haired old man in an out-of-style suit.

"Am I interrupting something?" Judge Ferris asked.

"Nothing important, Your Honor," Webb said. "We were just leaving."

"Don't mind me," Ferris said. "I just realized I needed to retrieve a legal brief. If you could move to one side or the other, young man?"

Vic sidestepped. Ferris walked past him to the file cabinet in the corner and unlocked it.

"Your colleagues have finished canvassing my home," Ferris said. "They are confident they have discovered and disabled all the traps which were set for me. It's really quite flattering that our city's criminal element considers me worthy of so much trouble. I've heard it said that if they're trying to kill you, you must be doing something right."

"Or something wrong," Vic said.

Ferris chuckled. "Excellent point, young man." His face grew serious again. "The funeral service for Miranda will be on Tuesday. Might I invite all of you to attend?"

"We'd be honored," Webb said.

"I understand you have dispatched the perpetrator?"

"More or less," Erin said.

Ferris raised his eyebrows.

"Rolf's the one who got him, Your Honor," she said.

"Yes, of course," Ferris said. "And from what I hear, he worked in the theater?"

"As a backstage worker," she said. "He was good with machinery."

"Indeed," Ferris said. "A strange and dangerous man. But I suppose he was merely an instrument. Whose hand wielded him?"

"Vincenzo Moreno," Erin said. "You're right, sir. You must be doing something right, because the Lucarellis wanted you out of the way to make Gabriel Vitelli's trial go smoother. They thought they'd do better with a different judge."

"Did they?" Ferris replied. "So this was a deliberate act to put their thumb on the scales of justice, not an attack based on revenge?"

"That's the way it looks," she said.

"And I would have been replaced by Pasquale Barberis," Ferris said.

"That's true," Erin said.

"You knew that," Ferris said, darting her a keen-eyed look. "Do you know something about one of my colleagues?"

"Nothing definite, Your Honor," Erin said.

"Someone in your profession surely understands how much damage suspicion alone can cause," Webb said. "We wouldn't want to go slinging unprovable accusations."

"You said 'unprovable,'" Ferris said. "Not 'unfounded.'"

"I'm not a lawyer," Webb said. "I'm a little sloppy with my words."

"Maybe," Ferris said thoughtfully. "You are keeping your own counsel, so I will do the same. But knowledge of this sordid affair might be considered grounds for recusing myself from the case anyway. Some people might think being targeted for assassination by friends of a defendant might prejudice me against that defendant."

"You think they'll bring that up on appeal if he's convicted?" Vic asked. "They'd have to admit their own motive and culpability."

Ferris nodded. "True. But as I understand it, Mr. Moreno recently suffered a misfortune of his own, not far from where we are currently standing."

"You don't have to worry about him anymore, Your Honor," Erin said.

"What happened to him?" Ferris asked.

"It's a long story," she said. "The short version is, he racked up some debts and the bill came due."

"With interest," Vic added.

"Then we'll say no more about it," Ferris said. "Will any additional assassins be calling on me in the near future?"

"Not on account of this case," Erin said. "I've got it pretty solidly from one of my sources on the street. You're not to be touched."

"I suppose I'll sleep easier knowing that," Ferris said. "But I shall keep my shotgun in my umbrella stand nonetheless and I shall keep it loaded." He walked to his desk and unlocked the right-hand drawer. "There's only one more piece of business before us."

"What's that, Your Honor?" Webb asked.

Ferris took out a jelly jar, the kind Erin's mom used for homemade jam. It was about three-quarters full of a clear liquid.

The judge laid the jar on his desk. Then he rummaged in the drawer and came up with four shot glasses. He filled the glasses and held the first one out to Webb.

The Lieutenant looked at it doubtfully. "What's this?" he asked.

"It's not water," Vic said, grinning.

"White lightning," Ferris said. "My own recipe. As I recall, Detectives O'Reilly and Neshenko didn't have the chance to partake the last time it was in front of them."

"We're on duty," Webb said, but he said it regretfully and kept looking at the glass.

"If you think three ounces of my moonshine will significantly impair you, I believe you may have a higher opinion of my distilling skills than they warrant," Ferris said. "In my capacity as a sworn officer of this court, I absolve you of this minor infraction of your Patrol Guide. I really must insist. I'm in dire need of a drink, now that this matter is concluded, and I'm damned if I'm going to drink alone."

Webb cracked a weary smile. "Fair enough, Your Honor," he said, taking the glass.

Ferris handed two more glasses to Erin and Vic, keeping the fourth for himself. "I don't have an appropriate beverage for your faithful companion, young lady," he said, glancing at Rolf.

"That's okay," Erin said. "I've got it covered." She reached into her jacket pocket and pulled out Rolf's rubber Kong toy.

The dog's eyes followed her hand intently. He cocked his head and stared.

"Here you go, kiddo," she said, tossing him the toy. He snagged it on the fly and started chomping.

"That takes care of all of us," Ferris said. "A toast, then. First, to Miranda Rodriguez, a woman who pledged her life to public service and whose tragic death served one final purpose, that of dragging a merciless killer into the light and ending his depredations."

The three detectives raised their glasses.

Ferris cleared his throat, blinked, and wiped the back of his hand across his eyes. "And to the New York Police Department," he went on. "More specifically the Precinct Eight Major Crimes unit, without whom I would also now be dead. May we share many more years of happy collaboration in the righteous business of putting malefactors where they belong."

"Cheers," Erin and Vic said. Webb nodded.

They clinked glasses and drank. Ferris was an excellent judge, but he would have been a superb bootlegger. It was the best home-brewed moonshine Erin had ever tasted. It went down smooth and left a fierce heat in its wake.

"Too bad we're on duty," she said. "Or I'd ask for another."

Rolf's rubber ball squeaked.

Chapter 26

Carlyle had a great poker face, but his eyes told Erin everything she needed to know. He'd already heard about Vinnie. He could hardly have missed it; the courtroom slaying had been all over the news. She darted a glance toward his apartment door. He nodded and slipped off his barstool.

"I wasn't expecting you so early," he said once the door was safely locked behind them and they were up in the living room.

"I told the Lieutenant I needed a little time to sort some things out," she said. "He told Vic and me to take the rest of the day, on account of the fatal incident."

"You didn't kill the lad," Carlyle said.

"No, but a guy getting his throat cut in front of you is a big deal, or so they tell me." She shrugged in what she hoped was a casual way. "I figured I'd better touch base with you. What's the word on the street?"

"The Lucarellis are in an uproar," he said. "Naturally enough, what with losing their second Don in a matter of months. It'll take some time to shake itself out."

"What about the O'Malleys?"

"I'm meeting Evan this evening to discuss that very question. No doubt he'll be looking for opportunities for expansion, but frankly, I think our wee arrangement will come to fruition before anything definite develops on that front. Evan's not likely to be in charge of anything at all, a few months from now. But tell me, darling. Are you all right?"

"Of course I am. It's not the first guy I've seen die."

He nodded. "From what they're saying, the Madonna lad did for Vinnie. Is that so?"

"Yeah," she said. "Garroted him right in front of the judge, some reporters, half a dozen Lucarellis, a pair of Marshals, Vic, Rolf, and me."

"It seems we underestimated the lad."

"You sound impressed."

"I am. Have you any idea how many gangsters have wanted to kill Vinnie Moreno over the years? Alfredo's the only one who got close, let alone succeeded, and he did it practically alone."

"That's only because he didn't give a damn about getting away afterward. Now the idiot's looking at the rest of his life behind bars." She sighed. "I was trying to look after that dumb kid."

"An assassin who doesn't care if he's caught or killed is hard to defend against," Carlyle agreed. "You did what you could for him. His fate's not on your hands."

"What about Vinnie's?"

"What do you mean?"

"If I hadn't intervened on Alfie's behalf, the Lucarellis would've killed him a while ago," she said. "I saved his life at least once, maybe a couple of times. Then he went and wasted Vinnie."

"Erin, you can't possibly think that's your doing," Carlyle said, laying his hands on her shoulders. "Every one of us makes our own choices. We're not responsible for anyone else's."

"I was going to kill Vinnie," she blurted. "That night I followed him and that crooked FBI agent into Jersey. I had it all planned out, how I'd do it, how I'd get away with it. I nearly did it."

Carlyle nodded. If he was surprised, it didn't show. "Why didn't you go through with it?"

"Because then I'd be a murderer!" she snapped. "I would've proved I'm not a cop, I'm just a gangster with a shield! But I might as well have done it. How many other guys died in the meantime, just because of that bastard and me dragging my feet?"

"Erin, darling," he said. "The way I'm hearing it, you'd a narrow escape. You didn't let the Oil Man drag you into the muck with him. You protected another lad, though he was a criminal too, and he repaid you the best way he could, by dispatching your enemy."

"I didn't ask him to do that," she said dully.

"Of course not! And you'd have told him not to, if he'd have listened."

"I did tell him," she said, remembering those tense seconds in the courtroom. "And you're right, he didn't listen. I don't think I've got much future as a hostage negotiator."

"Then perhaps, this time around, the universe rewarded your mercy by dealing with Vinnie through the consequences of his own actions. Be sure your sin will find you out."

She smiled sadly. "You're quoting scripture at me now?"

"As I've told you before, the world runs on favors, darling. You did one for the Madonna lad, he did one for you. You're square. And for what I'm hoping is the last time, you didn't kill Vinnie. He killed himself, through the life he led and the paths he chose. And there's an end of it."

She wrapped her fingers around the lapels of his coat and gave them an affectionate shake. "You're right," she said. "Who would've thought you'd be my moral compass?"

He bent down and lightly kissed her on the lips. "It's only fair. You've been mine more than once. I love you, darling. Did you know, they're calling you and Detective Neshenko heroes?"

"What? Who is?"

"The telly. Some blonde colleen on Channel Six is saying you heroically intervened, preventing greater loss of life."

"That's bullshit," Erin said. "Alfie was never going to kill anybody else, except maybe Valentino Vitelli if he'd had time. But I guess that Gardner chick isn't as big a bitch as I thought."

"You know her?"

"Yeah, I keep running into her."

"You may want to keep on her good side," he advised. "It's always grand to have good public relations."

Erin rolled her eyes. "As if I didn't have enough trouble dealing with psycho murderers and mobsters, now I've got to play nice with the media, too? No thanks. This is why I'll never make Captain. I'll leave that shit to Holliday and guys like him."

"As you wish, darling. Can I get you anything? You've had a short day, but a trying one."

"It's a little early for the hard stuff," she said. "Maybe just a pint of Guinness to wet my throat. I need to make a call."

"Nothing dangerous, I hope."

"I hope not."

"Your handler?"

"Worse. My dad."

* * *

"O'Reilly."

Sean O'Reilly Senior always answered the phone as if he was still wearing a shield. No "hello," no idle banter.

"Hey, dad," Erin said.

"Oh, hey, kiddo. Everything okay?"

"Yeah, everything's fine." It was close enough to the truth. "What're you up to?"

"Well, you know, deer season's about to open. So I've got my Remington out of the case and I'm giving it another cleaning, getting ready to go bag Mary some fresh venison in a couple of days. How about you?"

"Oh, you know, the usual. Perps and paperwork. Have you been watching the news?" She tried to make the question as casual as possible.

"Not today. I'll catch the six o'clock while your mother's cooking supper, just like I always do." Sean was old-school enough to view anything off the Internet as highly suspect. He watched the evening news and read the *Times* the next morning. If an event wasn't important enough to be in the *Times*, he'd said more than once, it wasn't worth knowing about.

"This'll be the leading story," she said. "Unless somebody sets off a nuke in the next couple of hours."

Sean's voice sharpened. "What's up, kiddo?"

"A Mafia boss got whacked," she said. "Vinnie Moreno, the Lucarelli boss. I wasn't directly involved. Well, maybe I was. It's complicated. Dad, another mobster practically cut his head off right in front of me."

"Jesus," Sean said quietly. It sounded more like a prayer than an oath. "Are you hurt?"

"No. I was just a bystander." She quickly explained Vinnie's last courtroom appearance.

"What do you need from me?" he asked when she was done.

"Nothing."

"Baloney," Sean said. "You wouldn't have called if there wasn't something I could do. From the sound of it, this is a slam-dunk of a case. You've got the killer in custody; hell, they were already breaking out the cuffs. You said it was a personal thing, not really a Mob hit, so that's all there is to it. Did you need to talk about it? I know you've seen guys die before, but that sounds like a bad way to go. Is it bothering you?"

"It's not that." She hesitated, searching for the right words. "I just... I needed to talk to my daddy."

That threw him for a moment. That had been what she'd called him when she was a young girl. "Absolutely, kiddo," he said, recovering. "I'm listening. What do you need to talk about?"

"These past couple of months have been rough," she said. "I think this part of it is over, but the way it ended... This kid, his dad got murdered and all he could think about was killing the guy who was behind it. I guess it got me thinking about what I would've done if anything... you know."

"Hey," Sean said. "Nothing happened to me. Nothing's going to happen to me. I'm right here. We O'Reillys are hard to get rid of."

"If some gangster had killed you, I might've wasted him," she said. "I... Dad, I had some close calls. I'm not talking about bullets. I almost did some bad things, and the more I think about it, the more I think it was just dumb luck that I didn't."

"Baloney," he said again. "There's plenty of bad cops out there, kiddo, and you're not one of them. I've never known anyone who wore a shield that I'd trust more to do the right thing when the chips were down."

"Of course you'd say that," she said, smiling into the telephone. "You're my dad. You're biased."

"I'm your dad and I know you," he countered. "You think the really bad apples have conversations like this? You think they worry about it? No way. They're out there doing the bad stuff, getting in trouble, not agonizing about it. You know what I think? I think it's your Catholic upbringing, all that going to Confession stuff."

"Dad, I was being serious."

"I know. What is it you're really worried about, kiddo? Because it's not me. I'm out of the game, have been for years. Nobody's coming after me all the way upstate, and if they did, Mr. Remington here and I would have something to say about it."

"Carlyle." The word was out of her mouth before she was aware of it. It hung there between them, in a silence that lasted ten or fifteen seconds.

"You're worried he's going to get killed, and you'll go on some sort of vigilante rampage?" Sean asked at last.

"We're almost done with that thing we're not supposed to talk about," she said. "I hope it's all going to go clean and smooth but..."

"But when does it ever?" he replied wryly.

"Exactly. If something happens to him, I... I don't know what I'd do."

"And if something happened to your mother, I'd go out of my head, and God help the bastard who hurt her," Sean said. "That doesn't make you a bad person. It means you love someone. I just wish you'd picked somebody else."

"Like who?" she asked.

"I don't know. Tom Hanks?"

"Isn't he already married?"

"A father can dream."

"Well, dad, Tom Hanks was taken. I guess I settled."

He chuckled. "Well, your guy isn't as bad as I thought he was. Even if he is named Morton. Dear Lord, what were his parents thinking? As if life isn't hard enough. My point is, the two of you have stood by each other through some pretty hard times already. I've got a feeling you'll make it through this. But if you do, he'd better put the biggest rock on your finger you've ever seen, or I'm taking him behind the woodshed."

"Dad! Did Mom put you up to that?"

"I'll take the Fifth."

"Didn't you tell me once that only guilty guys take the Fifth?"

"I'll take the Fifth on that, too. Isn't the Constitution wonderful?"

"Thanks for nothing," she said, but she was smiling as she said it. "I feel a little better."

"That's what I'm here for. Say, why don't you come up on the twenty-first? First day of the season. We could go out, just the two of us, and look for a nice buck."

"Tramp around the woods with a bunch of heavily-armed, trigger-happy, beer-drinking guys? Thanks, dad, but I prefer my recreation not to look quite so much like my day job. Besides, I need to work."

"Crimes to solve, Fives to fill out?"

"That's the nice thing about original sin," she said. "It gives cops great job security. Anyway, we'll be seeing you for Thanksgiving in a few days."

"That's right. Your mother still wants to host, but Shelley and Junior talked her out of it. I guess it makes more sense for us to come down, with all you kids still hanging around the big city. But Mary's bringing pie."

"Looking forward to it. Say hi to Mom for me, will you?"

"Absolutely. And stop thinking so much about sin. It's bad for the digestion."

"I love you, dad."

"Love you too, kiddo. And I'm proud of you."

Erin hung up the phone and slipped it back into her pocket. She looked at Rolf, who looked back with his serious brown eyes.

"You don't worry about sin, do you?" she asked him.

Rolf did not.

"That's one mob boss down," she said. "One more to go. You ready to get Evan O'Malley?"

Rolf barked. He had no idea what she'd just asked him, but he recognized the word "ready," and there was only one right answer to that question.

"Of course you are," Erin said, rubbing his ears. "I think we've let him go long enough. It's time to run him down and put the teeth in. Then we can all go home."

Rolf squinted happily and pressed himself against her hand. His mouth opened, his tongue flopped out, and he smiled. His tail started wagging.

Keep reading for a sneak peek from
Kamikaze

Here's a sneak peek from Book 21: Kamikaze

Coming 9/25/2023

"This is going to be a disaster. They're never all going to fit. We're going to crash and burn."

Michelle O'Reilly surveyed the room, hands on her hips, shaking her head.

"Nonsense, dear," Mary O'Reilly replied briskly. "It's only a few more guests than usual. We'll have plenty of room."

"It isn't the square footage I'm worried about," Michelle said. "It's the chairs. We don't have enough."

Erin O'Reilly looked from her sister-in-law to her mother, then back at the O'Reilly living room. She believed in adapting and overcoming whatever obstacles life threw in her way, but she had to admit Michelle had a point. Michelle and Sean

Junior's Midtown Manhattan brownstone was looking awfully full.

"Let's see," Michelle said to Mary, ticking off names on her fingers. "There's you and Sean Senior; Michael and Sarah; Tommy; Erin and Carlyle; Ian, Cassie, and Ben; and of course Junior, Anna, Patrick, and me. That's twelve people, and that's not even counting the dogs. Rolf, Miri, and Lucy."

"The dogs don't need chairs," Erin said. Rolf was lying on the carpet in the middle of the living room. The German Shepherd wore an expression of long-suffering patience. Erin's niece Anna was on one side of him, braiding little colored ribbons into his fur. On the other side, a fluffy Newfoundland puppy was tugging on one of his large, upright ears.

"Lucy! Stop that!" Anna scolded. "You can't chew on Rolfie!"

Lucy took no notice, continuing to pull. She growled low in her throat, thinking it sounded fierce. It didn't.

"Let's see," Mary said, tapping her chin. "We've got eight chairs in the dining room set. That leaves four. You've got one in the kitchen..."

"Another two folding chairs in the front closet," Michelle said. "And I guess we can use the swivel from Junior's office."

"There!" Mary said. "That wasn't so bad, was it? Just think, I raised twice as many children as you've got. We always found room for them."

The shrill beep of an alarm cut through the air.

"Oh no!" Michelle exclaimed. She spun and dashed into the kitchen to tend to an unspecified culinary emergency. At the same moment, a crash came from the living room. Patrick O'Reilly and Ben Jordan had been building a castle out of wooden blocks. They had apparently neglected a major structural support and the whole thing had come tumbling down. Miri, Ian's scruffy, nervous dog, twitched and scooted under the couch. Her snout protruded, quivering. Ian got down off the couch on one knee and began talking soothingly to her.

"Good thing Thanksgiving only comes once a year, eh, Mom?" Erin said with a smile.

"Get used to it, dear," Mary said. "One of these days this might be you."

"Give me a police station on a Saturday night," Erin said, but she was still smiling. The O'Reilly house was full of people she loved. She might complain, but she wouldn't be anywhere else in the world.

The O'Reilly clan always got together for the holidays. It was one of the only times Erin saw her brothers Michael and Tommy. She ran into Sean Junior more often than either of them would have liked; trauma surgeons and police detectives had an uncomfortable amount of overlap in their professional lives. But Erin's mom and dad had moved upstate after her dad had retired, and it was always good when they came down to visit.

This year, however, things had gotten a little out of hand. Inviting Morton Carlyle, Erin's boyfriend, was the obvious thing to do. Ian Thompson, Carlyle's driver and bodyguard, needed to be included. That would have happened anyway, as Ian had been made an honorary O'Reilly after he'd nearly died protecting Michelle and her kids. But now Ian had a girlfriend, and that girlfriend had a son from her first marriage, so Cassie and Ben Jordan were roped in, too. Next thing anybody knew, they had a dozen people crammed into the house.

Mary bustled out to the kitchen to help Michelle get the food on the table. Erin started corralling her brothers, collecting furniture, putting the extra leaf in the table, and trying to keep Lucy from eating Rolf's ears. By the time the turkey was placed on the dining table, golden-brown and steaming, the friends and family were seated. The dogs lurked under the table; Rolf and

Miri at the feet of their respective humans, Lucy wandering from one set of ankles to another, begging for treats.

After a few moments, Sean Junior took advantage of a pause in the hubbub. He cleared his throat loudly.

"We're going to say grace in a minute," he said. "But first, I just wanted to say how glad and… and grateful Shelley and I are to have you all here with us."

Erin heard the hitch in her brother's voice and caught the look in his eye. He and Michelle hadn't fully recovered from the events of the previous summer. Their marriage had strained to the breaking point, but it hadn't quite come apart.

"It's been a difficult year," he went on. "For all of us. But we've made it through. Now we're here together, enjoying what looks to be a fantastic Thanksgiving feast. I want to thank my mom for her famous pies—remember to save room, everybody— and Sarah for her sweet potato casserole, and Cassie for… what's this again?"

"Macaroni pudding," Cassie said. "It's one of Ben's favorites. It's kind of like mac and cheese's big brother."

"It looks delicious," Sean said. "And I want to thank Carlyle for the wine. I have to say, it's pretty great having a pub owner in the family. You took your time, kiddo, but you know how to pick 'em."

Erin smiled and shook her head. Carlyle wasn't quite in the family, not technically. But he certainly had a well-stocked cellar. He gave her a sly, subtle wink and squeezed her hand under the table.

"And as for all the rest of you," Sean finished, "you brought yourselves, and that's what matters most. We're so very thankful all of you are with us. And I hope all of us will be together again next year, and for many years to come."

"Hear, hear," Michael said, raising his wine glass.

Erin nodded. But looking at Carlyle and Ian, she was thinking about all the narrow escapes, the fear, the bullets, the blood, and the pain. They'd dodged death this past year and had only scraped past it by a razor-thin margin. They'd passed through a lot of dangers and close calls, but they weren't out of the woods yet. Her own hopes were much more modest than her brother's. She hoped they'd all live to see New Year's Day.

"If you'd like to say grace, Dad?" Sean said, turning to his father.

Sean O'Reilly Senior cleared his throat. His mustache shifted. "Bless us, O Lord, for these, Thy gifts, which we are about to receive from Thy bounty," he said. "Through Christ, our Lord. Amen."

"Can we eat now?" Ben asked loudly.

"I think we'd better," Erin's dad said.

*   *   *

"No offense, but I prefer my family gatherings to yours," Erin said as she steered her Charger through the Manhattan streets. Ian would normally have driven them, but he'd borrowed Carlyle's Mercedes to transport Cassie and Ben.

"You're referring to our meeting with Evan next week?" Carlyle replied.

"Yeah. Any idea what he wants to talk about?"

"I presume he'll be discussing some organizational changes, on account of recent headcount reduction," he said dryly.

Erin swallowed, feeling the two slices of Mary O'Reilly's homemade pie shift in her overfull stomach. Unable to choose between pumpkin and apple, she'd compromised and had one of each. She knew Carlyle was thinking about Veronica Blackburn.

Neither of them had liked the streetwalker-turned-madam, but they hadn't wanted her to die the way she had, either.

"The O'Malleys are running out of bosses," she said. "First Liam, then Mickey, now Veronica. That just leaves you, Evan, Corky, Finnegan, and Pritchard. If things keep going like this, we won't need to do anything. The whole gang's going to self-destruct."

"I've heard evil contains the seeds of its own destruction," Carlyle said. "But that's no great surprise. We're all of us rushing toward death, when you get down to it."

"That's a cheerful thought," she said. "Aren't we supposed to be feeling thankful today?"

"Oh, I'm grateful, darling," he said, laying his hand on her thigh. "Not least to your kin, who've welcomed me as one of their own. When your brother said I was one of the family, does he know something I don't?"

"No!" Erin said sharply, glad she wasn't a blusher. "I mean... we can't rush into things. With everything that's going on."

"Of course not," he agreed. "I'm merely glad your da's decided not to shoot me."

"He never would've shot you."

"You're certain of that? A gangster stepping out with Sean O'Reilly's only daughter?"

"Okay, he probably wouldn't have shot you. At least, nowhere vital. Maybe in the leg or something."

"That's a great comfort, darling."

* * *

The holiday season was a time of light, joy, and family. Sappy movies appeared on TV. Multicolored lights were hung from just about every horizontal surface. New York's drab concrete and asphalt were festooned with red and green. And the crime rate went up by about twenty percent.

Criminologists theorized this was because people carried more cash and crowds got bigger. Americans also liked to travel, visiting their relatives. That meant more empty houses and apartments, which made prime targets for burglars. But none of that explained why the murder rate also spiked on major holidays.

Vic Neshenko's theory was as terse and straightforward as Vic himself. In the Precinct 8 Major Crimes office the following morning, when Erin mentioned the uptick in homicides that came with Thanksgiving and Christmas, his answer was a single word.

"Family."

"Maybe your family, Vic," she said. "Not mine."

"I'm serious," he said. "Take your average American family. Chances are, two or three of them aren't on speaking terms. Maybe one guy is boinking his brother's wife. Maybe another guy borrowed money and never paid it back. Whatever. But they're going on with their lives, everybody's basically fine, until wham! It's Christmas and they're all gonna be under the same roof for a few days. Take your average American Joe. To get there, he's gotta go through a crowded airport full of bullshit security, the airline loses his luggage, he's tired, he's stressed. Now he's in a house with eight screaming kids, two of which are his own, he's using Aunt Edna's toothbrush because his suitcase got flown down to Fort Lauderdale or some damn place, he's sleeping on the fold-out bed with a metal bar across his spine so he wakes up with a backache. Then he's sitting next to his asshole brother-in-law, who he hates and who won't shut up about the Democrats or the Republicans or whoever. There's alcohol, lots of it, so he's more than half drunk. And right there at his fingertips is a nice, fresh-sharpened carving knife. Yeah, I got no idea why people get stabbed during the holidays."

"Wow," Erin said. "You've put some thought into this."

"I call 'em like I see 'em," Vic said.

"Neshenko's right, sorry to say," Lieutenant Webb said from behind his desk. "But we don't need to worry about any of those homicides. They're open-and-shut. The Homicide boys can sort them out in an hour or two, tops. I'd be surprised if we get anything big on our plates. Even gangsters like to go home for the holidays."

"Where they can murder their wives, girlfriends, and in-laws," Vic said.

"Right," Webb said.

"Black Friday," Vic said darkly. "Watch. We're gonna get some sort of weird-ass murder case. Some psycho's gonna be offing people in the Walmart checkout lines."

"You drink a lot during the Christmas season, don't you," Erin said.

"I drink a lot year round," he replied. "That doesn't make me wrong."

"Let me tell you what makes you wrong..." Erin began.

"Hold that thought," Webb said, raising a hand. In the sudden silence, the tinny notes of canned music drifted through the office air.

"Oh my God," Vic said. "I don't believe it. The Lieutenant changed his ringtone to 'Jingle Bells.'"

"Shut up, Neshenko. I need all the Christmas cheer I can get." Webb thumbed his screen and put the phone to his ear, mercifully cutting off the chorus. "Webb."

He listened to the voice on the line for several moments. "Copy that," he said at last. "Wait a minute. How come this is ours? Shouldn't it be NTSB? Oh. Yeah, I copy. Okay, we'll get right down there."

Webb put his phone back in his pocket. "Saddle up," he said.

"Where are we going?" Erin asked.

"Jamaica Bay Wildlife Refuge," Webb said.

"What's up?" Vic asked. "Are the waterfowl forming gangs? Ducks versus geese?"

"Plane crash," Webb said.

"Oh my God," Erin said. That explained Webb's question about the NTSB. The National Transportation Safety Board was responsible for investigating crashes. If they were calling in Major Crimes, it meant they'd already found signs of foul play.

"From JFK?" Vic asked.

Webb shrugged. "We'll find out when we get there."

"How many passengers?" Erin asked. She felt sick to her stomach, her thoughts filled with passenger planes packed with holiday travelers.

"That's the weird thing," Webb said. "None."

"Just the pilot?" Vic asked.

"Not even that," Webb said. "The plane was empty."

Ready for more?

Join the Clickworks Press email list
for the latest on new releases, upcoming books and
series, behind-the-scenes details, events, and more.

Be the first to know about new releases in the Erin
O'Reilly Mysteries by signing up at
clickworkspress.com/join/erin

About the Author

Steven Henry learned how to read almost before he learned how to walk. Ever since he began reading stories, he wanted to put his own on the page. He lives a very quiet and ordinary life in Minnesota with his wife and dog.

Also by Steven Henry

Fathers
A Modern Christmas Story

When you strip away everything else, what's left is the truth

Life taught Joe Davidson not to believe in miracles. A blue-collar woodworker, Joe is trying to build a future. His father drank himself to death and his mother succumbed to cancer, leaving a broken, struggling family. He and his brother and sisters are faced with failed marriages, growing pains, and lingering trauma.

Then a chance meeting at his local diner brings Mary Elizabeth Reynolds into his life. Suddenly, Joe finds himself reaching for something more, a dream of happiness. The wood-worker and the poor girl from a trailer park connect and fall in love, and for a little while, everything is right with their world.

But suddenly Joe is confronted with a situation he never imagined. What do you do if your fiancée is expecting a child you know isn't yours? Torn between betrayal and love, trying to do the right thing when nothing seems right anymore, Joe has to strip life down to its truth and learn that, in spite of the pain, love can be the greatest miracle of all.

Learn more at clickworkspress.com/fathers.

Ember of Dreams
The Clarion Chronicles, Book One

When magic awakens a long-forgotten folk, a noble lady, a young apprentice, and a solitary blacksmith band together to prevent war and seek understanding between humans and elves.

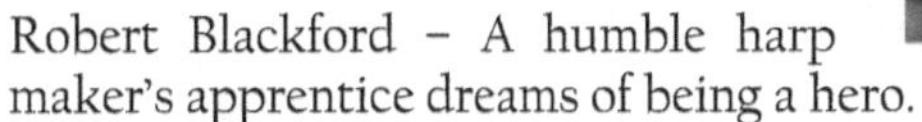

Lady Kristyn Tremayne – An otherwise unremarkable young lady's open heart and inquisitive mind reveal a hidden world of magic.

Robert Blackford – A humble harp maker's apprentice dreams of being a hero.

Master Gabriel Zane – A master blacksmith's pursuit of perfection leads him to craft an enchanted sword, drawing him out of his isolation and far from his cozy home.

Lord Luthor Carnarvon – A lonely nobleman with a dark past has won the heart of Kristyn's mother, but at what cost?

Readers love *Ember of Dreams*

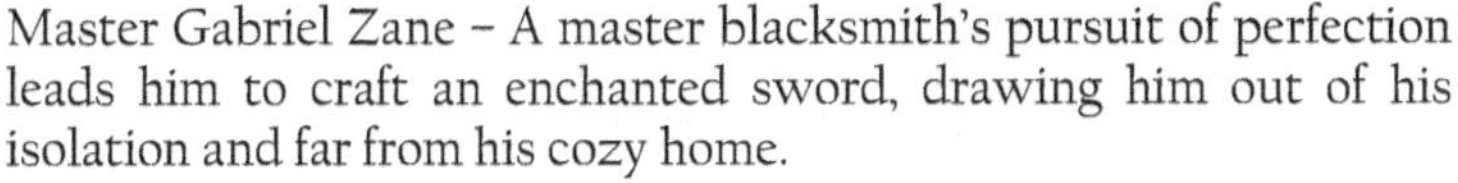

"The more I got to know the characters, the more I liked them. The female lead in particular is a treat to accompany on her journey from ordinary to extraordinary."

"The author's deep understanding of his protagonists' motivations and keen eye for psychological detail make Robert and his companions a likable and memorable cast."

Learn more at tinyurl.com/emberofdreams.

More great titles from Clickworks Press

www.clickworkspress.com

The Altered Wake

Megan Morgan

Amid growing unrest, a family secret and an ancient laboratory unleash long-hidden superhuman abilities. Now newly-promoted Sentinel Cameron Kardell must chase down a rogue superhuman who holds the key to the powers' origin: the greatest threat Cotarion has seen in centuries – and Cam's best friend.

"Incredible. Starts out gripping and keeps getting better."

Learn more at clickworkspress.com/sentinel1.

Hubris Towers: The Complete First Season

Ben Y. Faroe & Bill Hoard

Comedy of manners meets comedy of errors in a new series for fans of Fawlty Towers and P. G. Wodehouse.

"So funny and endearing"

"Had me laughing so hard that I had to put it down to catch my breath"

"Astoundingly, outrageously funny!"

Learn more at clickworkspress.com/hts01.

Death's Dream Kingdom
Gabriel Blanchard

A young woman of Victorian London has been transformed into a vampire. Can she survive the world of the immortal dead—or perhaps, escape it?

"The wit and humor are as Victorian as the setting... a winsomely vulnerable and tremendously crafted work of art."

"A dramatic, engaging novel which explores themes of death, love, damnation, and redemption."

Learn more at clickworkspress.com/ddk.

Share the love!

Join our microlending team at
kiva.org/team/clickworkspress.

Keep in touch!

Join the Clickworks Press email list
and get freebies, production updates, special deals,
behind-the-scenes sneak peeks, and more.

Sign up today at clickworkspress.com/join.

www.ingramcontent.com/pod-product-compliance
Lightning Source LLC
Chambersburg PA
CBHW020340010826
48970CB00012B/1868